No sooner did she hit the first notes than the full force of the Songstress Specialized Model rushed into Vivy's consciousness.

Something about the tone of the music brought on a wave of nostalgia. It was gentle, yet lonely. It made you want to sink into it, but it wouldn't let you. It was like something you had and then lost.

CONTENTS

VIVY

Prototype

NOVEL

3

WRITTEN BY
**Tappei Nagatsuki
Eiji Umehara**

ILLUSTRATED BY
loundraw

Seven Seas Entertainment

VIVY prototype volume 3

Seven Seas press and purchase enquiries can be sent to
Marketing Manager Lianne Sentar at press@gomanga.com.
Information regarding the distribution and purchase of
digital editions is available from Digital Manager CK Russell
at digital@gomanga.com.

Follow Seven Seas Entertainment online at
sevenseasentertainment.com.

TRANSLATION: Jordan Taylor
ADAPTATION: Leigh Teetzel
COVER DESIGN: Nicky Lim
INTERIOR LAYOUT & DESIGN: Clay Gardner
COPY EDITOR: Dayna Abel
PROOFREADER: Jade Gardner
LIGHT NOVEL EDITOR: T. Anne
PREPRESS TECHNICIAN: Melanie Ujimori, Jules Valera
PRODUCTION MANAGER: Lissa Pattillo
EDITOR-IN-CHIEF: Julie Davis
ASSOCIATE PUBLISHER: Adam Arnold
PUBLISHER: Jason DeAngelis

ISBN: 978-1-63858-821-4
Printed in Canada
First Printing: March 2023
10 9 8 7 6 5 4 3 2 1

Prologue

.: 1 :.

MUSIC SPILLED FROM THE STAGE into the audience. High-pitched, mournful singing gripped their hearts, drawing them in to the end of the story—a tale of lovers forever separated by war and death. Emotions rose with the crescendo as the music swelled with overwhelming power. The actors' grief and tears entwined with the song in harmony for this final, tragic moment.

Wet-faced, the lead actress laid flowers at her dead lover's grave. Once the flow of her tears finally stemmed, she smiled and said her farewell. The impassioned music faded ever so slowly, coming to an end as the curtain closed on the story and the stage.

It was the perfect ending.

When the curtain rose again, every actor was lined up, their eyes filled with the joy and satisfaction of a successful performance as they gazed out at the audience. They all joined hands, bowing. There were the leads who played the lovers, the one who played the stubborn father, the actress who played the sickly yet compassionate mother, the famous actor who played the lover's rival, and the rookie who played the role of the sniper who took the lover's life. Each and every one of them bowed graciously, looking utterly fulfilled.

It was the curtain call, the moment after the story's conclusion when the audience could express their admiration and feelings toward the passionate performance. Perhaps there were even those who—while they obviously enjoyed the show—had come to the theater for this moment alone. And the curtain call for this particular show was incredible.

For the first time since the show began, bright and cheery music played in the background, congratulating them on an emotional finale and on bringing this work to a close.

It was perfect. Absolutely perfect.

Or it would have been, if this were not a nearly deserted theater on the outskirts of town, if the seats hadn't been so empty that it was hard to find spectating eyes to look into, if the passionate performances of the actors who'd never really made it big were actually going somewhere, if the majestic background music didn't clash so obviously with the situation, if everything weren't so incongruous...

In that painful, dreary moment, there was one audience member clearly unable to read the room, one who clapped and cheered despite the sparse applause. If the actors on the stage were abnormal, then the audience members who went out of their way to come see them were even more so.

And in that disparate, mismatched scene, there was one little girl in a black dress hanging her head, standing off to one side away from the line of performers. Her voice was the only one that was *truly* perfect.

.: 2 :.

"HAVE YOU EVER SEEN something like that?! Have you?!" a fiery male voice boomed backstage as the curtain lowered for the last time and staff milled about. He repeated his shout three times, and though they were savage and commanding bellows of anger, everyone around reacted to the raging voice with slight smirks or even outright grins, as if this was some tired routine.

One actor even shrugged and said what everyone was thinking: "There he goes again."

"Hey, who was that just now?! It wasn't just anyone. It was you, wasn't it?! Hey, Mister Yanagihara! Did you say 'again'? Huh?! Just so you know, I'm gonna say it as many times as it takes!"

"Ack, shouldn't have fanned the flames," said the actor who'd spoken, hunching a little at having wound up as a target.

The charming mannerism only made the others nearby smile more. Snickers rippled through the staff members barely able to contain their laughter. They had no ill intentions, but their reaction only served to provoke the person—or rather, the AI—in the middle.

"And what are *you* laughing at?! I'm starting to question your sanity! Nice job putting on what might've been the best performance of your lives...in front of a few stragglers in this tiny, podunk theater! I seriously regret wasting some of the world's oxygen for this!"

"Aw, the best performance of our lives... I'm blushing."

"Don't! It wasn't a compliment! You may have been far more engaged with the script during this performance than during rehearsals, and I was impressed with how natural your tears seemed during the lovers' farewell, but I cannot stress this enough—that is *not* what this is about!"

The one ranting was a non-humanoid AI with a distinctly large, round frame. His massive, rotund body was equipped with arms for handling detailed work and legs so he could move, but his most prominent feature was the sheer number of audio devices installed throughout his body.

He was the sound designer, in charge of any and all things related to audio—aside from raw vocals—including background music, sound effects, environmental noise, mics, and the mixing console. This AI, MS4-13—aka "Antonio"—was in sole control of all the sounds that came together to make a show.

"I'm trying to tell you there's something wrong with your sense of danger! There's already a hole in the ship's hull, water is flowing in, and it's only a matter of time before we capsize! Yet all of you are standing on the deck chatting about what color we should paint the mast. How can you ignore this?!" He flapped his arms up and down (rather than side to side, in case he hit a staff member), and his body's eye cameras flashed red and green as he grumbled and complained.

Considering the size of the theater, the pitiful ticket sales, and the fact that Antonio's sound work was passionate and all-encompassing, the crew was kept to a minimum. All of them had been there a long time.

Antonio was the most recent addition to the array of long-term crew members. And since he was the newest member of the troupe, it was inappropriate for him to meddle in direction. He was well aware that he was committing a breach of etiquette, but he continued to point out faults he found in the crew and performers as they scraped by.

Several factors contributed to their current situation. For starters, a comparison of average values calculated from statistical patterns of past performances indicated that the actors' dramatic performances shouldn't have fizzled out in this small, backwater theater. Also, Antonio had higher specs than necessary for a sound manager in a theater of this size.

But there was only one reason Antonio would so desperately raise his voice.

"You should be aware of this, Ophelia!"

"Eek!"

"Did you just shriek?! What kind of reaction is that?!"

"Y-y-you s-surprised me..."

Antonio whirled around, his eye cameras fixing on the one he'd called Ophelia. The girl was clad in all black: black hair, black eyes, black dress. Except she wasn't a girl—she was another AI.

She shrank in the face of Antonio's menace while she explained her reaction, stammering significantly as she did. Despite the terrible condition of her voice at the moment, with its faltering and spluttering, it still managed to cut through the bustle of the backstage environment. She wasn't trying to make her voice sound beautiful, yet it was a gift to anyone who heard it. The other actors, likewise in the business of using their voices as instruments of emotion and storytelling, were visibly captivated by her sweet, melodious voice.

Ophelia.

The girl's voice was the reason Antonio had overstepped the bounds of his role as well as his duty to serve humanity, and the reason he so strongly demanded an improvement to the situation.

The small theater was on the edge of town, had little presence, and was horribly unknown. The performers loved to act and gave every show their all. The crew were eager to bring success to the stage, even in these hard times. The soundmaster AI utilized the power of music to its fullest to support the plays. He was the best one there and wholly unsuited to the place.

But not nearly as unsuited as Ophelia's voice was.

"You get it, don't you, Ophelia? Your talent is not something to be wasted in a piddly theater like this, doing original works written by some no-name playwright. There's a stage out there that would suit you better. Do you understand what I'm saying?"

"Um, uh, w-well…"

"Keep up! Get it through your head! God, I can't *believe* how slow the links are between your thought calculations and your emotional expressions! You are a serious wreck when it comes to anything other than singing. There's not a single thing I can compliment you on other than your voice! Singing is all you have! Do you get that?!" Antonio pressed closer to Ophelia when her reaction was too slow, and her eyes darted away. It was quite the scene: a massive, non-humanoid AI looming over a small girl.

Seeing that, one of the crew members rushed to put himself between them. "C'mon, calm down, Antonio. Ophelia's doing her best. Her singing is honestly amazing, and she even got a lot of applause from the audience."

"Don't coddle her!" Antonio shouted. "Ophelia's got more potential than this! Most of the applause was coming from one regular making a fuss! Are you really judging her success off a fan like that?! I have a responsibility to Ophelia!" Antonio gestured to his body and stared at the staff member. "Besides," he said shortly, "I'm a soundmaster AI designed to support Ophelia. As her partner, my entire purpose is to draw out the full beauty of her voice."

"I guess that is true, but—"

"But *this* member of the Songstress Series has absolutely no self-awareness!" Antonio leaned around the crew member to glare at Ophelia, who was hunched over, hiding behind the man's back. If Antonio were human, he'd be heaving with rage.

The crew member let out a sigh, scratched his head, and said, "Ah, fine. I'll leave the post-performance review meeting to the two of you. Everyone else, let's tear down the set!"

Calls of "Good job, everybody!" rose up around them. Ophelia merely stammered her acknowledgment. After some claps and cheers, everyone quickly bowed and dispersed. The crew put back the props and cleaned the stage while the actors removed their makeup and changed out of costume. As everyone busied themselves, Ophelia was left alone with Antonio.

Gathering her courage, Ophelia began, "Um, I—"

"We're both AIs," Antonio said harshly, glaring at her up close. "I'm pretty sure you get what I'm saying, but I'm going to put this in no uncertain terms."

"O-okay..."

"Ophelia, you are an experimental AI whose capabilities in all areas except singing have been sacrificed. That inarguably makes you defective. As your partner, I guarantee it."

"..."

"Because you lost all the abilities that your average AI would have, your potential use became extremely limited, and you were dumped off as registered equipment for this gaggle of nobodies. You've shown no development or expansion of your consciousness since then. You're stuck. Calculators have made more advancements than you have."

Antonio laid into Ophelia in fits and starts, telling her she needed to open her eyes and see what was happening, that she couldn't stay like this forever. If any of the troupe members had heard his stern speech, they would have reprimanded him for going too far. But Antonio never went easy on his partner. When necessary, he would give whatever advice or criticism he saw fit—even if that meant creating a rift in their relationship. An AI found meaning in constantly improving things and moving forward.

And how did Ophelia respond to the lecture?

"Hee hee hee..."

"Why are you laughing? I don't think that's an appropriate emotional pattern for this moment."

"It's just you, Antonio. You're the only one who always, *always* values my singing," she said, her lips turning up in an emotional pattern of happiness.

Antonio was confused by her response. He narrowed the shutters of his eye cameras and struggled to find anything to say.

"Everyone says nice things about my singing. They all say I'm fine the way I am. You're the only one who says I can't stay this way."

"Just to be clear, I'm not talking about your singing. It's everything else that's terrible! You've got so many areas you can improve, and hardly any of them have to do with your singing. Well, not zero, mind you! Just hardly any. You know that, right?" Antonio poked her forehead.

Ophelia looked at the tip of his long arm and nodded. "Yeah, I know." She then turned her black eyes toward the stage, the cameras inside them whirring. "One day..."

"One day what?"

"I'll work hard so I can live up to your expectations, Antonio."

VIVY

Prototype

CHAPTER 1

The Songstresses' Festival

. : 1 : .

PROGRAM INITIATION CONFIRMED. *Consciousness conversion activated.*

Vivy was waking up just as Diva was going to sleep.

According to procedure, Vivy did a self-scan. No abnormalities were found. Recently, she had briefly activated several times in order to escape danger, but this activation was not one caused by an extreme situation. It fit all normal activation patterns.

In other words, the Singularity Project was starting up again.

Vivy tucked that information in one corner of her consciousness and began tackling her list of tasks, beginning with the highest priority: securing communication with Matsumoto. She opened her transmission circuit as she determined her current environment. At that moment, a voice reached her audio sensors.

"...but I digress. It's seriously an honor to be here with you, Diva. I am so excited for this performance. I guess that doesn't sound very AI-like of me, does it?"

Someone was talking to Vivy as she activated. Or really, they were addressing Diva. Vivy's eye cameras swept in the direction of the speaker, an energetic-looking AI with blue hair cut into a neat, short bob. Using the AI's external features and the shape of her wired earpiece, Vivy searched for a name. There was a hit: DTM9-12.

"Could you call me Katie? That's my designated name. Don't you think using designated names or nicknames is way friendlier than model numbers, A-03?"

"Friendlier, you say? You're probably right."

"I'm glad you're so straightforward. Oh gosh, look at me. I'm over here preaching to you and you're, like, way more experienced than the rest of us. So very sorry, ma'am." DTM9-12—Katie—brought her hand up to her forehead in a salute and gave a smile.

Her smooth enactment of the emotional pattern caused slight ripples in Vivy's consciousness. Time had flowed on since the last Singularity Point, and AI technology had evidently made great leaps in the time since she'd last activated. Katie's fluid movements just proved it.

"..."

Katie's skill with expressions wasn't unique to her either; Vivy recognized it in the behavior of all other AIs around them. The whole lot of them had been loaded into a trailer used for transporting AIs. Vivy, Katie, and the others were being moved somewhere else. The cargo area had seats installed, and each AI was sitting in their respective seat. They had also been provided with standby terminals for charging and datalinks.

The thorough considerations made it seem less like a shipping vessel for AIs and more like a shuttle for VIPs. Even the decorations had been placed with comfort in mind, which sparked an odd disturbance in Vivy's consciousness—something analogous to discomfort.

"You look kind of annoyed," Katie said. "Are you not a fan of small talk?"

"No, that's not it. I just don't operate outside the park often. It requires more calculations than normal," Vivy replied.

"Oh, that's right. You always sing at NiaLand, don't you? Wow, to stay in one place... I'm actually a little jealous you have your own home. Me and the other songstresses are always on tour." Looking cheery, Katie stretched her long legs out.

Vivy frowned. "There are a lot of girls like that these days, it seems."

Her discomfort stemmed from an aversion to being treated like a human, but neither Katie nor any of the other AIs appeared to mind it. Vivy referenced some data and determined that there were twelve AIs in the trailer, including herself. They were from all different manufacturers and had been made at different times. There was only one thing the diverse group of AIs had in common, which led her to a theory about why they were all there.

"You know what, it's grand to see so many songstresses squeezed into one vehicle. Don't you agree, Vivy?"

The transmission came not as a sound but as a delivery of data straight to Vivy's consciousness, as if the sender had been perusing Vivy's internal logs. At the "voice's" interjection, Vivy performed an emotional pattern akin to a sigh. It was an automatic response based on past experiences, but it most likely would've looked like an organic sigh of relief to onlookers.

Vivy was incredibly annoyed to be perceived as such, so she kept her thought processes in check as she replied, *"Looks like we're kicking things off in another strange situation, Matsumoto."*

"I guess you could call it strange. Anyway, it's better than activating to find yourself falling from a height that would result in inevitable destruction, or flung onto a freeway with a four-ton truck barreling down on you, or surrounded by dozens of guns pointed at you, or onstage at the height of singing the catchiest part of a song—"

"What about the risk of being hated by my junior songstresses because I forgot what they were just talking to me about?"

"In that case, wouldn't the best solution be to make full use of your veteran customer-service personality and whip out the tricky skills a hundred-year-old clunker like yourself has in order to win their respect back?"

"I haven't been operating for a hundred years."

"At this point, you're old enough to be in the ballpark of a hundred with a bit of rounding."

At least she didn't have to contact Matsumoto now. For better or worse, friendly banter was not a thing between the longtime friends. They used their blunt jokes to get a rough idea of each other's situation, and it was clear Matsumoto's sarcasm hadn't dulled.

A hundred-year-old clunker. As much as she'd found it an exaggeration, the Singularity Project had been going for several decades. AIs had seen astounding progress in that time, and the newly created AIs were leaving old models like Vivy behind. The passage of time and advancements in AI technology had led to this moment.

"Today is the Zodiac Signs Festival, which will bring twelve songstress AIs together to celebrate song!"

.:2:.

WHILE IT MIGHT HAVE BEEN an exaggeration to say that the twelve AIs in the trailer represented a century of songstress history, they *were* from various time periods, and the enormous Zodiac Signs Festival was meant to celebrate that history. Each AI would be assigned a zodiac sign and perform on a stage of starry skies.

"I hear this event got so much attention, people were going around saying they'd get a ticket even if they had to pawn off their own family members for it!" Matsumoto said.

"They'd pawn off their own family?" Vivy replied, skeptical.

"I have no idea how this happened, but the event is being held on Christmas, of all days! I mean, Jesus Christ! Literally! In other countries, people gather with their families on Christmas to commemorate Jesus's birth. Yet over here, we've got people trying to peddle their nearest and dearest just so they can go see some AIs sing... It's a scary world we live in, Vivy. God save their souls..."

"Enough talk about selling family members. Let's move on."

"All right, all right. Our good lady Diva, the eldest songstress, was bequeathed the tremendous honor of taking part in this prestigious event. I daresay the zodiac sign she's been assigned is the most important one—Aries, that is."

"What's with the old-timey speech? You're making me feel like an antique."

"Goodness, I appear to have ruffled your feathers! Never mind the trifling details, my dear girl. This is an honor because it proves that out of all the songstresses in the world, they recognize *you* as the crème de la crème. Hard to believe you aren't letting it show on your face, but...all the pampering and recognition isn't so bad, is it?"

Vivy had entered her personal Archive, and Matsumoto was there with her. He changed freely into a dapper outfit as he spoke.

The personalized space formed in the data field of an AI's positronic brain was the manifestation of their Archive. Each space's interior depended on the AI responsible for it. Diva, an AI songstress, had an Archive modeled after a school music room. It was not a real place, however; it had been compiled from online images of music rooms.

It was a bit odd that both Vivy and Diva, two AI personalities, used the same Archive.

"Vivy? Hellooo, Vivy? Are you ignoring me? Well, that's no good. You're the only person I have to talk to! I'll die of boredom if I can't even make fun of you."

"You won't die. And what's with all this talk of recognition?"

"Hm? Oh, you mean the whole 'crème de la crème' bit?"

"Yes. That is a product of Diva's achievements. It has nothing to do with me."

Even though they were in a digital space, they didn't hold back with their emotional patterns. Vivy's shapely brows furrowed, and Matsumoto's eye camera shutter opened and closed like he was blinking.

"I wouldn't say that," he said. "It is entirely due to your work that Diva's body has made it to this era in one piece. I salvaged data that showed Diva trying to destroy herself ten years ago, and you stopped her by the skin of your teeth. Humanity nearly came to an end."

"But that was just one result of her suspecting I was up to something. All I did was cover for myself. I can't take credit for solving a problem I created."

"You might not be perfect, but I think you're blaming yourself too much. Also, I don't recommend that you consider yourself and Diva to be separate individuals. You and I have been at this for nearly a hundred years. My original era will be upon us before you know it."

Matsumoto's voice seemed to fall, and Vivy pursed her lips.

He was right. The Singularity Project, this mission the two of them had embarked on together, was coming to a close. And the end of their journey meant Vivy's role was almost over.

"If that's the case, we have to hurry up and fix this Singularity Point," said Vivy. "The Zodiac Signs Festival was probably a big event for Diva in the original history, right?"

"Of course it was. I didn't think I needed to point that out, but it's also why I don't want to ruin the event."

"The next Singularity Point takes place near the festival, then."

"Bzzt! Nice try, but you'll only walk away with a participation trophy for *that* answer. Our target location is, in fact, the very site we're en route to now... The Zodiac Signs Festival!" He sounded like he'd been holding out for the right moment for the big reveal.

Vivy said nothing. If this Singularity Point had something to do with the Zodiac Signs Festival, then Diva—who was taking part—couldn't be disregarded while they went about their business.

Matsumoto's eye camera adjusted with a whir. Perhaps he knew what was going through Vivy's mind. "Allow me to give you a little more detail. Back in the real world, the truck you're on is arriving at the venue. Then come rehearsals and such, with the actual festival taking place this evening. Since you have been activated, Diva will not be able to rehearse, so please be careful."

"You're not giving me much to—"

"I don't like it either, so let's keep working in two places at once."

At that moment, Vivy's consciousness was flung from her own Archive even as she tried to cling on. It was absurd that Matsumoto could just chase her out of her own territory if he so desired. She registered dissatisfaction in her logs as her consciousness was transferred back inside the transport truck.

Just as Matsumoto had predicted, they had arrived at their destination. This festival of dreams bringing together twelve songstresses was being held in the Touto Dome. The truck pulled up and parked at the staff entrance, after which an event staffer approached and addressed the AIs.

"You've all had a *long* trip! Everyone come inside and get ready in your dressing rooms. Rehearsals will start right on schedule, so please don't be late!"

Vivy disembarked as directed and made for the employees-only area of the Touto Dome, simultaneously referencing any and all data on the venue. Processing the sheer size of the stadium drew heavily upon the resources of her consciousness. The venue had the capacity to seat over fifty thousand people, making it one of the largest event venues in the entire country. Even though Diva had starred on NiaLand's Main Stage for years, this number was over ten times greater than her normal audience of three or four thousand.

Katie strode up beside Vivy, who had unintentionally stopped in her tracks. "I've sung at loads of venues, but this one's in a whole different league. No matter how many times I come here, it always gets me pumped up," she said, shooting Vivy a wink.

Quite a few of the songstresses had already gotten the chance to sing at the Touto Dome. Even Diva's many years of experience paled in comparison to what those AIs had accomplished. And that was doubly true considering that Vivy was not even a songstress but an AI with a whole other mission.

"I'm definitely out of place here," Vivy said.

Katie rushed to encourage her. "Hey, hey! Don't be so down on yourself. You're the eldest songstress. With your background, you're absolutely fit to sing in this place. You'll knock it out of the park." Although she'd made an incorrect assumption about Vivy's character, Vivy accepted the encouragement.

From the outside, Katie was indistinguishable from a human. Her smile, her mannerisms—every move was precise down to the last detail. Vivy didn't have the resources necessary to determine whether that was a good thing.

"Diva? What's wrong?" Katie asked.

"It's nothing. You're just a nice girl."

"Girl? I'm not that young... But I guess from your perspective I am. All right, here's some advice from a rookie to a veteran: If you're nervous, write 'AI' three times on your palm and then lick it with your tongue sensor."

"I don't think a human superstition will have any effect on an AI."

"That's better!"

As Vivy chatted with Katie, she could almost imagine herself talking to Matsumoto instead. He was an amalgamation of the technology in the near future, but Vivy didn't want to think about how all AIs would become like him as they advanced.

"Well, she was given Pisces as her sign, meaning she's the newest songstress model. The oldest songstress right next to the newest songstress. I don't know who decided on the seating arrangements, but they're a bit cruel, aren't they?"

Matsumoto's voice cut into Vivy's consciousness, imperceptible to anyone but her. She suppressed an outward reaction, then sent a curt transmission back to her partner to express her discontent.

"You're right to be upset," replied Matsumoto. *"But you've cultivated a history and reliability. Is it because this girl is young and clever? In the end, she's a star you only ever watch from the other side of a screen, like a flower high in the mountains you can never reach. You, on the other hand, are the kind of idol people can go see, like a pretty wildflower growing in a playground. You two are at odds with each other in that way."*

"Are you trying to pick a fight? Or are you making a jab at me? Because if you are, it's not working. Quit it and just support me on the Singularity Project." Vivy brushed aside the ineffectual wireless message and scanned her surroundings.

The twelve songstresses had exited the trailer and were being led toward their dressing rooms, where they would prepare for rehearsals. They lined up as the staff members stared at them, eyes burning with envy or passion. Evidently, a number of them admired the songstress AIs. Katie waved at them, causing them to blush with excitement or even let out quiet cheers.

"I'm sure they were careful with their staffing, but it does look like songstress AIs are quite popular," Matsumoto noted.

"It's an honor to accept a role in this history," Vivy said.

Selection for the festival wasn't just down to how good the AIs looked or sounded. It was also down to the confidence people had that they would do their job well.

Normally, Vivy and the other songstresses wouldn't need to rehearse because they had the data for the set list installed. It was the human staff members who needed the rehearsals—unlike AIs, humans needed to check how things would go on the real stage and prepare for anything that might go wrong. Most of these roles had been automated by this era, so the need for this sort of preparation was declining.

"Even NiaLand is making the bold move to swap a portion of the cast for AIs in the future. They'll steadily streamline most of the work that used to be handled by human staff," said Matsumoto.

"Am I an old clunker for not being able to see that as a good thing?"

"This isn't something I should be commenting on as an outsider."

A car came to a stop next to the truck, breaking up Vivy and Matsumoto's heavy conversation. The door opened, and someone stepped out into the employees-only area. Several of the staff members gasped the moment they recognized the interloper. They were just as excited as when they'd seen the twelve songstresses arrive.

"..."

The AI who'd exited the car was slight of frame and wearing a pitch-black dress. Her black hair was perfectly straight, without a strand out of place. Her eyes were black as a sunless sky. She was styled in pure black from head to toe—a rather bold color choice.

Her black heels clicked on the ground as she walked over. One wrong step, and she would make a garish example of herself. Yet the AI made such a striking impression that any onlooker would've been hard-pressed to criticize her. Her grand entrance seemed appropriate somehow.

It wasn't just the staff members whose eyes were glued to the AI's arrival; the songstresses were also lost for words. Even the bubbly Katie was gazing in wonder, her attention stolen by the AI striding toward them.

Katie's narrow, shapely lips trembled, and a name slipped out like a breath. "Ophelia..."

The black-clothed AI heard the small exhalation. Her eyes, rimmed with long lashes, looked in Katie's direction. She took a step closer to Katie, and...

"Urgh!"

...she tripped on the hem of her dress and toppled forward.

"Ow..."

A panicked staff member dashed over. "Ophelia, are you okay?! Are you hurt? Is the dress damaged?!"

"I-I'm sorry. Um, I'm okay. I-I fall a lot...so my dresses are special. Th-they're hard to tear..."

"Your nose is red! Someone call a stylist!"

The AI squatted down and pressed a hand over her nose, her spellbinding impression from a moment ago gone to who-knew-where. Now she had a completely different air. The staff members ignored her explanation as they checked her and the dress in a flurry, clearly worried her fall would impact the concert.

Vivy said, "Is that...?"

"Ophelia. A Songstress Specialization Model and the Black Angel of the Small Theater. Diva, she's your cute little sister," Katie told her, smirking a little as she eyed the AI in the middle of the commotion. "Listen, I don't know how this'll come off, but you and her both seem like totally different people once you step onstage."

Hearing that, Vivy checked the data again and verified what Katie had said. Ophelia was the most recent addition to the Songstress Series, meaning she was one of the Sisters—Diva being the eldest. She had also been specifically crafted to maximize her role as a songstress.

The constellation she'd been assigned for the Zodiac Signs Festival wasn't one of the twelve zodiac signs. It was Ophiuchus. She was the secret bonus act, the real shining star of the festival.

And she was the star of something else as well.

"Ophelia is the source of this Singularity Point," Matsumoto said.

"What are we going to do to her?" Vivy asked.

He didn't reply right away. The role this "sibling" of Vivy's had to play would determine the success or failure of the Zodiac Signs Festival. How would Vivy need to handle the situation surrounding her youngest sister? Would she speak with her as she had Estella? Would she stand against her like she had Grace? What was the necessary approach?

Vivy observed Ophelia, surrounded by staff with a hand still pressed to her nose. Her voice had been incredibly smooth and clear. What would Vivy have to do to that girl in order to save humanity?

"Our goal is to save her," said Matsumoto.

Vivy blinked rapidly, taken aback. Thinking she might have misheard, she said, *"Save her?"*

"Yes. She committed an act that would have a huge impact on AI history after the festival: her suicide. Our mission this time is to stop her from killing herself."

.: 3 :.

THE FOURTH SINGULARITY POINT, the turning point in history that Vivy and Matsumoto now faced, was an event known as "Ophelia's Suicide."

"Ophelia's Suicide changed AI history," Matsumoto explained. "I mean, we're talking about the suicide of an AI, a construction that supposedly has no life or soul. She broke the AI 'no self-harm' rule and destroyed herself... An incredible story, don't you think?"

He was surrounded by music stands in Vivy's Archive. The shutter of his eye camera narrowed as he looked at Vivy, who was sitting in front of the piano.

After Ophelia was escorted inside the venue, Vivy and the other Zodiac Heroines had gone to their respective dressing rooms. Vivy and Matsumoto were using the brief time before rehearsal for a strategy meeting.

"My initial thought was *not* that it was incredible," said Vivy. "Actually, I find it absurd. AIs can't break the rule preventing damage to themselves. Are you sure Ophelia destroyed herself in the original history?"

"Public opinion leaned toward suicide. Personally, I think it's nonsense. All anyone can say for certain is that it was self-destruction caused by some sort of system error. Then again, humans can be arrogant enough to play God."

Matsumoto's sarcastic comment referenced how humans viewed AIs. Humans gave AIs names, the right to marry, and even the "free will" to choose suicide—but they weren't real choices for the AIs. Humans had installed and permitted those things. Although the sentiment was dark, Matsumoto implied that humans mistakenly thought they'd reached godhood by giving AIs what some believed God had given humans.

"Can you finish flaunting your acerbic wit and tell me everything about Ophelia's Suicide?" Vivy asked.

"I guess there's really no point chatting with you. I already explained the gist. During the festival, the Songstress Specialization Model, Ophelia, threw herself from the roof of the venue where the songstresses were gathered, resulting in her destruction. AI rights groups used Ophelia's so-called suicide to claim that her breaking the rules and killing herself meant she had a soul."

That half-baked conclusion wouldn't even fly with conspiracy theorists or the most romantic of thinkers. "All that from just one AI destroying itself? That's a stretch."

"Agreed. What is this 'soul' of Ophelia's supposed to be? And she could have just tripped and fallen from the roof. Humans! Always got their heads in the clouds. Or...so I wish I could say. But after the incident, a series of AIs destroyed themselves, and Ophelia's Suicide was pointed out as a major contributing factor."

"..."

"That was what the AI rights groups were really reacting to. Ophelia's Suicide provided AIs with an option they hadn't had before: the choice to take their own lives. That isn't just 'self-destruction,' and this interpretation proves that AIs acknowledge their own lives. In other words..."

"They'd gained the 'will' to act, even if it meant breaking rules."

"Exactly."

Matsumoto shuffled the cubes making up his body, entertaining himself as Vivy processed what he'd said. She glanced at him out of the corner of her eye. Something dark seeped into her consciousness as she considered the shocking consequences of Ophelia's Suicide. If only one AI had committed the act, then it could have been chalked up to a simple system error. But Ophelia had become a catalyst, causing other AIs to destroy themselves as well. Vivy feared infection by a malicious virus or perhaps the spread of a fatal system error, like a disease making its way into positronic AI brains.

"Does that mean our job is really just to stop Ophelia from killing herself?" she asked.

"I know what you're thinking. You suspect this chain reaction is a malicious virus or the result of code operating unexpectedly, right? But I can tell you that law enforcement and the AI corporations of this era put plenty of consideration into those theories as well."

"It didn't go anywhere? Does that mean there were no abnormalities found in Ophelia?"

"None. And it wasn't just Ophelia—not a single one of the AIs who killed themselves had any abnormalities. An investigation concluded that no malicious force had caused them to destroy themselves, and there was no serendipity involved either. In that case, what could have pushed them to take that last step?"

"A soul?"

"Indeed. But souls don't exist. We have to prove that to the world."

Both Vivy and Matsumoto were AIs—they had functions that enabled thought and something akin to emotion. However, if you looked closely enough, you would find nothing but arrays of calculated numbers. Their thoughts and actions were brought about by human knowledge and technological understanding. They had no souls.

Preventing Ophelia's "suicide" would prove that no AI did.

.: 4 :.

OPHELIA WASN'T in her dressing room, so Vivy went to the stage in search of her. Everyone was buzzing in anticipation of the big event, but one black-clad figure stood still in the middle of it all, staring at the stage from the audience seats. She seemed so ephemeral, as if she stood frozen in the middle of a wasteland.

"..."

Vivy questioned whether this was the same individual who'd had such an overwhelming aura when she first appeared. If it was, perhaps it wasn't surprising that humans found something special in her. Vivy's positronic brain gave her the impression that the songstress's small shoulders carried the weight of their expectations.

"Ophelia," Vivy called.

"..."

"Ophelia?"

There was no response. As she peered at Ophelia's profile, Vivy's long hair spilled over her slight shoulders. That, combined with Vivy's stage outfit with its bold back cutout, gave her a resplendent and sensual appearance. The staff members scurrying around looked at the two songstresses, side by side in their dresses, and Vivy could tell their expressions had softened. To a passerby, it might look like an intimate moment between the two sister AIs— even if it was actually the younger sister ignoring the elder.

"Oh. Yes? Sorry, did you say something?" Ophelia asked suddenly, just as Vivy was calculating whether to call her name again.

Vivy hadn't been built very tall, but Ophelia was particularly short for a humanoid AI. She had to turn her dark eyes up to look at Vivy. Her eye cameras, which looked no different than a real human's eyes, adjusted to focus on Vivy. A soft sound came from between Ophelia's lips. "Oh..."

That reaction was so utterly human.

"..."

Ophelia's response shocked Vivy—not because of how natural it was but because of the specific sound of her voice. When she spoke, the AI perfectly replicated 1/f noise—aka "pink noise." Pink noise appeared often in the natural world and was thought to be capable of soothing human hearts, relaxing listeners by providing a pleasant stimulus. Vivy could feel the effects, even when Ophelia had barely let out any breath at all.

"Diva-oneesama..." said Ophelia in that perfect voice of hers, though she sounded equally taken aback.

Hearing the honorific one might use to formally address their elder sister, Vivy's brow furrowed. She brought a finger to her lips. "You called me 'oneesama.'"

"Oh, uh, s-sorry! Is it, erm… Is that inappropriate?"

"No, that's not it. I was just surprised. I'm just not used to being called that." Vivy couldn't help being flustered when Ophelia referred to her as such. Even though she had encountered other Sisters several times before, none of them had genuinely acted like a little sister with her. This was a new experience.

"Well, all the Sisters you met before—Estella, Elizabeth, and Grace—hardly looked like your little sisters. You couldn't help noticing it," came a transmission from Matsumoto, but Vivy made the healthy decision to ignore it.

If sisterhood was determined based on outward appearances alone, Vivy wouldn't have necessarily passed as the eldest. Years of operation had to be considered. Ophelia was the first Sister who both was younger *and* looked younger than Vivy, although it didn't make Vivy feel any particular sort of way. Had it been Diva standing here instead of her, the songstress would've probably felt some sort of kinship or joy.

"You can call me whatever you like, Ophelia. I'm glad I get to perform with my sister today," said Vivy.

"M-me too. I always sing solos. Oh, but I think I might be nervous… My system is all backed up…" Ophelia flapped her hands, like her consciousness couldn't keep up with her actions. While it didn't make her less humanlike than other more fluid AIs, she seemed a bit slow in comparison.

Vivy quietly contemplated how to interact with her. *"This is way different than dealing with Diva or Katie,"* she told Matsumoto via transmission.

"Variety's the spice of life and all that. Actually, nah, that's a lie. There is a good reason for her witlessness, though: She's a Songstress Specialized Model. Her design concept is quite different from yours, the Sisters', and all the other songstresses."

"Specialized Model, you say...?"

"All of her specs are curated to maximize her singing capabilities. She's equipped with only the most basic operational and interpersonal abilities of modern AIs. Her positronic brain does learn but barely. She's a strange one," Matsumoto said. Ophelia's "genius" was created at the expense of all her other specs. *"Anyway, humans can't create an omnipotent being. No matter how much they analyze the highest limits, it'll be a long time before they ever reach perfection. I wonder...what's humanity's endgame with all this?"*

"That's not something for us to think about."

This time, it was Matsumoto's sentimental comments that stood out, but Vivy wouldn't engage with him. He was always intentionally creating chaos in her consciousness. Right now, they needed to prioritize Ophelia, who hadn't moved. With nothing else to do, she stared at the stage, whiling away the time until rehearsals.

Perhaps Vivy's gaze kept her from truly relaxing, because she snuck a glance at her and said, "Um, Diva-oneesama, a-are you going to see the other girls too?"

"Am I bothering you by being here?"

"N-no! Not at all... B-but I'm not really good at talking. I thought maybe you would get bored."

"Ophelia, you were originally sent to be a member of an opera troupe at a small theater, right?"

Ophelia's long-lashed eyes opened wide, and she nodded several times.

Matsumoto had given Vivy a rough overview of Ophelia's history. A0-17/Ophelia was a modern songstress designed to be the latest addition to the Sisters Series. However, since she was created with all her specs geared specifically toward singing, the result was a unit far worse at general-use applications than the other Sisters. Her designers had initially hoped for her to operate in the same way as the other songstress models, but her extremely limited application was deemed problematic. She was passed from her developing company, OGC, to someone with connections to the company, then added to the opera troupe at the theater he owned. Records indicated she continued to sing at the theater for several years, though her career never really took off.

"S-singing at the theater was fun," Ophelia said. "The troupe didn't sell many tickets, but the actors, and the staff, and the troupe leader were all really nice..."

"Did you talk to people in the audience much?" Vivy asked.

"No. Th-they would be disappointed with me. It's the same now, even though I left the small theater and sing in front of more people."

"Why did you leave?"

"There was an important person who happened to see me sing, I guess. If only...it'd been sooner, then this wouldn't have happened..." Ophelia muttered, her pleasant voice expressing something deeply unpleasant.

Modesty and humility had deep roots in the positronic brains of many AIs, but they were like an illness in Ophelia. A positronic brain's development and personality were greatly influenced by the AI's early environment and their life afterward, but while humans could make AIs who performed the reactions humans wanted, they couldn't make AIs with the *consciousness* they wanted. Ophelia's individuality had been shaped by her days with the troupe.

"Diva-oneesama, are you...disappointed when you talk to me?"

Apparently, Ophelia was somewhat critical of her own individuality. Vivy hesitated to answer the unexpected question.

"W-we're both from the Sisters Series, but I'm a failure. Yet you... Well, you're the first songstress ever, and you're still singing in your original role. It's the same for all the other Sisters too," Ophelia said.

"If you mean they all left a mark on AI history, then yes."

Estella and Elizabeth had been made out to be the heroes of the Sun-Crash Incident in the modified history for preventing human casualties, even though they had been the original targets of the attack.

Then there was Grace, who was meant to be the first AI to marry a human, like in the original history. In the modified history, she became the core of Metal Float, where it was believed she went on a rampage and caused an epic battle between humans and AIs. In this era, however, people didn't know the truth about Grace's contributions to Metal Float. Saeki and others claimed she had given her all to solve the Metal Float problem.

Those three were Vivy and Ophelia's sisters, and they had all left their mark on history. In fact, the Sisters had contributed far more to history than any other AI series.

"By the way, I hear there's a saying that goes, 'And you're not even one of the Sisters!' Apparently, it's a common phrase when an AI produces results far beyond what was expected," said Matsumoto.

"And I'm at the top of the Sisters Series?"

"You are the eldest, so people have their eyes on you. Having said that, people think OGC opted not to issue a full recall of the Sisters after Metal Float because of what you and the other Sisters have accomplished. Considering OGC knows what happened there, you're not that ordinary either."

"..."

"Besides, it's not common for an old clunker to keep going for nearly a hundred years. That in itself should be plenty to prove you're something special. Have some confidence, will you?"

"My—or rather, Diva's—value doesn't matter right now. Ophelia's the one talking about it, and she's going to end up writing her name in the history books too, if things keep going the way they are."

Vivy and Matsumoto spoke privately inside her consciousness, away from prying ears. They knew the future, and thus they knew that despite Ophelia's inferiority complex, her self-evaluation was wrong. If Vivy didn't do anything, Ophelia's name would go down in AI history later that night, and it would function as one of the triggers for the war between AIs and humanity.

"Ophelia, is there someone you want to be?" Vivy asked then.

"Huh?" Ophelia's brows shot up. She rolled the question around in her positronic brain, finally settling on a response. "Not someone else, no. I-I want to...I want to be 'me.'"

"..."

Ophelia's next words were clear and free of stammers: "I'm sure that's what my partner would want."

Even that was an extreme thought process for an AI. The fact that AIs were allowed to voice their wishes and implement them was a sign the rules of AI existence were changing. Moreover, Diva—and therefore Vivy as well—had probably received updates to her system in accordance with changes in law. Vivy could also voice her wishes, if she tried. But she wouldn't. She had made the decision not to.

"Ah..."

Just after their exchange, both Vivy and Ophelia received the same transmission. Preparations for rehearsal were complete, and all Zodiac Heroines needed to report backstage. Vivy looked up to see the setup crew waving at her and Ophelia.

"Um, Diva-oneesama...do you want to, er..."

"Let's go together. I'd like to talk more with you, my fellow Sister. Unless you'd rather not?"

Ophelia's eyes sparkled at Vivy's reply. "H-how could I not?! I mean, I-I'd like that."

Witnessing that emotional pattern of raw joy reminded Vivy of meeting a child at NiaLand. Ophelia really *did* feel more like Vivy's little sister than any of the others she'd met, and Vivy was overcome with the urge to protect her.

"Well, that's unexpected," said Matsumoto. *"Were you hungry for big-sisterhood?"*

"Be quiet."

After shutting him down, Vivy headed backstage. Ophelia joined her as she walked off, looking ahead and in a seemingly great mood.

"Agh!"

And then her feet caught on the skirt of her dress, and she hurtled forward again. Vivy helped her up. Ophelia's nose was red from hitting it a second time, and Vivy conducted the sigh emotional pattern.

"Are you absolutely certain Ophelia's Suicide wasn't just her slipping and falling?" she asked, finding the thought frightening.

Matsumoto's response lacked conviction. *"There's no way. Probably. It couldn't be. You don't think...?"*

They could only pray Ophelia's clumsiness wasn't the spark that would light the fires of war between AIs and humanity.

.: 5 :.

CONCERT PREPARATIONS in large venues typically took weeks or even months. The venue staff would be busy setting up equipment and obtaining materials. The star performers would be practicing their music and dance moves. The set list had to be made, and there was a whole slew of other tasks that needed doing.

But with the rise of the AI songstress, performances began to change. AI performers didn't need to practice, and there was no concern that they'd forget the set list or make a mistake on the day of the show. That was why rehearsals weren't for the AIs, but for the human staff supporting them. This resulted in rehearsals that went smoothly, with surprisingly few snags along the way.

After her rehearsal, Katie walked into the wings, mopping her forehead despite the absence of sweat. "Well, this is a new experience. It's been a long time since I've shared the stage with someone else. Stepping back after my piece is done sort of feels like skipping class." With ample cheer, she approached Vivy and Ophelia, who were on standby.

Vivy faced Katie, her lips turning up in a soft smile as she said, "Good job. Your acrobatics performance was really interesting."

"It's the job of a modern songstress to captivate her audience by leaping and bounding across the stage," Katie said. "Though… that kind of sounds rude to say to the two of you, since you don't leap and bound." Katie playfully poked out her tongue and apologized. The gesture was wonderful, filled from end to end with perfectly calculated cuteness.

Katie's programming was one factor in her impeccable performance, but it was really the result of her own experiences and the corresponding expansion of her positronic brain. She was less like a songstress and more like an idol.

"Y-y-your performance w-was so, so good," Ophelia gushed, joining in on Katie and Vivy's conversation.

"Huh?" Katie blurted. Vivy had seen the girl planning compliments in her periphery, so she wasn't surprised by it, but Katie appeared to be caught off guard. Her eyes widened as she froze in place, and only once her expression returned to normal did she reply, "Oh, thanks. Makes me really happy to get a compliment from you, Ophelia."

"Y-your dancing was really pretty too. And so skillful! Your singing carried a long way, and your stage outfit is so cute, and— agh!" Ophelia bit down hard on her tongue.

Vivy had never heard of an inarticulate or clumsy AI, but humans might have wanted some to appear that way, since they preferred a few charming flaws over total perfection. She wasn't sure if it was a good thing for a songstress, though.

Ophelia blushed, visibly shocked. "Oops..."

The mechanism that changed an AI's face color in response to emotional patterns was the masterpiece of renowned AI researcher Karen Anderson, who had the friendly nickname of "Red Face." The function came standard in many AIs, and even Vivy herself was equipped with it. She didn't have many opportunities to make use of it, but her face could turn red.

Ophelia's cheeks flushed deeper scarlet in her embarrassment.

Katie was taken aback to see it happen right in front of her eyes, and she let out a snort of laughter. "Ah ha ha! Wow, you're way friendlier than I thought you'd be, Ophelia. I had this impression you'd be hard to get close to—and pickier. A bit of a letdown, actually."

"I-I'm sorry for being such a disgrace..."

"Not at all. I'm actually kind of relieved now that I've gotten a glimpse of your personality." Katie patted her chest, glittering in her glamorous stage outfit, and let out a sigh of relief. Ophelia shrank away as Katie smiled at her.

Setting aside whether Ophelia was approachable, Vivy had now seen that Ophelia could carry a conversation, so it struck her as odd that everyone had given the girl such a wide berth when she arrived at the venue. Vivy had no idea where the overwhelming presence she'd felt during Ophelia's arrival had come from. While she didn't find it peculiar that Ophelia was surrounded by helpful people, like those who had come to her aid when she tripped on her dress, Vivy thought it unusual for an AI to be at the center of such a commotion.

"Diva, you're up next for rehearsal. Please take your position!" said a staff member, interrupting Vivy's contemplation.

"Understood," Vivy replied before walking onstage.

Unlike the modern songstresses' performances, which involved leaping and bounding, Diva's performance was a simple solo. It was the same as her shows at NiaLand—except the venue, costumes, and staging were of a different order of magnitude. The AIs experienced something akin to being deeply moved, even if they didn't feel nervousness.

"I imagine it's a fresh experience to look out at the seats from a new stage," Matsumoto said.

"You're not wrong. I'm blessed with this experience because Diva has continued to sing. I have those memories too," Vivy replied.

She followed the director's orders, making minor corrections based on the data she received. A festival of this size would be tweaked based on how all the songstresses' performances turned out, and Vivy quietly implemented the necessary changes as she prepared for her festival solo.

"You're taking this very seriously even though it's not even your role to sing," Matsumoto said.

"That's exactly why I have to take it so seriously."

Diva's performances had gotten her invited to this event. Plenty of people would be looking forward to seeing her sing on this very stage. Vivy had stolen this valuable experience from Diva, and so she had to perform in earnest.

"All right, Diva," the director said. "Give us a quick run-through of your song. Then we'll move on."

||||||||||||

Even though Vivy had been certain until then, she froze the moment she got the order to sing. She faltered for reasons she didn't understand. Oblivious to Vivy's hesitation, the background music for her solo began to play, bringing her cue closer and closer.

"..."

She asked herself why she was wavering. It was just as she'd calculated before. This performance was for Diva, but Vivy was

THE SONGSTRESSES' FESTIVAL   47

doing the rehearsal in her stead. She had to do it well. The more
her calculations ran through that fact, the more errors filled her
vision, blocking it out and burying her viewscreen. Every error
said THIS IS DIVA'S PERFORMANCE.

"*Matsumoto!*" Vivy called to him as if spurning the first lines
of song that were coming right at her.

He reacted immediately, interfering with the venue's equipment. The music stopped, and Vivy's scheduled rehearsal was
forcefully overwritten.

"Huh? Why'd the music stop?" asked one staff member.

Another cut in, "Augh! Stop, stop! We're behind schedule on
the rehearsals—we can let Diva get by without one. She's been
doing this for decades, and she's not one of the dancing songstresses anyway."

"Uh... Well, I guess that's true. Okay, then. Diva, your rehearsal's over. Give us a good performance tonight!"

While some of the staff puzzled over the music stopping, they
accepted the orders and moved on. The schedule and concert
program were handled mostly by machines, which created an
environment where few humans ever questioned what was written in the data. That, and Matsumoto's hacking skills were still
top-tier, even in this era.

Vivy walked off the stage, as if nothing out of the ordinary
had happened, and returned to Ophelia and Katie in the wings.

"Oh man, it sucks that we're so behind you can't do your rehearsal," said Katie. "I really wanted to actually hear you sing... I
wonder if we're running late because I was jumping around? Sorry."

Katie made a cute little bow of apology, but Vivy shook her head. Katie hadn't done anything wrong. In fact, Matsumoto was largely responsible for the hiccup. Vivy felt guilty being on the other end of Katie's apology—although there was no room in her consciousness for it to linger.

"Don't you think it's sad, Ophelia? We can't hear the eldest—uh, Ophelia?" When Katie turned toward Ophelia to lighten the mood, her brows shot up.

Ophelia's whole demeanor had changed, and she hadn't spoken since Vivy had come back. She paid no attention to Vivy or to Katie. Her wide, black eyes were fixed on the stage without so much as a glimmer.

"Ophelia, you're up for rehearsal," the director called.

Her intense concentration gave Ophelia an air that didn't suit an AI. She walked onstage without another word, then stopped in the center and faced straight ahead. The plan was for her to perform a solo like Diva's—or rather, Vivy's—where she moved very little, instead showcasing her singing. However, Ophelia's performance would go ahead as planned without interference from Matsumoto. The musical accompaniment began to play, and Ophelia waited for the right moment to sing.

No sooner did she hit the first notes than the full force of the Songstress Specialized Model rushed into Vivy's consciousness.

Vivy whispered, "Oh..."

Ophelia's voice, which produced pink noise, synthesized the very best modern singing technology in a way that made full use of AI capabilities. Her voice was literally perfect—that was all there was to it.

If you broke down a song into its simplest components and examined them, you could theoretically arrange them into a high-quality product. But listening to Ophelia's song sparked something like the enjoyment you'd get from eating good food, the emotional roller coaster of a story, the thrum of your heart when you studied a painting.

This wasn't about logic. This was what it meant to be entranced.

Vivy, an AI created to be a songstress, immediately began gathering data to master her own singing function. And she wasn't the only one; Katie was beside her doing the exact same thing. A songstress AI—or really any AI—was fated to hone their skills as much as possible in order to serve humanity, which meant their consciousnesses became enraptured by extraordinary things. Ophelia's voice was one of them.

｜⊪⊪⊪⊪⊪｜

It didn't matter that this was just a rehearsal. Ophelia gave the song her all, leaving everyone—AI or human—spellbound and unmoving even after she finished. Only the mechanical AIs that lacked consciousness were unaffected. They performed their automated tasks to ensure Ophelia's performance went off without a hitch, adjusting the lights and operating the stage equipment.

After a short silence, Ophelia expressed something else in that pink noise voice of hers: a mutter of self-derision. "This isn't it..."

Only then did the listeners snap back to their senses.

.:6:.

THE ZODIAC SIGNS FESTIVAL rehearsals concluded without issue. Now that the songstresses' set lists had been confirmed, they only needed to wait a few hours for the event to begin. Unlike the other songstresses and staff members, who were wound ever tighter as opening time drew near, Vivy's consciousness was branded with Ophelia's voice—and the enigmatic expression she'd made at the very end of her rehearsal.

"The number of times you've referred to your memories is abnormally high, Vivy. And in such a short time too. It's unlike you."

"Matsumoto?!"

Vivy had returned to her dressing room and was about to make a wired connection to the terminal there when she heard a familiar voice. She showed her surprised emotional pattern and whirled around. There, she saw a male humanoid AI she didn't recognize standing in the doorway. His model was that of a young man, somewhere around twenty years old in appearance. Notably, his voiceprint data had Matsumoto's digital signature, and he wore an event staff T-shirt. Vivy narrowed her eyes and glared at the male AI, wondering if this was some tasteless joke.

"Huh, you don't seem that surprised," he said. "I didn't tell you about this because I was hoping to give you a shock."

"It doesn't matter what form you're in—you are always *you*. But...what's with that body?"

"Oh, you know, I took over the positronic brain of some AI walking around outside... Just joking. I wouldn't do that, so don't worry. I just borrowed a body from an OGC warehouse before it had its positronic brain put in. I'm basically controlling an empty-headed frame remotely, since it's hard for me to physically follow you in this situation."

"Uh, isn't that always the case?" Vivy furrowed her brows in suspicion, wondering why Matsumoto would go out of his way to come to the venue in a humanoid frame.

The only reason he avoided acting in public was because his base technology didn't exist in this time period. He and Vivy could only exert influence on history in the narrow scope of the Singularity Points. There seemed to be an unwritten rule making it impossible for them to go beyond that.

Thus, Matsumoto had largely only been able to follow Vivy behind the scenes up until now.

"Things are different this time," said Matsumoto. "One of us has to be with Ophelia at all times in case she tries something when she's alone."

"So we can prevent Ophelia's Suicide?"

"Correct. And the way to ensure that would be to—"

"Destroy her before she can kill herself?"

"You're still holding a grudge about Estella and Grace, aren't you?" Matsumoto's temporary body flashed a humanlike lop-sided grin. It was smooth, but the borrowed frame just couldn't fully recreate Matsumoto's expressiveness. Oddly, Vivy couldn't help thinking his cube form was more expressive than this one. "Anyway, I've already modified the venue's staff list and put myself on it as an AI staff member. If you run into any problems, just call good old 'Inaba' here."

"Inaba...? All right. Also, if you're going to be working in that frame, you should avoid doing anything extreme. The venue staff know their AI models, so they'll probably notice you acting differently than expected."

He nodded, his next smile just as lacking as the first. "I'll store that tidbit away in my brain. Not that this frame *has* a brain." Matsumoto was just as long-winded as ever.

She watched him, but her questions remained. Why was Matsumoto going to the effort of preparing a borrowed frame this time? Why did he want to be so involved?

"Is there...a songstress you want to meet?" she asked.

"Vivy, you are the only songstress for me. Ooh, does saying that make your maiden circuit run at high speeds? Does it make your chest grow hot?"

"I've never heard of a maiden circuit, nor do I have one. Stop avoiding the question."

Vivy preferred not to be the target of such flattery or to be treated like a proper songstress—especially after she'd heard Ophelia sing. To compare herself to one capable of producing a perfect voice, while she hadn't even been able to carry out her rehearsal, was a travesty deserving of divine punishment.

In spite of her internal conflict, Matsumoto just shrugged.

"As you already know, the best way to prevent Ophelia's Suicide is to keep an eye on her. Considering your position in this event, it'll be hard for you to be with her all the time. That's where I come in."

"She probably leapt off the roof to escape the torture of being stalked by a creepy AI."

"There are a lot of time travel books and movies that turn into that sort of 'chicken or the egg' situation. But don't worry about that. At least with me here, we'll always have eyes on Ophelia."

"I feel like it would've been fine if you hadn't bothered to come and I kept an eye on her myself."

"You had your rehearsal to focus on, to say nothing of your performance later. What would you do about that?"

"Worst case, I just don't go on stage. I need to prioritize the Singularity Project over a single performance. It should be easy for you to modify the records."

They did have the option of eliminating Diva's performance by making up some excuse before she went on, like mechanical failure. The Singularity Project was more important to her than singing—it was her mission. That mindset was the only thing that had brought her this far. And yet...

"I'm here so you don't have to do that," said Matsumoto. "Vivy, please take the stage today. You should sing."

"Why?"

"Well, in the original history, Diva carried out her solo in the event. If we leave a hole in the program, it'll have a knock-on effect and eventually impede the Singularity Project. You're getting your priorities backward if you're losing sight of the long-term in your rush to accomplish a short-term goal."

"…"

He was right. Vivy's resistance to performing had nothing to do with Matsumoto, and his input was logical enough. Rather, her hesitancy stemmed from the doubts and considerations nesting in her own consciousness.

Just as Matsumoto had said, they could surveil Ophelia without any gaps as long as they worked together. Since Matsumoto had already modified the staff list, and he was already here wandering around in a borrowed frame, no one involved in the event would question his presence. He wasn't the problem—Vivy was.

Could she even sing? When it was Diva's time to take the stage, could Vivy sing in her place? She couldn't escape the conundrum.

"Tell me everything about Ophelia's Suicide," she said.

"Of course. But we're short on time, so let's do it in The Archive."

As Matsumoto suggested, the two sent their consciousnesses into the created world. Conversations conducted in there took only a moment in real time.

"Now then, time for my beautiful, lovable self to come out!" Matsumoto said, appearing in his cube form in the middle of the music room. "You know, this form is so comfortable. It's like coming home."

Vivy ignored him and opened the sheet music on one of the stands to view the data regarding Ophelia's Suicide. The data that materialized on the paper's surface was just a repeat of what Matsumoto had already told her.

During the Zodiac Signs Festival, Ophelia—the newest addition to the Sisters Series—jumped off the roof of a building near the arena with the intent to kill herself. She was no longer operational by the time she was found. Her shoes were neatly set side by side at the spot from which it was assumed she jumped, but there didn't appear to be a note or message of any kind. Two things remained a mystery: why she had done it, and what had allowed her to break cardinal AI rules against self-harm.

"Ophelia becoming nonoperational led to a debate on whether AIs had lives and souls," Vivy said.

While she examined the data, Matsumoto described the incidents that followed according to memory. "After Ophelia, a spate of AIs committed 'suicide.' Considering how fatally flawed their judgment was, you could potentially argue that volunteering to destroy themselves was actually their way of giving one last service to humanity. It's just..."

When he trailed off, Vivy understood why. Her eyes passed over the same information, and she drew in her chin.

"Is there a chance it wasn't suicide but murder?" she asked.

"It would actually be 'destruction of property,' but the destruction of AIs is a worse crime than that, so perhaps it was already treated as destruction of valuable property in this era."

This wasn't the time to be arguing semantics, but Vivy couldn't help grimacing at his words. According to the data, suspicions of murder surrounded Ophelia's Suicide, although the investigating authorities in the original history would likely have discovered some sort of proof.

"Ophelia committing suicide was more convenient for the AI rights groups," Matsumoto explained. "Besides, people love tragedies. If they can't change what happened, they want it to be as dramatic as possible. Humans don't want to know if it's true or not."

"But if Ophelia was destroyed by someone, then—"

"As a fellow AI, it makes me angry to consider. She was made to sing, not to be propped up as propaganda."

Vivy quietly closed the sheet music. She knew basically everything there was to know about Ophelia's Suicide. There had been one suspect after the incident, but the authorities lacked sufficient evidence to charge him, and he'd disappeared after he was released. The investigation dried up there.

"That suspect was a man named Makime Ryousuke," Vivy noted.

"He's our current prime suspect too. We'll need to be wary. Just to let you know, he does have a ticket for today's festival. He'll be here."

"Will he destroy Ophelia?"

"I personally believe that to be the most likely outcome. He also evaded the investigation somehow, which is how the incident was ruled a suicide. But if he didn't do it…"

Matsumoto trailed off into a meaningful silence. He looked at Vivy, the shutter of his mechanical eye camera narrowing with complex emotion.

"Then the stories about Ophelia's Suicide may very well be true."

CHAPTER 2

The Songstress and the
Ones Who Love Her

.: 1 :.

VIVY AND MATSUMOTO CAME BACK to the dressing room, their secret meeting complete. Their conversation in The Archive had taken only a few seconds in real time. That was one benefit AIs had when communicating with each other. Nothing had changed yet, but they had a good deal of information about the situation. They still had to hurry in order to save Ophelia.

"Did our peerless songstress Ophelia kill herself, or was it murder? We'll find out...after this commercial break!" Matsumoto said, stepping out of the dressing room.

Vivy hurried after him, speed-walking to match his long strides. "Don't joke about something like that."

The AI named Inaba had a right to be in the venue, so no one took issue with Matsumoto accompanying Vivy. Nevertheless, a weight resembling fatigue sat heavy on Vivy's consciousness.

"..."

She stored the invisible sensation in her logs as she came to a stop, noticing a section of the Touto Dome that had been turned into a gallery of some sort. There were a variety of curious objects on display, as if this were an exhibition of a child's toybox. Vivy had to wonder what the space was being used for. The doors weren't yet open for the event, so there wasn't anyone around except for staff, but soon the space would be packed with guests.

"It's a record of the songstresses," Matsumoto said, sounding impressed. He'd stopped beside her to gaze at the same thing. He stood up a little taller, tilting his head. "I feel a bit like a fish out of water in this frame... Anyway, the twelve songstresses are the headliners of the event. This display shows off their roots. It makes sense that people would be interested in what made the songstresses who they are today. Actually, there was a museum in my era with an exhibit on AIs, including the Sisters."

"Did that include my—Diva's frame?"

"It did. The oldest songstress was one of the crown jewels of the museum's collection. They claimed it was a triumph of human innovation that the old clunker maintained her original form for such a long time."

"Hm."

"Also, people marveled that she was treated with such care as to survive all that time. Something along those lines, anyway. I won't tell you the details, since it's related to history."

"Mm."

Vivy kept her eyes fixed on the array of artifacts, unconcerned about the additional information. Even if all twelve of them were categorized as songstresses, the scope of their work and their methods were so varied. This was apparent in the way they sang onstage.

These days, AIs who danced around as they sang—like idols—
were quite popular. Katie was the leader of the pack among those
modern songstresses, a rising star. She had been given a larger
portion of the exhibition space than any other songstress.

By contrast, Diva's section seemed small and plain. She was
recognized like the rest of them, but her singing style was old,
left behind by the changing tides of time. Even her music selection lacked the power needed to excite younger generations. Still,
Vivy felt she caught glimpses of the staff's devotion through the
way they carefully prepared her items, but maybe she was just
being sentimental.

All of the objects on display for Diva were, as expected, things
Vivy had strong emotional ties to as well. There was the standing
mic she'd used at her very first performance, her very first letter
from a fan, and handmade trinkets and accessories. There was
even the medal she received from the Prime Minister, honoring
her accomplishments at NiaLand. Those were the sorts of in-
valuable objects documenting her life. She could probably view
records about each and every one of the items if she looked at or
touched them.

But Vivy only silently gazed at them from a distance. She
didn't approach the artifacts, let alone hold any for herself.
Matsumoto stood beside her, a puzzled expression on his face.
Before he could ask, Vivy spotted another figure in the space and
said, "Isn't that Ophelia?"

A single glance was enough to tell her that the black-haired,
black-clothed figure was indeed Ophelia, even if they were seeing

her from behind. She was standing completely still at the very back of the exhibition area, unaware of Vivy and Matsumoto's presence. If the size of each display correlated to the public's expectations of its songstress, then what Ophelia was looking at represented the one carrying the highest hopes of all.

It was in fact the peerless songstress Ophelia's section, and the enormous memento there resonated with purpose: A giant, non-humanoid, multipurpose frame had been put on solemn display. The engraved nameplate below marked him as "Antonio."

"Antonio..." The moment after she saw him, Vivy's consciousness brought back the data she'd viewed in The Archive.

Antonio. That name carried an importance that couldn't be overstated in discussing Ophelia. The soundmaster AI named Antonio had been designed to push Ophelia to even greater heights. He had been her partner. As all of Ophelia's specs had been curated toward her role as a Songstress Specialization Model, Antonio's job had been to support her in any musical aspects besides singing. Records indicated he had been by her side for years, since she first began operating.

But that had come to an end.

"Antonio stopped functioning several years ago," Matsumoto explained as he watched Ophelia. "The cause was assumed to be a defect in his positronic brain, but the source of that defect remains a mystery even in my time... He was also the reason the world wanted to believe the lie of Ophelia's Suicide."

Vivy's eye cameras narrowed as she realized the reason people yearned for tragedy in the original history: They wanted to believe

Ophelia had followed her partner, Antonio, into death. Even though Ophelia's partner AI had stopped operating for reasons unknown, she had bounced back from this misfortune until she was bathed in the spotlight of every stage imaginable. And yet, during the event that was supposed to be the pinnacle of her career, she somehow broke the rule preventing AIs from self-harm and hurled herself into a cold, snowy night with no one watching. The story lit a fire in the hearts of anyone who believed AIs had souls. It was simple irony that this fire also sparked the war between humanity and AIs.

Once Vivy was done reviewing the data, she made up her mind to act. "Ophelia!"

"Oneesama?" Ophelia turned to Vivy, her expression tense—almost disbelieving.

"What's wrong? Why are you making that face?" asked Vivy.

"Um, well, it's just... I-I'm a bit surprised."

"Surprised?"

"Wh-when everyone saw me sing, the other girls and the staff... They didn't really come near me after that. So, erm, I thought...y-you wouldn't either..." Ophelia stammered, her long-lashed eyes aimed at the floor.

Her words made Vivy think back to the atmosphere after Ophelia's rehearsal. She'd shown off an overwhelming voice and power appropriate for a real show. Immediately after, she expressed disappointment in herself. There was something horrific about hearing a voice so magnificent—and then hearing the singer disparage it as though it were nothing. The staff had pulled themselves together afterward and ended rehearsals. Ophelia had left the stage, and even Katie hadn't been able to manage an encouraging word. Vivy had also been swallowed by Ophelia's voice, but not because she felt threatened by it or because she was afraid of how Ophelia had acted afterward.

"Your singing at rehearsal was incredible," said Vivy. "So incredible, I couldn't move. My learning function was in overdrive."

An AI's programming was constantly updating so they could improve themselves. They took in stimuli from humans and other AIs to store and examine experiences with their learning function. When the stimulus came from a field closely related to an AI's identity, their processing power could be affected. Vivy was greatly influenced by other songstresses—as was Diva, of course. That influence was even stronger when it came to Ophelia, a songstress deserving of her "peerless" reputation.

"The other girls also needed some time to stabilize after the stimulus, that's all," Vivy went on. "I'm sure they'll want to talk to you again soon. Don't worry."

"Maybe. You're just special, Diva-oneesama. That's why you've already..."

"It's probably just because I've been operating for so long. There's not that much room left for improvement in me."

"That's not true!" Ophelia's voice rose, and she stepped closer to Vivy. It was a stark change from her former unsteadiness.

Vivy had accidentally chosen words more suited for talking to Matsumoto, and she was surprised by Ophelia's sudden ferocity.

Ophelia paid it no mind as she said, "I gathered all the video and audio recordings of your performances at NiaLand. I listened to every single song I could get my hands on. I mean *all* of them, from your very first performances in the year you started operating to the ones from this year. And they're—well, they're totally different. Your singing's still getting better, yet I..."

"..."

"I'm not changing at all. Not one bit..."

Ophelia's expression was racked with fierce pain rather than sorrow. There was no sign of the weak, unreliable songstress from before. She was now expressing a tenacity so powerful it made her tremble—an insatiable obsession with singing, a thirst for improvement.

ılıı||||ıılıı

Vivy was so shocked that her consciousness momentarily blanked. Ophelia probably hadn't only gathered Diva's data in her quest for improvement. She looked so threateningly determined that Vivy could easily believe she'd collected and listened to data on all the other songstresses in the festival, or even all the songstresses in the world whose data she could get her hands on.

There was a despair in Ophelia that only she understood. She put in so much effort, yet she never reached the standards she set for herself. Vivy sensed that her emotions were dangerously powerful. Powerful enough to make Vivy wonder if the story about Ophelia's Suicide was true. If an AI felt emotional patterns this powerful, perhaps they could become pessimistic enough about their future to be able to throw themselves off a building.

Vivy changed tack, trying to pretend the thought—one hardly appropriate for an AI—hadn't just flitted through her consciousness. "What kind of AI was Antonio?"

Ophelia's eyes grew round, and her agitation subsided. "Antonio," she said, the name sticking in her mouth. "He was my partner. His mission was to be my soundmaster..."

"I know that. He was an audio AI modified just for you... But you made it all the way to this stage without him. I get the feeling you exceeded everyone's expectations," Vivy said, making a guess based on reference data since Ophelia had only given her a surface-level response.

There actually hadn't been high expectations for Ophelia and Antonio in the beginning. The Songstress Specialized Model and her support AI were an experiment, and often considered a failed one. Putting too much emphasis on her singing ability had resulted in her being far inferior in other areas when compared to standard AIs. It also had had an impact on her incomplete disposition, creating a shyness unusual in AIs.

As a result, the two were sent to a small theater, far from the grand stage they wanted, and Antonio stopped operating before he could ever make it out of there. Ophelia's incredible progress had all happened after Antonio became nonoperational.

"Your specs were designed with the presumption you'd be with your partner, yet you've actually been able to make better use of your functionality since he ceased functioning. It's almost like—"

"Like Antonio was a dead weight?"

"I wouldn't say that..." But Vivy also couldn't help making a similar assumption based on what Ophelia was accomplishing these days.

If Ophelia were human, one could argue she had been spurred on by the death of a loved one and the desire to honor his memory, and that the tragedy had acted as a catalyst for her improvement.

"We're AIs. Miracles like that don't happen," Vivy muttered.

"You're right, my voice isn't much different with or without him. It's just...*where* I'm performing has changed, and so has the way I think about it."

"..."

"Antonio was the only one who ever believed we'd spread my voice throughout the world. And I always just said, 'One day...' He was the only one who was serious." There was a hint of nostalgia in her voice as she looked at Antonio's frame. There was also some longing for the days with her partner at the small theater. Her narrowed eye cameras, made to resemble black eyes, showed the change in emotions.

Watching her, Vivy could tell Ophelia still had some regrets regarding Antonio. But from an AI perspective, it was unbelievable that her feelings toward her partner would be the trigger that sent her to join him in death.

"Let's make today's performance a success. For him," Vivy said.

"Oh..."

Vivy reached out to the display of Antonio, picked up one of the artificial flowers decorating his stand, and tucked it in

Ophelia's black hair. The white petals stood out, adding a final pop to her all-black ensemble.

"Hm, maybe it'd be better to take a piece of Antonio with you?"

"If we did that, it might cause trouble for the staff. Thank you." Ophelia touched the flower and smiled.

Vivy felt an emotional pattern similar to relief seeing the change on Ophelia's gloomy face.

"Er, by the way, Diva-oneesama..."

"Yeah?"

"Wh-who's that fellow? The staff member who's been watching us from over there the whole time..."

Vivy whirled around with a suspicious look. Matsumoto was standing near the entrance to the exhibition space, looking bored. When he noticed Vivy and Ophelia staring at him, he offered a weak smile and a wave.

"Is he...a staff member assigned to you, oneesama?"

"He's one of the venue staff. I talked to him a bit because he looked new to the job. If he's bothering you, I'll get rid of him."

Vivy hadn't been speaking loudly, but Matsumoto enthusiastically jumped in the moment he became the topic of conversation. "Wait, wait, wait! Just a moment, please. That's a bit much!"

Ophelia blanched as Matsumoto scurried over, but he stood in front of her before she could escape.

"I apologize for not introducing myself earlier," he said. "I was waiting for the right moment, hoping Diva would be so kind as to introduce us, but the opportunity never presented itself. You know, I was just thinking to myself how strange it was that someone like me, blessed by their creators with life, would suffer such misfortune. I nearly gave up!"

While Ophelia reeled at his hasty approach, Vivy stepped in front of her with a meaningful glare at Matsumoto.

"I don't get what you're up to," she said. "What do you gain by meeting her?"

"Please don't reduce relationships to simple gains and losses," he replied. "Am I so awful for interrupting your precious sisterly date?"

"You're awful for other reasons."

"Wowie! A simple 'no' would've been more than enough." Matsumoto's shoulders slumped in a weary, comical way. Considering he appeared to be a fairly respectable male AI, the gesture made him look like a buffoon.

Even though he was in a different form, it was obviously still Matsumoto. As he made great use of his conversation skills, Vivy glanced over her shoulder, afraid of how Ophelia was reacting. She was a rather withdrawn AI, and Vivy hoped she wasn't afraid of Matsumoto. Luckily, Vivy's concerns were unfounded.

"You seem to be close with oneesama, umm...?"

"Call me Inaba. I'm on staff for the Zodiac Signs Festival today, so feel free to make use of my services, Ophelia-sama." Matsumoto knelt before her. "I will triumph through any hardship to accomplish whatever you ask of me, even if it costs me my life. Not that I'm alive," he added in an exaggerated fashion, like a court jester might.

"Hee hee. Thank you, Inaba-san."

Vivy was surprised by how adaptable Ophelia was in her reactions to Matsumoto.

When she asked about it, Ophelia smiled and said, "I used to sing in operas and at the theater. That's why...having Inaba-san do this sort of, um, playacting, is something I'm..."

"Used to hearing? Seeing? Even though it's totally unrealistic," said Vivy.

"I'm not sure if I should take that as a compliment or an insult," Matsumoto said with a grimace. His expression made Ophelia's smile grow wider, and Vivy couldn't help a little smirk of her own at that.

Watching Ophelia engage in such open conversation was surprisingly pleasant. Evidently, Ophelia was able to be herself in front of Diva, the eldest of their Sisters Series. There was definitely something special there, as there had been when Vivy was with Estella and Elizabeth, and she could understand why they felt like sisters.

"We shouldn't let ourselves get swept away for too long," Vivy said then.

"What?"

The longer Vivy enjoyed the moment, the more the familiar error logs piled up inside of her, creating an unnecessary buildup for Diva. Vivy was carrying out the Singularity Project. She was an AI who would destroy AIs in order to save humanity—no more, no less.

"We have some free time until the performances, but I think I should head back to my dressing room. I'm sure you have your pre-performance routine too, right, Ophelia?"

"Ah, yes... I have to review the video of my rehearsal..."

Vivy had a feeling Ophelia wouldn't just be viewing that rehearsal video a couple of hundred or a couple of thousand times, but tens of thousands of times.

"Oh, right! Inaba-san, did you hear my rehearsal?" asked Ophelia, the idea seemingly coming to her as they moved away from the exhibition space.

Matsumoto's eyebrows shot up, like he was being attacked with his defenses down.

"..."

The truth was that he hadn't been physically present at the rehearsal but had heard the whole thing through transmission with Vivy. Even if he hadn't, he knew Vivy had reviewed her recording of Ophelia's rehearsal several dozen times. He couldn't talk his way out of this one.

"Well, Inaba-san?" Ophelia prompted.

"Uh...of course I heard it. I heard everyone sing, but you were by far the most incredible. There's no doubt that out of all the songstresses present, you are the peerless songstress, taking the music awards in every single category!"

"Peerless songstress...? In that case, can I...ask you something?"

"Yes, yes, of course! What is it?"

Vivy was impressed by the unbroken stream of compliments that came out of Matsumoto's mouth. The silver-tongued AI looked at Ophelia expectantly.

She waited a moment, then asked, "Did my singing make you cry?"

"Make me *cry*?" Matsumoto's eyebrows rose again, as did Vivy's as she listened to their conversation.

AIs didn't cry. There were fewer differences in how humans and AIs looked nowadays, and AIs had gained many functions allowing them to better replicate humanity, but certain mechanisms were considered taboo: They couldn't bleed a red liquid if injured, and they couldn't cry a clear liquid if they became emotional.

Blood and tears were both important components of a human body and were treated as off-limits when it came to AIs. The first, blood, wasn't allowed in AIs because it could muddy important judgments at the scene of an accident. The second, tears, were considered just as important to the human identity. Even after all these decades, Matsumoto's joke about a robot that shed neither blood nor tears was still accurate. It was just a matter of fact regarding AI composition.

And so, Ophelia's question seemed ridiculously off the mark. There were some AIs who underwent illegal modifications allowing them to shed a clear liquid from their eyes during a sad emotional pattern, but they were very rare exceptions.

"Well now! If my frame were equipped with a function that allowed me to cry, then I absolutely would've had waterfalls pouring down my face during your rehearsal! My flowing tears would have turned into an ocean that swept the entire arena away! Oh, how lucky we are I don't have it!"

In his usual way, Matsumoto used far too many words and a roundabout path to get to his point, but it was a passable attempt at talking himself out of the situation. In the end, there was no other way of answering the question, seeing as it was unlikely Ophelia was trying to determine if Inaba—an AI she just met—had undergone illegal modifications in order to cry.

Ophelia's response came as a shock to both of them.

"I knew it... My singing's absolutely worthless..."

Her voice was a curse upon the whole world. Just as she had during rehearsals, she expressed loathing toward her peerless voice, like it was some sort of inescapable nightmare.

.:2:.

"**D**ID I SAY SOMETHING WRONG?" Matsumoto asked once they returned to Vivy's dressing room after walking Ophelia to hers. He was second-guessing himself after Ophelia's extreme reaction, but Vivy didn't know what the right answer would have been.

"Maybe you should have jabbed your finger into your eye camera and let the protective fluid in your skull run out of your eye socket?"

"That is terrifying, Vivy. I don't want to get crazy with this frame, since I'm just borrowing it. Inaba might not have a positronic brain installed yet, but I would like to return him safe and sound to the warehouse he came from." Matsumoto was having an easier time moving around by now, and he seemed more comfortable in his artificial skin.

Vivy glanced sideways at him and thought back to what Ophelia had said, contemplating what thoughts could have possibly been going through the girl's consciousness.

"Did my singing make you cry?" Her question alone had been absurd, but she'd asked Matsumoto of all AIs—one incapable of crying.

"..."

Vivy had access to memories from when Diva was operating and was aware that some humans cried when overcome with emotion at her performances. Moments like that, when she elicited such an intense response, gave her a sense of accomplishment toward her ultimate goal as a songstress.

But that was a completely different story from an AI crying. AIs didn't have the mechanism to cry. So then, was Ophelia's question just a theoretical one? If so, Matsumoto's answer that essentially boiled down to "if I were human, I would have cried," should have passed with flying colors.

"But your answer made Ophelia decide her singing was worthless... Maybe she took what you said as a poor attempt at flattery?" Vivy suggested.

"Hold up just a second. I won't argue with the fact that maybe I go a little overboard compared to the average value for word selection in AIs, but I really don't think this has anything to do with a failure on my part. Maybe she's just the kind of person who likes to make fools of others by telling riddles."

"I don't think she's the type to test other AIs. She's more likely to test herself."

"You're saying she's predisposed to wanting capability beyond her specs? If that's the case, things are going to be difficult." There was a hint of worry in Matsumoto's voice.

Vivy thought back to Ophelia's obsession with singing and nodded firmly.

"It's normal for AIs to want to hone and master their skills," Matsumoto continued, "but it's a different story when they start to want something beyond their limits. That phenomenon's more likely to occur when an AI has another AI to compare themselves to, but Ophelia seems to be a special case."

There was a phenomenon called "ambition-induced grief"— a condition that could occur in AIs because of the different characteristics in each positronic brain. Explained simply, it was when an AI became locked into calculations in an attempt to close the skill gaps between them and other AIs.

The phenomenon typically occurred in individuals from the same series between older and newer models. In those cases, it didn't matter that they were both made with the same concept in mind—the newer model would inevitably demonstrate more excellent characteristics. And, as an AI couldn't go against their programmed directive of self-improvement, they might begin to desire abilities beyond the limits of their specs. They'd become stuck in a loop of calculations and eventually overheat. It was sad enough if that caused a temporary freeze, but they didn't always get away that easily.

"Sometimes the positronic brain catches fire, which makes the AI permanently nonoperational," Vivy said.

"Perhaps Ophelia's Suicide was caused by her desire for an ideal she couldn't achieve. If that's the case..."

"Yes?"

"Your suggestion that we destroy her to prevent her suicide becomes more realistic."

"..."

That suggestion had come out as a joke while they'd been chatting, but this time there was a weight that meant all joking was done.

What the Singularity Project was concerned with, and by extension what Matsumoto was concerned with, was not Ophelia's Suicide itself but the change in public opinion and the suicides of several AIs that followed. If they didn't eliminate the underlying cause of Ophelia's self-destruction, there was a chance it would still happen during the Zodiac Signs Festival. The danger existed as long as Ophelia continued to operate.

"But even if an AI predisposed to an obsession with improvement reached the end of their calculations, they couldn't give up on existence and throw themselves off a building," said Vivy.

"..."

"If they managed that, we would have to acknowledge the possibility there is a soul. That can't happen with us AIs. Right, Matsumoto?"

Matsumoto didn't immediately reply. His silence surprised her—and, moreover, sowed seeds of doubt. She had the odd feeling she was forcing her opinion on him. They had the option to destroy Ophelia and make it so her suicide never happened. That was a completely valid strategy and the same one they'd ultimately chosen when dealing with Grace on Metal Float. Despite that, Matsumoto seemed hesitant to do it again, which didn't make any sense to Vivy.

"They say there's no limits to humans' growth," he said at last. "Is there really a limit to AIs' growth? What do you think, Vivy?"

"What are you talking about?"

"An AI's abilities and specifications are all decided at the design stage, and it's not possible to surpass that. You can't lift something heavier than your arm's strength rating, no matter how much you struggle against gravity. But...that's the same for humans, isn't it? The human body can't exhibit capabilities beyond a certain limit. Why, then, would people encourage humans to surpass their limits but deem AIs' to be concrete? It doesn't make sense."

Pessimism hung over him as he continued to talk about something that seemed wholly unrelated to their current conversation. Vivy's brow furrowed as she listened, but she didn't interrupt.

In the end, he seemed slightly frustrated, his face an expression of remorse easily read in his humanoid form. He said, "Maybe Ophelia's pursuit of improvement—even though she has no one to compare herself to—will show AIs a revolutionary way of existing. She's someone who tries to move beyond her limits. Or that's the motive."

"What motive?"

"If suicide wasn't the reason she became nonoperational, then the only other explanation is murder. The AI rights groups used her death as a reason to argue the existence of AI souls, but there were other suspicious aspects. The investigation into Makime Ryousuke, for example."

Vivy grimaced when she heard the name. Makime, the prime suspect in Ophelia's murder, might come to try and destroy

Ophelia. There was a reason why Matsumoto was suspicious of him.

"Does your suspicion have to do with the investigation hitting a dead end pretty early on?" Vivy asked him.

"Yes. Even considering that the investigation into Ophelia's Suicide was abnormal, the leads dried up quite early. I have no doubt there were politicians and activists who supported the AI rights groups at work, but OGC was the biggest contributor."

"OGC... That's the company that develops the Sisters."

"OGC basically bullied their way into recovering Ophelia's frame after she became nonoperational. There are also signs they applied pressure on law enforcement to prevent any further investigation. Makime was arrested as a suspect but then released due to insufficient evidence... It's all just a little too tidy."

It was as if everything surrounding the incident had pushed the conclusion to be suicide. Everything swirled about, keeping everyone from the truth, pushing them further away.

"Let's find out the truth. We'll destroy Ophelia if we run out of all other options," said Vivy.

"Agreed. I have no desire to help those who benefit from making her destruction a 'suicide.' It's irritating."

"..."

"She was designed to sing. She definitely wasn't created so someone could destroy her for their own benefit."

Vivy was fully convinced by Matsumoto's words. Now that they were both on the same page, they could move on to take control of the situation. And, unlike with the situation at Metal

Float, they were going in with the hope they could avoid destroying another Sister.

"Matsumoto, tell me what you know about Makime Ryousuke."

"As of right now, he is the prime suspect. Even if he was working under OGC's orders, there would be no arguing he carried out the crime."

As he spoke, Matsumoto transferred data from his real body to Vivy. She opened the data to find a pudgy, overweight man: Makime Ryousuke. He was thirty-two years old and worked in AV equipment sales. In terms of his relationship with Ophelia, he'd been a fan of hers since her days singing at the small theater. He remained an ardent follower of hers who attended every performance she gave. They met when he visited the small theater for work. He became entranced with her appearance and was always there for her, even when her performances weren't selling. He was the epitome of a diehard fan.

"Even though he was a huge fan of hers, he didn't cross a line. He always maintained a healthy distance and has never caused a problem at an event," said Matsumoto.

"Perhaps so he could avoid drawing attention until the critical moment?"

"In reality, any fans considered dangerous are rejected when they try to buy a ticket. That's not just for Ophelia. It's the same for the passionate fans of all twelve songstresses here...including yours."

"..."

"And Makime Ryousuke is among those who passed that vetting process. He'd be the perfect person to pull off the crime."

Vivy studied the image of Makime Ryousuke while Matsumoto talked. He looked harmless, but a human's personality wasn't reflected in their appearance. With all that in mind, they had to come up with their plan.

"Where is he currently?" she asked.

"He booked a hotel in the city, and there's record of him checking in. Considering he'll be coming to the Zodiac Signs Festival, I imagine it's about time for him to leave."

"Can you follow him through security cameras when he does?"

"In this day and age, you almost never have to worry about blind spots in the security camera network. Long live surveillance companies! Or whatever. We've nearly reached a world where crime can be prevented before it happens!"

"That's not our goal."

After their conversation, Vivy and Matsumoto went their separate ways. Matsumoto would monitor Ophelia, who was still in her dressing room, and Vivy would use her position as a songstress to investigate the movements of the other songstresses and related figures. They kept their transmission circuits open, allowing coordination at any point.

Vivy probed into the movements of people in the venue as she exchanged casual comments with Matsumoto. When she spotted a familiar neat blue bob, she said, "Katie, do you have a moment?"

Katie spun around. "Oh, Diva..." The corners of her mouth stiffened when their eyes met.

Absorbing that humanlike reaction into her own systems, Vivy came to stand by Katie. The other songstress was staring at the main stage, where rehearsals had been held not long ago and where they were currently running final checks.

"Is it part of your routine to check up on the stage before the event?" asked Vivy.

"Yeah, it is. Seeing the staff work so hard gets me pumped up! My consciousness goes 'Yeah, let's make this show happen!' At least, it normally would..."

"Normally? But not now?"

"I'm kind of feeling beaten down. Like I've hit this impossible wall as a songstress." Katie scratched her cheek in a self-conscious mannerism.

Vivy guessed the true nature of this "wall," this feeling of failure she was having, based on her tone. The reason she could was because Diva—inside Vivy—felt something similar in response to Ophelia's performance.

"Hearing Ophelia sing got me thinking," Katie went on. "People have been calling me the rising star of the songstresses, and I think it went to my head. I'm an AI made to sing, but... Ophelia's singing is in a totally different league. You felt it too, didn't you, Diva?"

"I did."

"And her voice was so amazing, but she still wasn't satisfied with it. I...I think I'm using my capabilities to their fullest, but Ophelia's different. She's trying to go *beyond* that."

"..."

"So then, what's the point of the songs I've sung so far? Like, if a songstress is supposed to be aiming for whatever Ophelia's got her eyes set on, then my songs are just..." Katie wrapped her arms around her slender shoulders, her voice and eyes trembling.

This was the thought-processing error that occurred at the extreme end of a demand for improvement, when an AI compared themselves to another unit with the same "concept" and began to question their existence when they didn't match up. At the end of that road was a positronic brain that crashed—or worse—when it lost its reason for being.

"I can't get Ophelia's singing out of my mind. At this rate, I'm—"

"You and Ophelia were designed with different goals in mind. There's no need to compare yourself to her, even if you are both songstresses," said Vivy.

"What...?"

There were only two ways for an AI to avoid their positronic brain crashing when their reason for existence collapsed. The first, and the one many AIs chose, was to shut down their positronic brain. The other was to eliminate the AI they were comparing themselves to. This solution came up as an option under the pretense of the AI protecting themself.

In Vivy's eyes, Katie was standing on the verge of that decision, but neither solution would actually prevent Katie's definition of self from collapsing. If she went with the first option, she would shut down permanently. If she chose the second option, she would be disposed of for being a faulty AI.

As far as Vivy could see in the data on Ophelia's Suicide, Katie didn't shut down and she wasn't disposed of in the original history, which meant this problem was new. Surely if Vivy, acting as Diva, hadn't interacted with Katie and Ophelia, then Katie wouldn't have seen Ophelia's rehearsal. Thus, Vivy was the source of this issue, and she was handling it with that in mind. Thankfully, she'd already prepared the necessary logical argument to fight back against those thoughts for none other than herself.

"You and Ophelia have completely different approaches to your music. She's supposed to improve according to cutting-edge singing technology, while you're supposed to make humans happy."

"..."

"Ophelia's a Songstress Specialized Model. She is different. Don't mix that up."

Vivy was dangerously close to relying on the weight of words like "specialized" to drive her point home, but this sort of logic—which would have fooled a human child—was crucial to AIs. Ophelia's singing voice had shocked Vivy too, to the point that her consciousness was still reeling from it. As it had for Katie, it rocked the foundations of her sense of self as a songstress. She'd only been able to withstand the impact because she had stepped out of the role of a songstress to focus on the Singularity Project.

What if it hadn't been Vivy but Diva who heard Ophelia sing? Diva was part of the Sisters Series just like Ophelia, and the eldest at that. How would she have reacted?

The answer lay with people: Diva's fans, her audience members at NiaLand, and anyone else who listened to her music.

Diva didn't sing for some god of music who might not even exist. She sang to reach all of her fans, and she could see them right in front of her when she sang. She knew they existed.

As part of Diva, Vivy felt an incredible loneliness in Ophelia's song. For what—or whom—did the peerless songstress sing with that incredible voice?

Katie's eyebrows shot up. "Wow, Diva... You were seriously, like, a legit mentor just now."

"A mentor...? Well, thank you for saying so."

"For real, though. I mean it." Katie closed her eyes as if digesting what she'd heard, nodding over and over. "My songs are meant to make people happy—to be heard. They are there so the people who listen to them can have fun. That's...that's the role of Katie the songstress."

"Did the advice from your 'legit mentor' help calm you down?" Vivy asked playfully.

"Yeah... Totally. It absolutely did. I can sing too." Katie brought a hand to her delicate chest, let out a sigh of relief, and smiled sweetly. "I was about to lose myself. I was even afraid for Ophelia."

"She was upset that everyone was staying away from her after hearing her rehearse. You should talk to her the next time you see her. I'm sure that'll be enough to make her feel better."

"I will, right after the concert. Diva...thank you. You really are everyone's oneesama."

"..."

Katie shot Vivy a wink and jogged away, seemingly back

to normal. Watching her go, Vivy figured she wouldn't have to worry about Katie acting erratically before the concert. Who knew what would have happened if they hadn't spoken?

"It's the same feeling you get when you plug a hole in your boat to stop a leak," Matsumoto cut in.

"Ophelia's singing has such an extreme effect."

"It's a threat. Especially around so many AIs who define their existence through their music. I hope Katie was the only one showing those scary symptoms."

"I agree."

As far as Vivy knew, she and Katie were the only two who had heard Ophelia sing, but there was always a possibility some other Zodiac Heroines had been listening. Vivy and Matsumoto had no way of knowing how the other songstresses might respond, so they had to consider the dangers.

"Matsumoto, I have a favor to ask."

"Oh God, what did I get myself into? Actually, this is the first big favor you've asked of me in decades! I think I could manage to use some elbow grease. I'll take care of checking on the other songstresses."

"Thank you."

Matsumoto was piloting Inaba's frame around to investigate the movements of their prime suspect, Makime, while still maintaining surveillance on Ophelia. On top of that, he had to check the stability of the remaining ten songstresses' consciousnesses. He was undoubtedly busy, but Vivy didn't say anything to him other than a short message of support. Over the near-century they'd worked together, Vivy had developed enough trust in him to know he was perfectly capable. Thus, she took it upon herself to head to the next destination—somewhere Matsumoto couldn't reach.

At the arena entrance, Vivy noticed a security guard talking to a middle-aged man. She stopped in her tracks.

"My apologies. Ophelia's given strict orders to not let anyone go in before the concert. I really am sorry, but I'm going to have to ask you to leave."

Something about the exchange triggered an uncanny sensation in her consciousness.

.: 3 :.

"**D**O YOU KNOW OPHELIA?" Vivy called out to the man at the entrance.

"Hm? Uh, and you are...?" He looked perturbed for a moment, then appeared to recognize her and broke into a smile. "Oh, you're Diva! Am I right?"

The man was tall and had to be in his forties. He had pronounced facial features and long, slender limbs. Most notably, his voice carried extremely well. He was an orator, or an actor perhaps. Vivy put the pieces together and concluded that he was from the small theater where Ophelia used to work.

"Should a star of today's festival really be wandering around right before the concert? AIs have their routines before getting on the stage, don't they?" he asked Vivy.

"My routine includes interacting with as many people as I can, even if it is just before the concert. This comes from being a member of the cast at NiaLand. It helps me relax."

"That makes sense. They're scoring against me here, telling me I can't see one of your co-stars." His smile was so friendly, Vivy had to smile back.

While they were talking, she received a transmission from Matsumoto with details on the man.

"You're Ootori Keiji-sama, aren't you?" she said.

"Oh, you're just full of surprises. I can't keep up with a world fast enough to search up us D-list actors in an instant."

"You're the chairman for the theater Ophelia belonged to." Vivy bowed elegantly. "Thank you for looking after my little sister."

"Little sister? Ahh, that's right. I remember now!" He smacked his knee, clearly used to theatrical gestures. "Now *you're* scoring against me too." Smiling pleasantly, he looked around to see a bench just outside the venue and asked Vivy to sit with him.

Vivy accepted his invitation, and they took a seat on the bench.

"Didn't think I could smooth-talk you into this! You're significantly friendlier than I imagined, songstress."

"As I mentioned, I'm a cast member at NiaLand before I'm a songstress. Interacting with people is my duty too. Was it not the same with Ophelia?"

"She's really shy... She opened up quite a bit with the other members of the troupe, but she'd still only make eye contact with a few people. She wouldn't have kept it together if it hadn't been for Antonio." Ootori leaned back against the bench's backrest.

Vivy narrowed her eyes, thinking there was something lonely about him. He was also a potential suspect who knew Ophelia, and his life's work was acting. She had to determine whether he was being honest.

"Have you come to see the Zodiac Signs Festival?" she asked him.

"Well, it's more like I came to see Ophelia. I got a ticket for a reserved seat as a gift from someone involved with the event. I get the impression they kept it a secret from Ophelia, but I'm worried she'll get quite a shock if she sees me in the middle of her performance. Might make her choke."

"You really think she would make a mistake like that?" Vivy blurted out, surprising herself.

Ootori chuckled and scratched his head. "Guess you don't? Thankfully, even though I wasn't able to go in and see her, they did tell her I was here. I think that's probably good enough... Diva, do you think she's incredible too?"

"..."

"You're a songstress AI like her... Actually, you're her older sister. Do you think her singing's so perfect that she couldn't possibly mess up in the middle of a performance?"

Vivy let some time pass before she answered the probing question. When Vivy thought about how focused Ophelia was when she sang, she didn't seem likely to crumble if she looked out into the audience and saw a familiar face—but there was something else about his concern that bothered her.

"It's an unnecessary concern for AIs, Ootori-sama. It's not just

Ophelia either. None of the songstresses here can experience a slipup like that."

"Ah, a blunt answer. To be honest, I agree with you. Part of me even thinks it's an insult to AIs to be worried like that." He paused for a moment. "Yeah, you're right. It's probably just something I hoped for."

"..."

"She probably won't fall to pieces if she sees one of us. I was afraid of what might occur if I saw it happen, so I figured I'd ask you to get it out of my mind... Enough about me, though. What do you think, Diva?"

"This conundrum is difficult to interpret. It's a complicated concern, which is very human."

"And different from you guys—AIs, yeah? Anyway, thanks. I learned something."

Vivy found it difficult to guess at the complex emotions Ootori was experiencing. Wanting to do something, or wanting others to do something, were taboo desires for AIs. Man-made beings weren't allowed to open those doors, yet humans sometimes closed them out of humility or restraint. Vivy perceived Ootori's reason for trying to see Ophelia as coming from a similar place.

Ootori stretched his back out while Vivy was thinking, then beamed and nodded. "I couldn't meet Ophelia, but I still got something out of the attempt. Next, I just need to be there to see her perform and deal with whatever happens."

"What did you want to talk to Ophelia about?"

"Heh. Digging right in, aren't you? I think my intentions have become clear to me after my self-analysis a moment ago. It might not sound fancy, but the main thing I wanted to do was give her a pep talk before the big show. As for the other matter...well, that's not the kind of thing I should talk openly about." He flashed a wide grin, which made him look significantly younger. Vivy felt it suited his position as a chairman, as someone who had others' eyes on him.

"..."

Having seen Ootori look so upset about being asked to leave, Vivy almost suggested they find a way to get him inside. She could probably bring him and Ophelia together if she worked on it. Getting the two to talk would, at the very least, shift some of the reservations she could still see in him. But that hadn't happened in the original history.

Vivy's careless interactions had almost led to fatal errors in songstress Katie. Though she was past that now, Vivy needed every argument at her disposal to resolve the problem. If she recklessly caused another problem, she'd be busy cleaning up her own messes everywhere—and that was a bit too sloppy for the AI upon whose shoulders rested humanity's future.

"What led to Ophelia's departure from the theater?" Vivy asked instead.

Ootori's eyebrows rose. "Well...Ophelia was originally borrowed from the corporation that developed her, along with her partner, Antonio. He was a soundmaster AI. The old man who used to own the troupe had some connection to the company.

The troupe wasn't that big at the time, but the owner used his connections to get a famous musician to come see a show."

"So Ophelia caught the musician's eye and was whisked away from the troupe?" Vivy assumed it was a simple Cinderella story, but Ootori shook his head and smiled ruefully.

"You'd think, wouldn't you? Actually, it was the other way around. He didn't have a favorable impression of her at all. Maybe it upset her, because she went and applied to every music award for AIs there is and scooped them up one after another. That was the birth of the Black Angel, the songstress everyone wanted a piece of."

Rather than a Cinderella story, Ophelia's tale involved her coming up in the world—with a bit of a twist. With his toothy grin, Ootori bowed like he would after a performance. Vivy caught a glimpse of loneliness and worry in his smile.

"I know there's no point in telling an AI not to forget their roots," he said, "but this is such an important show, and I wanted to say it to her beforehand. I just feel like Antonio would have wanted that."

"Ophelia's partner would have?"

"Yeah. They seemed completely mismatched, but they really did suit each other. Antonio had a habit of saying Ophelia would be absolutely worthless without him, and she'd just smile and listen." Ootori looked up at the sky overhead, the same sky that hung over Ophelia's tragedy in the original history, and Vivy felt she'd heard something like this before.

Night was steadily approaching, and with it, the concert. Vivy had nothing to say in response to him and his lonely words.

.:4:.

AFTER VIVY PARTED WAYS with Ootori, Matsumoto reached out. *"Good decision putting the brakes on Mister Ootori meeting Ophelia."*

Evidently, Matsumoto had been discreetly monitoring them. He was multitasking to prevent the tragedy surrounding Ophelia, but he'd assigned some resources to listening in on Vivy and Ootori's conversation.

"I didn't say anything because there was no need for me to barge in," he added. *"I think you made the right call."*

"There's no need to go out of our way to make something happen that diverges from the original history," Vivy said.

"It's better to have as few variables as possible. Right now, one of our few advantages is that we have an idea of what will happen and how, to a degree. Our other advantage is none other than yours truly, the super AI sent back from the future supporting you with my incredible powers."

"As good as your advance reviews might be, I don't remember any of the Singularity Points being easy to modify."

"Huh? Did the transmission lines get crossed? I can't hear you. La-la-la, I can't heeear you!"

Vivy imitated a sigh of annoyance with Matsumoto, who was quick to quip when things weren't going his way. She then reviewed the data she received from Matsumoto, which he'd dug up while she was talking to Ootori. It consisted of everything directly related to the Zodiac Heroines. Thankfully, it didn't appear that any other songstresses had heard Ophelia sing during rehearsals, and none were showing errors like Katie had. Vivy wouldn't need to use her mentor-esque standing as a veteran songstress to encourage a mental revolution in any more of them.

"Vivy, Makime Ryousuke has left his hotel."

"..."

Matsumoto had hacked into the surveillance cameras throughout the city and was following the movements of their prime suspect, Makime, and giving brief updates to Vivy. His report made the alert level in her consciousness jump up a notch.

Makime's movements were proof that the Zodiac Signs Festival would be starting soon. While AIs didn't especially *feel* nervousness, they did experience a stress on their systems from the sheer amount of calculations.

"This is the same Makime Ryousuke we talked about during our pre-incident meeting..." Matsumoto added.

"Can you go meet him in your humanoid AI form? Although I do think the fastest way to deal with him would be for me to go find and restrain him..."

"Don't make me repeat myself, Vivy. We need you—well, Diva— to participate in the Zodiac Signs Festival. If it takes us longer to modify the Singularity Point than planned, it'll be you on the stage, not Diva."

This was the third time Matsumoto had emphasized the importance of Diva being part of the festival, forbidding Vivy from doing anything outside the venue. Vivy understood that Matsumoto was right, which highlighted a problem with something else.

"*There's no point in me working on the Singularity Project,*" she said. "*If you're taking care of both surveillance and dealing with suspicious people, then why am I even here?*"

"*You could get information directly from Ophelia, and you already helped Katie when she was reaching her breaking point. I'd even say that not letting Mister Ootori meet Ophelia was fairly good work. That's not enough for you?*"

"*There's not a single AI who wouldn't be upset when they couldn't fully carry out their mission.*"

"*...*"

"*What's wrong, Matsumoto? You've been acting weird since we came to this Singularity Point. I feel like we're even less in sync than usual.*"

In fact, there were a lot of things Matsumoto had said or done over the last several hours that didn't seem quite right: for example, his plan to have an alternate frame for himself brought in—which he'd never done before—and his insistence that Vivy take the stage. There was no end to how wrong it all felt to her.

Matsumoto stayed quiet for a moment, the static over the transmission the only sound. Then he said, "*I was just thinking about our missions. I was created for the sole purpose of carrying out the Singularity Project. I play a very limited role. And I have such high specs that I can do incredible things, but what I* can *do isn't the same as what I* should *do.*"

"*Our reason for being and the things we should do are important to AIs.*"

"And when I calculated that, I found I could honestly say I was doing what I longed to do. But you... What about you? I looked back at records from the last Singularity Point, and I felt something like emotional pain."

The last Singularity Point was at Metal Float, with Grace at its core. Being made into the core of Metal Float had taken Grace away from her original mission, but she did what was needed of her because she was an AI. Vivy was an AI meant to save humanity, and she'd destroyed Grace in the name of fulfilling her own mission, forever silencing Metal Float.

Vivy didn't regret the outcome. AIs weren't capable of emotions as high and mighty as regret anyway. Both she and Grace were just carrying out their missions in service to humanity. If they were to ever question their reason for being, their service to humanity would come first, and all other missions would follow after. For Diva, that meant serving humanity was the highest priority, and singing came second.

"You don't need to worry about me, Matsumoto. The first thing you and I ever agreed on was that worrying about that would be an insult to us, the AIs carrying out the Singularity Project."

"I'm not sure it's the first ever. Probably one of the first, though, considering how we miraculously seem to disagree on every course of action."

"Matsumoto, you're being so..." She trailed off, a realization dawning on her as they had this remote conversation where neither could see the other's reactions.

She thought about Matsumoto's intentions, about what

he wanted from her. Most likely, Matsumoto was fretting over whether Diva would make it all the way to the future after the Singularity Project was over, like she had in the original history. The AI known as Diva had to make it to Matsumoto's time period in order for the Singularity Project to be executed, and she had to comply with the Project's policy, which instructed them to limit the effect they had on history to only those factors that led to the Singularity Points.

Perhaps he was even trying to be kind. He might want his partner—who had come on this one-hundred-year journey with him—to resume her original activities once it was over.

If that was what this was about, Vivy felt he shouldn't worry. She had already anticipated what would happen once the Singularity Project was over and was acting with that outcome in mind. She hadn't spoken openly about this with Matsumoto, which meant she had mixed up her priorities if that had caused this misalignment.

"Anyway, Vivy, just do what we agreed on in the meeting. I'll hold back Mister Makime. You take my place monitoring Ophelia in her dressing room."

"Understood. Let's make sure to trade information once we're done."

"We'll both go to sleep right after we finish modifying the Singularity Point...but okay. If we can, we'll talk in The Archive." With that, Matsumoto donned his disguise and left the venue.

Having switched spots with him, Vivy was now continuing the surveillance of Ophelia in her dressing room to make sure there were no changes in her consciousness, despite the steadily increasing tension as the concert's start time approached.

There was a high risk of her being found by someone if she kept an eye on Ophelia in person, so she hijacked the video from the surveillance system and used that to spy. Connecting her earring to the terminal in her room, Vivy streamed the camera feed from Ophelia's room directly into her consciousness.

"She's being really quiet," Vivy said to herself.

Ophelia sat in a chair in the room, stock-still, waiting for the concert to start. She looked like she was just passing the time, but even now, her consciousness was likely replaying the video of her own rehearsal as well as the records of all performances past— thousands, if not hundreds of thousands of times—in order to advance her learning.

For her performance in the real concert, she would adjust all the little unsatisfactory details and unleash her music. Every human in the venue would probably be captivated by her. That is, if only she stood on the main stage and not the roof of a building.

"…"

Having thought through that much, Vivy's calculations pivoted in a different direction. Ophelia was pursuing the ultimate heights of singing, a goal no human or AI could ever reach, and her desire to improve was tireless. But who was she singing for?

"…"

Vivy—or rather, Diva—sang for all the guests at NiaLand. Katie and the other songstresses sang for the fans who came out to the concerts and the audiences who gathered to hear them sing.

Who was Ophelia looking at when she sang? She'd left the theater troupe and honed her abilities to the extreme all by herself, even trying to surpass her limits...and for whom?

Her singing enchanted everyone who heard it. She alone lamented her imperfections. Did she sing for herself? Or was the one she wanted to hear her voice most of all no longer in this world?

"Antonio..."

Vivy thought back to Antonio's unmoving frame in the special exhibition area. He had been Ophelia's partner, but he stopped operating before she made her way to the limelight. The unfortunate soundmaster did not stir, not even today of all days. Ophelia had talked about how devoted he was, and Ootori had reminisced about the days when the two AIs were together. Surely Antonio had been an indispensable guide as Ophelia forged her place in the world in accordance with her reason for being.

It was similar to what Matsumoto did for Vivy as she worked on the Singularity Project.

"Hm?" After calculating that much, Vivy started to feel something was wrong with the video feed she was monitoring.

Ophelia was engrossed in her pre-performance routine, not moving in the slightest. Vivy searched her mind to find what exactly it was that had sparked that feeling of wrongness. Soon enough, she found it.

"Augh!"

A groan slipped from the mechanism in Vivy's throat, and she rushed out of her room toward Ophelia's. She ran down the hallway, emptied of people so the songstresses could prepare in peace, and flung open the door to Ophelia's dressing room. If the surveillance camera footage was accurate, Ophelia would be sitting in the chair and look up in shock when Vivy opened the door.

Instead, there was no sign of Ophelia.

"Ophelia!"

Vivy ran over to the terminal and accessed the same camera she'd been watching from earlier. It showed Ophelia's dressing room with Ophelia still in it, focused entirely on her routine. It didn't show the room empty, and it didn't show Vivy, who had burst into the room.

It was a video loop.

The video recording of Ophelia continued to cycle over and over, deceiving any who might be monitoring her. Ophelia had left her dressing room long before Vivy realized it. The dead giveaway was that the white flower Vivy had tucked into Ophelia's hair was missing. Vivy doubted someone like Ophelia would remove a decoration given to her by her sister without asking first.

"This is bad…"

The surveillance footage had been modified, and Ophelia had disappeared. Vivy suddenly felt there might be some truth to Ophelia's Suicide. Had she and Matsumoto made a horrible mistake? No, there had to be more to it.

"Who set up the looped video?"

There was no point in placing a video loop unless the perpetrator thought someone was going to access the surveillance footage. Besides, it wouldn't look odd for Ophelia to get up and walk around the venue. Nobody would imagine she might kill herself, nor would they try to prevent her from acting of her own accord.

So then why go to all this trouble? The only way someone would decide this was necessary was if they knew there was someone spying on Ophelia's dressing room.

Vivy opened her transmission circuit. *"Matsumoto! Ophelia's disappeared from her room! What's Makime doing?"*

"..."

"Matsumoto?"

The response to the emergency situation wasn't Matsumoto's casual voice—just static that grated on her ears. Their transmission line had been cut. Was this a poorly timed accident? No. Someone was targeting them and the Singularity Project. With that calculation, Vivy immediately gave up on coordinating with Matsumoto. "Argh…"

Vivy searched Ophelia's dressing room for a clue and found something that didn't belong in an AI's dressing room: an ashtray with the burnt remnants of a piece of paper inside. The scraps left behind by the fire were unreadable, but Vivy could tell someone had burned the paper to get rid of it. She concluded that it had something to do with Ophelia's disappearance.

"Since it was a direct letter, I can't view the contents in email history."

The practice of sending paper letters was nearly extinct in this era. Diva received countless presents throughout the year for her work at NiaLand, but she still only got a couple of handwritten letters a year at most. She got hundreds, if not thousands of times as many emails.

A physical letter—like the one in Ophelia's dressing room—was easier to slip under AIs' noses and easier to destroy. This evidence wasn't in the data regarding the original history, almost certainly because it'd been missed by the police. Who doubted and distrusted the capabilities of law enforcement and would allow those emotions to explode out in frustration?

"I need to find Ophelia right now."

Vivy was the only one moving freely through the venue halls. Matsumoto was probably already formulating a solution on his end, considering the transmission interference. This was an attack by someone clearly hostile toward the Singularity Project.

Without another word, Vivy sprinted out of the dressing room to search the places she thought Ophelia might have gone. The first possibility was the roof of the building believed to be where she jumped from. There was a chance that whoever was planning this had already changed their plans if their first option was discovered, meaning—

"Huh?"

Just as Vivy was ready to hit the ground running with her theory, something impossible—or rather, *someone*—flitted across the edge of her vision, stealing her attention. She picked apart the visual information, wondering if she'd seen incorrectly, but there were no abnormalities. What she saw was a person moving away from her down the corridor, no doubt about it.

"Wait!" she shouted, her feet pounding the floor as she chased after him.

Complex calculations whirled through her positronic brain. She forced them aside and pressed forward. The figure wasn't directly connected to Ophelia, but Vivy knew they had to be related. There was no way they weren't involved in the surprising turn of events. After calling out to the man, Vivy rounded a corner, and her eyes flew wide open.

"Your voice is as nice as always, songstress."

"..."

The interloper stood there, right in her way. Then, faster than any AI could perceive or react, he struck Vivy at the base of her neck. White light seared through her positronic brain.

"Agh..."

It was an intense magnetic pulse, like a stun gun. The pulse slowed the operation of positronic brains, causing a temporary loss of consciousness in AIs. Vivy's system forced a shutdown in order to protect itself. She lost balance and pitched forward. The man who'd struck her scooped her up before she hit the ground.

"You're..." she mumbled weakly as her positronic brain deactivated.

He didn't reply, but his face was enough of an answer. This man was the enemy of the Singularity Project. He had a youthful face, but there was a composed dignity about him that made him seem like a veteran who'd spent decades on a battlefield. She knew this contradictory young man all too well.

"...Kakitani."

He was a member of the anti-AI organization Toak, and Vivy and Matsumoto's adversary for many years. The image of this man who looked exactly like a young Kakitani was reflected in her eye cameras as her consciousness sank into darkness.

.:5:.

AS VIVY WAS ENSNARED by a treacherous ploy, Matsumoto was struggling with his own obstacles.

"Vivy, Vivy, please respond. Something weird is happening!" he called.

"..."

The humanoid frame controlled by Matsumoto grimaced at the static coming over the transmission, and he held his head in his hands. *"Dang it! Splitting up has really come back to bite us, Vivy! Someone's got us right where they want us!"*

Matsumoto had been monitoring Makime Ryousuke's approach per the strategy he and Vivy had agreed on—that is, until he saw something wholly unexpected and realized something he never could have imagined. This new piece of information had the potential to capsize the entire Singularity Point. He needed to tell Vivy right away so they could come up with an emergency solution. Just as he reached out to her, however, the interference hit. Something was clearly up.

"Come on, it's me we're talking about here," Matsumoto muttered to himself. "I'm like, a hacking wizard in this time period!

I've got walls in place, and no one should be able to knock down even one of them."

Lying low was one of Matsumoto's essential skills. He'd come into this Singularity Point with all due precautions, just like every Singularity Point before, but someone had managed to interfere with their transmissions. This should not be happening. He came to the same conclusion Vivy had: An unknown actor was sabotaging them and the Singularity Project.

"It's a bit rude, but I think I'll dump Inaba's frame and use a terminal to get back to my real body..."

Matsumoto looked around and, luckily, spotted a public-use terminal. In the distant past, there were things called "phone booths" all over the place, which were used to make a call in exchange for a couple of coins. They'd seen a resurgence as connection points for AIs.

Matsumoto's real body was currently operating in the background while the majority of his consciousness was in Inaba's frame. It was kind of like having a piece of external hardware plugged in, and he couldn't guarantee there wouldn't be some sort of error if he disconnected without following the proper procedure. One might call him pedantic, but it was his nature not to cut corners on processes.

It didn't work out as well as it usually did this time.

"Oof...!"

As he was hurrying over to the access point, something hit him from behind. It was a soft blow, as if a passerby had bumped into him on the street, but he had been rushing alongside the road at the time. The slight impact was enough to send his frame sprawling into the road.

Realizing the danger he was in, he ran through all 163 possible reactions to the situation. He evaluated each one in detail, simulating their ability to resolve the issue in front of him.

Then something smashed into his frame, crushing it.

Metal parts bent and broke from the intense impact, the sounds tearing through the air. The driver of the large semitruck that struck Matsumoto had immediately recognized the abnormal situation and slammed on its breaks, but the massive tires had already mown down and crunched up Matsumoto's borrowed frame.

Screams filled the air. People stopped to stare when they noticed the tragedy. Even with his battered body, Matsumoto could still tell people were pointing the cameras of their handheld terminals at him, though he had no intention of criticizing the rubberneckers. That wasn't as important as the fact that he would never be able to connect to his main consciousness again.

But just before the frame known as Inaba disappeared forever—just before his duty was brought to an end—he saw something. In a twist of fate, he saw this at the exact same moment that his partner, Vivy, was passing out in the arms of a man they both knew.

"Ah... Gurgh..."

His voice wouldn't take shape. He watched helplessly as a small figure wound its way through the crowd, moving farther and farther away. It was an AI with a white flower in her black hair. Matsumoto watched her disappear into the throngs of people, and then static filled his vision before it cut out.

A bleak shadow had been cast over the Singularity Project.

Human

.:1:.

HE FIRST TOUCHED A PIANO when he was barely old enough to form memories. It wasn't like he was born into a family of musicians; he simply had a fascination with the black and white keys that produced sounds when he pushed them. His parents were happy to give that to their only son.

In the beginning, he just liked to make noise. Soon he found joy in playing music. Eventually, he was on the road to becoming better, more advanced, and he aimed to perfect pieces he once could only polish. It might sound trite when put into words, but he worked so hard that he bled.

He sat with a piano for more than ten hours a day, honing his precision on a single song. Music flowed through his veins. He was alive only to press the keys on the piano, and his eyes' sole purpose was to read notes.

By the time he turned sixteen, more than a decade after he first touched a piano, he was so proficient that no peer could rival him. His hard work had paid off. The results came in the form of several opportunities to stand on a podium and proudly accept a trophy. But every time he took the step up, he heard the same thing:

"Guess that's the most we can expect from a human performance."

He bled to achieve that skill, and it was surely worthy of praise—but only when referring to what *humans* were capable of.

It was already the golden age of AI technology. Advancements weren't just made in many industrial fields but in music and the arts as well. AIs performed the music and notation exactly as they were laid out on the page.

AIs provided exemplary results in fields where there was a correct, established answer. In seconds, they could learn how to use their metal fingers to gently press the keys in a way that took most pianists thousands of hours of practice to master. And once they had that skill, they never again made a mistake when playing. Before long, there were whole programs of songs that implemented techniques only AIs could use. A clear divide began to form between "human music" and "AI music," in the same way there was one between children and adult musicians.

It was almost as if they were trying to protect fragile human pianists, to keep them from breaking against the wall of AI potential.

"You can't win against AIs."

Many people shared that belief, which was quickly becoming common sense. The idea that humans were inferior to their AI creations was spreading fast, but the boy challenged that notion.

You can't win. You can't do it. It's impossible.

Who was it that decided these things? Why had they built

this boundary around him without his permission? He wouldn't lose. *Humans* wouldn't lose. He was plenty capable of competing with AIs.

"You're so optimistic, Yugo. It's wonderful."

He'd had the same piano teacher for a very long time, and the fellow complimented him on his outlook. The piano teacher had never given up on Yugo, even when he couldn't play very well or lashed out with a nasty attitude. His teacher was the only person who never made fun of him no matter how foolish his ideas were. Instead, he would think it through with Yugo and try to figure out a way to make it possible.

And whenever Yugo managed to leap over a hurdle that had been in his way, his teacher would give him a gentle pat on the head. Those fingers were made of cold steel, with no blood flowing through them.

"Someday, I'll be better than you," Yugo said once as his teacher patted him on the head. "I'll give you a performance that'll knock your socks off."

Yugo's teacher was an AI. He was an experienced AI instructor that Yugo's parents had brought in to help their son when he was still young. Piano quickly became Yugo's near-exclusive pursuit as he devoted himself to learning, and his teacher had been with him from the beginning, meaning he was by Yugo's side even more than Yugo's parents.

Yugo declared he would play better than an AI. Most people burst into laughter when they heard his goal, and not even his parents believed he could reach it.

His teacher never laughed. Instead, he would nod and say, "I look forward to it." And he would smile, and Yugo would smile back.

Without reservation, Yugo promised his teacher he would do it. He had no idea he wouldn't be able to keep that promise.

.: 2 :.

YUGO WAS DIAGNOSED with osteosarcoma when he was eighteen years old. He'd been complaining for weeks that his right arm was swollen and the pain wasn't going away. He thought it would heal if he left it alone, but the pain only worsened. Eventually, it became so great he was having trouble enduring it, and he went in to get it checked out. That was when he got the diagnosis.

The disease would only get worse if left alone, and there was no treatment other than removing the tumor along with the affected area, so the surgery was scheduled right away. He had to say goodbye to his right arm after eighteen years together.

None of it felt real to him. It was like having a bad dream. The entire process from discovery to surgery moved so fast, it felt as if someone had orchestrated the whole thing behind the scenes. When he awoke, he was in a white hospital room. His parents were hugging him and crying with joy that their son's life had been saved. He was crying too, though he didn't know why.

It would be easy to imagine what became of a pianist who lost one of their arms, but reality was different. Times had changed.

Even if someone lost an arm, they could get a matching prosthetic that connected to their nervous system. The advancement of AI technology was tied to numerous other scientific fields, and it led to big changes in people's lives. It didn't matter if the issue was congenital or developed later in life—no shortcomings in the human body caused a permanent handicap when supplemented by the power of machinery.

Yugo's right arm was no exception. His parents were wealthy enough that they'd given him a piano and an AI teacher, so they could immediately pay for his large-scale operation. They'd already acquired a high-quality right arm for him.

You couldn't tell it was a prosthetic just by looking at it. It was an excellent piece of work that completely mimicked the appearance of a flesh-and-blood arm. Because it was connected to his nervous system, he could perform minute movements all the way to his fingertips, making it feel as if he'd never lost his arm.

The arm was a sign of his parents' love for him, and he was grateful for that, but what brought him the most joy was the knowledge that he wouldn't have to abandon his dream of being a pianist, a dream that had nearly disappeared along with his arm.

During his first piano lesson after he recovered from surgery, he discovered something that utterly shocked him: With his new right arm, he played far better than he ever had before. He had expended blood, sweat, and tears to get to his previous level, to say nothing of the time he spent hunched on that bench in front of sheet music.

The anxiety, the urgency of pushing himself to reach new heights faster and faster was all smashed in an instant by the impeccable movements of his artificial limb. His new right arm, the fake arm, was perfect. It was so perfect it made it painfully obvious how imperfect his music had been, how imperfect *humans* were.

"Yugo, you can come play piano whenever you want. I'll wait for you."

His prosthetic arm was good, his piano performance was amazing, and his passion faded appallingly fast. Instead of feeling excited that he was able to do something new, he was disappointed in himself for not being able to do it before and discouraged that he'd accidentally gained the ability. His love for it was gone.

He drifted away from the piano, and for a while he didn't play at all. His heart felt heavy every time his teacher contacted him, and he often ignored the messages. A strange sense of guilt took root inside him, along with a mounting frustration that had no outlet.

This was the first time he'd gone so long without playing piano—other than when he was in his mother's womb—but he just kept telling himself there was nothing he could do in an attempt to make himself feel better. His frustration continued to build, and he excused his inaction by willfully believing that energy would eventually rekindle his passion. Then he'd be a pianist again. And until it did, he tried to make himself more multifaceted, engaging with all the things he'd sacrificed in order to hone his piano skills.

He would keep his promise. He meant to keep his promise. Yugo licked his wounds by telling himself he hadn't forgotten, and that he would someday be forgiven for the delay.

About a year later, he heard his teacher had been destroyed in a building collapse while trying to rescue people at the site of an accident.

.:3:.

A SEMITRUCK PLOWED into a children's home. The building was ruined, but miraculously, there were no casualties. An AI named Cainz had been invited to the children's home to play piano. He'd quickly evacuated the children and saved the people inside. After he pulled out the final child, the ceiling collapsed on him, bringing about his end.

While holding a funeral for an AI might have seemed strange to some, it wasn't uncommon in this time period. Many of the children under his tutelage had gone on to become great successes, and their families tended to be wealthy and generous. No one was opposed to holding a funeral for an AI like Cainz, who'd finished his duty while saving humans. It was a grand affair attended by many. Yugo wasn't sure he if he'd have the confidence to show his face, but he went anyway.

Most of Cainz's broken parts had been picked up from the scene of the accident, and he'd been repaired to look good as new. In fact, he merely appeared to be sleeping. Whoever had prepared the AI *could* have simply swapped out the parts inside and restarted his positronic brain, allowing the frame to operate just like it had before, but no one involved wanted that.

Yugo also resisted the idea, though he didn't really know what to call that feeling. He just didn't like it. It was an instinctual rejection many humans experienced, and he was relieved to not be the only one. As the funeral trudged on, he felt some of the cracks in his dried heart healing. He started to sort through the memories he had of his teacher, and then it began.

In Yugo's nineteen short years of life, there were three things he deeply regretted: One, getting ill and losing his arm. Two, drifting away from piano after getting his new arm. And three, coming to his teacher's funeral.

A screen at the funeral displayed Cainz's memories from before he was destroyed, as well as his activity logs. Those records left nothing uncovered. It was everything about how Yugo's teacher, the AI named Cainz, had lived. The people around Yugo cried as if reliving memories of a deceased person. Yugo found himself stuck in the center of it all. He struggled to breathe, and sweat poured down his face.

There were records of every single child Cainz had ever taught. Some people laughed through their tears as they saw how much they'd changed since they were young. Others laughed because they hadn't changed at all. Nestled among those memories were clips of Yugo, their moments together, Yugo's promise.

"Someday, I'll be better than you. I'll give you a performance that'll knock your socks off." The image of him on the screen made that unfulfillable promise to his teacher.

"I look forward to it, Yugo," came his teacher's kind response when he heard the promise that would never be kept.

Seeing that overwhelmed Yugo's heart with self-reproach and a horrifying shame. When he closed his eyes, all he heard was his own voice belittling him, boiling up in an infinite torrent that flooded his heart. He didn't want to remember that promise. He didn't want to see it like this. The hope and expectations he'd had for himself had vanished as he'd moved away from the piano, but now they burned him up.

Then, he realized the most horrifying, appalling, and overwhelmingly terrible aspect of it all: Because Cainz was an AI, there were still logs from the very moment before he was crushed below that ceiling.

There was no such thing as instant death for an AI. They could be broken, shattered, bent, and forever irrecoverable, but Cainz would have been aware of his coming death and all sorts of things must have gone through his consciousness in the short time before he was destroyed.

Maybe Yugo's promise was one of those things. In the very last of last moments, as his consciousness was fading, had his teacher thought about Yugo's promise? Everything in him was telling him he didn't want to know. If he learned that Cainz had thought about it, he'd want to die. And if he learned that Cainz hadn't thought about it, he'd still want to die.

The truth would put him in a headspace he didn't want to be. He couldn't help feeling it was forbidden knowledge. Put another way, he didn't feel he had the right to face his teacher. Everything

he'd done as a student was shameful. He wished he wasn't quali-
fied to know his teacher's last thoughts and feelings.

Why were people allowed to do this—to see the last
moments? If Cainz had been a person, if he had crossed that
impenetrable barrier between the living and the dead, then no
one would have even considered exposing those secrets. And yet,
the moment the deceased was an AI, it became fine to go there?
It was utterly revolting, atrocious, loathsome.

In Cainz's final logs, he apologized for his inability to help
Yugo keep his promise.

.: 4 :.

DEATH SHOULD HAVE taken everything. How disgusting
and shameless was it to sweep up all the remnants and
patch them together? To Yugo, the most messed-up thing was
that no one seemed to question it.

"You regret it, then? Witnessing that lingering attachment?"

Yugo went back to the hospital for the first time in a long
time when his emotional state became unstable, and his mental
exhaustion started showing in his actions. The person questioning him now was a therapist in his golden years. He listened
thoughtfully and patiently to Yugo's faltering, nonsensical words,
working diligently to pull out the hopeless stagnation within.

Even the therapist's diligence wasn't enough to mend Yugo's
heart. He felt like giving up. There was no one who could possibly understand what he was going through. He began to look

down on others because of this revelation—not out of arrogance but because he thought he was the lowest of the low. Thinking himself foolish and disgraceful for looking down on other people, he loathed himself more. He stood now at the intersection of revelation, surrender, and despair.

"I see... I know how you feel. Humans and AIs really shouldn't get too close."

Yugo's eyes opened wide when he heard the therapist's unexpected words. He snapped back from the precipice of giving up on anyone understanding his mentality. The therapist's eyes crinkled as the corners of his mouth turned up in a smile, and his expression said he understood everything.

"I'd actually like to talk to you about a most enlightening subject. How about it? Do you have some time this evening, Kakitani Yugo-kun?"

VIVY
Prototype

CHAPTER 3

The Songstresses and Their Choices

.: 1 :.

...

......

....

SYSTEM REBOOT CONFIRMED. RESTRUCTURING CON-
SCIOUSNESS FROM IMMEDIATELY BEFORE SYSTEM SHUTDOWN.
REINITIALIZING THOUGHT SEQUENCES.

....

......

...

RESTART CONFIRMED. SINGULARITY PROJECT REINSTATED.
Vivy slowly opened her eyes, and her blurred cameras focused
on the world around her. They immediately adjusted to the dim
lighting, clearing her vision. She found herself in a dirty, white-
walled room she didn't recognize. She was sitting in a hard chair
in the center of that room, her head hanging from when she was
offline. There was nothing else in the square room, which made
it feel even drearier.

Just as the visual information was guiding her to an understanding of her situation, someone said, "You take a long time to wake up."

Her consciousness fixed on the speaker immediately. The pupils of her eye cameras contracted, and the man's face came into focus. He was smiling.

"Can you see me?" he asked with a little wave. "Seems you can hear me, at least."

His metal folding chair was turned backward so he was leaning on the backrest, facing her. He looked to be in his early twenties, but if this was the same person whose name she had recorded, he couldn't possibly be that young. She had first met this man, Kakitani Yugo, more than seventy years ago. Even if she nudged her initial estimate, he couldn't have been younger than ninety now. And what Vivy knew about the appearance of people in their nineties didn't match how this man looked. She didn't even need to spend time thinking to know that much.

There was only one thing to ask. "Are you the Kakitani Yugo that I know?"

"Uh-huh, so the thing that interests you most the moment you restart is my identity. That's a surprise."

"..."

"Let me ask you this: What do you want to hear? Should I say, 'Thanks for taking care of my grandfather. I'm not Kakitani Yugo—I'm his grandson, Kakitani Yudai,' or something like that?" The man's face twisted with irritation.

His way with words carried the weight of years on the job,

contrary to the inexperienced impression she got from the youth-
fulness of his voice and appearance.

Vivy came to a conclusion based on that additional information. "I've concluded you are the real Kakitani Yugo. But what's
with your appearance?"

"I'm not going to joke about finding a magic anti-aging crystal.
Think it through properly. There's only one possible explanation."

"A full artificial body transfer. Are you saying you put your
brain in an AI cranium in place of a positronic brain and abandoned your original body? But for you, switching over to a frame
would be—"

"Inconsistent with our beliefs? We—or at least I—have no
intention of rejecting human scientific advancements. I won't say
no to people swapping parts of their body for mechanical ones if
it'll extend their life or fix an impairment." He paused for a moment to pinch his cheek and pull the skin. "Then again, I didn't
just swap out a part of my body. The doctors tried to scare me by
saying the human brain rejects the swap in 80 percent of cases...
but I gambled and won. Ironically, it looks like I'm pretty compatible with your AI frames." As he talked, he moved his fingers
from his cheek, a smile growing on his face.

This frame was a reproduction of his natural human body.
And yes, it was indeed a frame. Seeing him in an AI frame, Vivy
made an expression mimicking admiration. Her eyebrows rose,
and the pupils of her eye cameras contracted in surprise.

A full-body transplant was still an experimental procedure
with a low success rate, even in this era of advanced AI technology.

Kakitani said he'd had an eighty percent chance of dying, and that was no exaggeration. You could actually argue those were fairly optimistic odds.

It was possible in this time period to swap out the majority of a person's organs with machinery, so the technology to remove the brain and place it safely into a frame did exist, as long as the right conditions were met. But in the vast majority of cases, the brain rejected its new host. The person could fall into a coma or suffer brain death.

That was why many argued that humans were unable to abandon flesh-and-blood bodies for mechanical bodies to attain immortality. With the high risks of the surgery, you could probably count the survivors of full-body transplants on one hand. And yet, Kakitani had taken that risk, and his determination had paid off.

Vivy couldn't see any obvious malfunctions in the operation of his frame. His surgery looked to have been a perfect success.

"By the way, that grandson of mine, Yudai—he really does exist. You even met him once at NiaLand, more than ten years ago. Are you surprised, Diva? Or should I say..." He stopped talking and fixed her with a fierce stare, his eyes narrowing. Then, in a gleeful voice, as if he'd been waiting for this moment, he said, "Are you surprised, Vivy?"

He called her by the name she only used during the Singularity Project.

"..."

Vivy's consciousness was instantly buried behind a wall of error messages. A constant static encroached on her systems like a warning as she considered the meaning behind Kakitani's words. She closed the error messages one by one, thunderstruck at hearing her name from his lips. Never before had she imagined her identity might be exposed.

Although she was loath to admit it, Matsumoto's technical skills were extraordinary, given that he'd come from the future. He had scrubbed her existence from every terminal and device, so there wasn't a single record of Vivy's work on previous Singularity Points. It was as if Vivy/Diva hadn't been there at all—so no one should have known her as Vivy except Matsumoto.

"You seem a little thrown off. Are you going to be all right?" Kakitani asked her.

"What do you mean?"

"Doors opened at five, and the Zodiac Signs Festival starts at six. Not much time left before you've got to go up and sing."

"…"

Kakitani's statement restarted Vivy's process of gathering information about the current situation, which had been pushed to the edge of her consciousness. She checked the time: half past five. Doors had opened at five o'clock sharp for the Zodiac Signs Festival, which meant the audience would be filtering in, buzzing about the special exhibition space or buying merchandise.

It had been just past four o'clock when she went to Ophelia's dressing room. She'd been unconscious for over an hour. Luckily, it didn't seem like anything had been done to Vivy's frame while she was out, beyond transporting her to an unknown location. Though that was a problem in and of itself.

"A whole lot of people are going to be disappointed if your performance gets delayed," said Kakitani. "Songstress AIs might be a dime a dozen, but Diva's definitely the frontrunner of the Zodiac Heroines. There're probably people looking forward to seeing you perform who haven't even seen you at NiaLand, and—"

"Is that what you're after?"

"Hm?"

Vivy interrupted Kakitani's fluid, impassioned speech. When Kakitani looked at her in confusion, she bit her lip in an expression of anger and said, "Taking me away and preventing the Zodiac Signs Festival. Is that your goal? Toak's goal?"

Kakitani stared back at Vivy, his lips clamped shut and his eyes wide.

His organization, Toak, was a group of anti-AI extremists. Toak had gotten in her and Matsumoto's way on several occasions during the Singularity Points. They'd been around for a long time now, and Kakitani had apparently been some sort of leader during the last Singularity Point at Metal Float. So long as their policies hadn't changed, their goal was the total eradication of AIs.

Vivy could only imagine how much they would hate an event like this, where numerous AI songstresses and their frenzied fans had gathered in one place. Perhaps their plan was to take Vivy away and create a hole in the event program. Regardless, they had plenty of opportunities to turn the Zodiac Signs Festival into a stage for tragedy. Maybe Toak even had their hands in Ophelia's Suicide. Maybe it was the result of some scheme of theirs.

"Pfft…"

"…"

"Ha ha… Ha ha ha! Ah ha ha ha ha ha!"

Vivy's suspicions and the silence were shattered as Kakitani burst out laughing. He hugged his stomach, chortling as Vivy watched. His reaction was so powerful, Vivy had to overwrite the sullen, angry impression of him she'd built up over their many interactions. He seemed like a zealous man who had sacrificed his everyday life to throw himself into Toak's mission of destroying AIs.

But Kakitani now laughed shrilly, his palm over his face, destroying the dour image of him in Vivy's consciousness. He leapt up from his chair, took a deep breath, and said, "Right, I see now. That's how it is. This is really, *really* interesting. Man, just learning one thing can totally change your perspective."

"The intention of your statement is unclear. Please explain. What do you mean?"

"I'm talking about the fact that you're operating based on records from the future."

Vivy froze. Her consciousness blanked and then whited out completely, her positronic brain overheating as it attempted to process the unexpected situation. Even as it reached maximum capacity, she couldn't come up with a reasonable course of action.

Of course she couldn't. They'd never assumed that information might leak out.

"You don't lie, and you're slow to deal with unprecedented situations. Those are some of the fatal flaws in AIs. Thinking about it, Beth was the same," he said.

"Elizabeth?"

"Yeah, I remember that much. Really, how could I forget? I recall what happened on Sunrise like it was yesterday," he went on, ignoring her. "Actually, I remember everything down to the first time I met you. That was at the OGC data center, when we were trying to off Assemblyman Aikawa... That was the first time our paths crossed."

"..."

"They crossed again in space, then at sea... On Sunrise and on Metal Float. How unlucky were we that you always managed to throw a wrench in Toak's plans? And now I've finally realized why. It's incredible—you cut us off from the *future*." Kakitani let that final word hang in the air, then shrugged.

Kakitani had seen his plans thwarted at every turn by AIs using information from the future, a move that should have been against the rules. And yet, Vivy didn't sense as much contempt, revulsion, or disappointment in his voice as there seemed to be in his words.

She couldn't deny it any longer: Kakitani knew everything. He knew what Vivy and Matsumoto were doing, and he knew about the Singularity Project. He had even realized that they were referencing records from the future to plan their moves. Perhaps that was the *only* conclusion he could've come to when he thought about everything up to this very moment.

Vivy had been thrown off by the surveillance feed loop when she was monitoring Ophelia. That wasn't something that could've been done as a contingency; someone would've had to have known definitively that Vivy was observing her in order to set that up. In all likelihood, Kakitani didn't just know about Ophelia's Suicide and the Singularity Project—he might even know about the impending war between humanity and AIs too.

On one hand, Vivy and Matsumoto were essentially devices that modified the Singularity Points to guide this world to rightful peace. On the other, they could be the triggers for worldwide chaos and terror if that information was disseminated. This was the gravest outcome Vivy could find in any calculation.

"Don't be so pessimistic," Kakitani cut in, shaking his head as Vivy thought the worst. "God, you always assume the worst possible outcome and limit your own actions. That's another flaw of AIs. Unlike humans, you have no optimism." Her brow furrowed as she wondered about his true intentions, and he continued, "I don't plan on telling people you're working to change the future. Who would even believe me? I'm just special, I guess."

"..."

"Obviously, I haven't told anybody in Toak either. They'd just lose faith. Might even make them go off the deep end." He shot her a reproachful smile and shrugged again. "It's just me."

"Kakitani..."

"I'm the only one who's run into you all these times over the years. The only one who will believe you." He brought a hand to his chest, and Vivy went quiet.

There was logic in what he said. Vivy had imagined the worst-case scenario and worried about the coming future, but who would believe such an absurd story? What human would believe two AIs were using information from the future to change the present?

With that thought came another question. "If that's the case... why do *you* believe it?"

"..."

"It does sound ridiculous, you can't argue with that. AIs getting information from the future and acting on it to change history? No one would believe it. But you did... Was it because of all the interactions you and I have had?"

Vivy had constantly interfered with Toak's plans, so it must have felt like a revelation when Kakitani learned the truth—but that just sparked even more questions. Vivy could accept that Kakitani believed in the existence of the Singularity Project. The question was, who had told him about it?

"Why did I figure you were working off stuff from the future...? Hm, I think you're probably right. My interactions with you were a big part of it. You kept getting ahead of us, always avoiding critical damage. That was all the proof I needed."

"I can accept that. But who—"

"You want to know who told me? Hmph. I don't actually know. Got any bright ideas?"

Vivy was taken aback. "What?" She wondered if he was messing with her, since his tone was rather flippant.

Yet he didn't take back what he'd said. He nodded a few times and replied, "Sorry, I'm not trying to joke around. I honestly don't know. There were no hints about where the information came from. It was delivered by anonymous email. Both the looped camera footage and the transmission interference software targeting you were gifts from the same person."

"And you...trusted it?"

"Is that really surprising to you? You've trusted information from the future for the past seventy years. It makes sense to me that you two have an enemy who also knows the future."

An enemy who knew the future? Kakitani said it in such an offhand way, but it filled Vivy with dread. That was it; it had to be. This mystery person had leaked information about the Singularity Project to Kakitani. They knew what Vivy and Matsumoto were up to and were planning to put a stop to it. Either that, or another AI like Matsumoto had been sent back from the future, operating in accordance with the will of those who'd started the clash between humanity and AIs.

"Doesn't really matter, though." Kakitani clapped his hands loudly in front of Vivy, who was experiencing disturbances in her consciousness. Then he clutched his hands in front of his chest, confirmed that Vivy was looking at him with her eye cameras, and met her stare. "Like I said, this has nothing to do with Toak. I'd also like you to believe me when I say I have no plans of interfering with the Zodiac Signs Festival. I came here as a lone human named Kakitani Yugo. There may not be blood flowing through my body, but I am human."

"Why did you come?"

"I plan to kill someone," Kakitani told her, calm as anything.

Vivy had lost count of how many times he'd shocked her.

With another nod, he said, "Today, I will kill a human. I'll do it while the Zodiac Signs Festival is going on. Now that you've heard...what will you do, Diva, the AI songstress?"

.: 2 :.

KAKITANI BEGAN by explaining his premeditated murder. "It'll be right in the middle of the Zodiac Signs Festival. What time? Hmm... Let's go with 7:30 p.m. That's about when you should be onstage, right?"

If the festival went according to schedule, Vivy—or Diva— was supposed to take the stage at 7:37 p.m. Kakitani probably had the schedule for the festival. It sounded like he was trying to test her. But test what, exactly?

"Diva... Actually, I'm going to call you Vivy. You were Diva to me for so long, but it seems the AI I've been obsessed with this whole time was you, Vivy."

"Obsessed with...?"

"For better or worse, you and I have stood against each other for a long time. It's not surprising I would develop some emotional attachment to you. If an emotional attachment can be positive, it can be negative too."

"In other words, you hate me?"

"Hate, huh? I hate all AIs. But you... Hrm. What would I call it?" Kakitani stepped back, thinking.

It was quite easy for Vivy to guess why Kakitani hated her, why he saw her as an enemy and wanted to do her harm. He'd said it himself: The Singularity Project was getting in the way of his and Toak's plans, preventing them from coming to fruition. He had managed to avoid death on Sunrise and Metal Float, thanks to the actions of Vivy and the other Sisters, but she doubted he was grateful for that. Kakitani had lived his life with AIs twisting what he wanted on several occasions.

"Are you interfering with our goals in order to get revenge?" asked Vivy.

"Ah, you've got that wrong, Vivy. I don't want revenge. I have no reason to interfere with your plans. I'm not even concerned about the danger in the future."

"Your actions contradict what you're saying. If you really know our goals, you should know the future we're trying to prevent is the same thing you were trying to avoid."

"You're right. We can't avoid a clash between humans and AIs. That's why we should stop AI advancement. But like I said, I'm not working with Toak's ideals in mind right now."

He placed a hand on the chair he had been sitting in, used his foot to fold it up, then leaned it against the wall and dusted his hands off. Vivy wondered why he was acting like he was cleaning up as he turned back to her.

"All right. I've basically told you everything I want to. I think I'll be on my way. Do you have any questions for me before I go?"

"I don't understand your intentions. You kidnap me, warn me you're going to kill someone during the Zodiac Signs Festival, and then set me free? Why?"

"Simple. I'm making you choose," he said.

Vivy's eyes widened. Kakitani was relaxed, almost like a burden he'd been carrying for years had been lifted from his shoulders. His shoes clacked against the floor as he walked to a metal door at the back of the room. He really was about to walk out without a care in the world.

"Wait!" Vivy shouted, finding herself unable to let this go. She reached out toward him, but she couldn't reach. Her feet wouldn't take her more than three steps from her chair.

"Based on my calculations, it should take you more than fifteen minutes to break out of that case, even with the output of your frame. You can't catch me here," he said confidently over his shoulder, and Vivy's arm bounced back off the wall in front of her.

Vivy had been surrounded by a special transparent case from the moment she woke in the chair. It had allowed them to see each other but kept her separated from Kakitani. She was sealed off from her surroundings—so thoroughly that if she hadn't been an AI, she might've suffocated. As Kakitani said, it would take Vivy some time to break the case, even if she attacked it violently enough to damage her own frame. She could only watch as he escaped.

"Kakitani Yugo! What are you trying to do?!"

"Once you break the case and get out, you can do whatever you like. I stuck a map to the outside of the door. Go ahead and check it; I won't interfere anymore. If you hurry, you should have just enough time to make your performance. But it'll mean you won't be able to stop me."

"Who are you going to kill and why, Kakitani?! What is the point?!"

"Look, I'm not going to tell you anything more—not who I'm going to kill, not why, and not the point of my actions. But, uh...I guarantee this person's death will have no impact on the future."

"..."

"You're free to go back to the venue and accomplish your goals, or you can carry out your mission as a songstress AI. Do whatever you want, Vivy. I've tossed the coin."

With that, Kakitani vanished through the door. It closed with a *thud*, creating another barrier between the two of them. Complete silence settled over the room, and Vivy immediately started handling the emergency situation. Her hand went to her left ear, and she attempted to send a transmission to Matsumoto, something she'd been trying for a long time. However, the interference was still in place, cutting them off from each other.

"I still can't reach him."

If Kakitani had been telling the truth, this was all some complicated plot by an unknown figure who had told him about the Singularity Project and provided him with several methods of getting in Vivy's way. Their accuracy was terrifying, given that their schemes were quickly encroaching on Vivy's—and humanity's—future.

She couldn't expect help from Matsumoto. She had to get out of this on her own.

Vivy grabbed the chair she'd been sitting on and smashed it into the wall with all her might. Her arms rebounded, and the folding chair bent pathetically. But she adjusted her angle, adjusted her strength output, and bashed the chair into the wall over and over again. As she attacked the case, her consciousness raced with calculations on what to do next.

The Singularity Project was still in progress. No matter what Kakitani said, he would probably put the Project—and therefore humanity—in jeopardy. But how likely was it that he was involved in Ophelia's Suicide? He was so obsessed with Vivy that he'd cast aside his human body to become almost entirely machine. If that obsession could spur him to commit murder, then their clashing throughout the Project had everything to do with it.

Was there really no connection between him and Ophelia's Suicide, a turning point in history that occurred with no influence from the Singularity Project? If that were the case, someone at the venue could stop Ophelia's Suicide. Vivy was unable to contact Matsumoto, and there was somebody out there bold enough to attack Vivy and the Singularity Project.

Who would save humanity from the threat of destruction?

"Oh!"

The cracks in the case suddenly expanded, spreading out like a spider web. The folding chair in Vivy's hands had completely lost its original shape after being smashed into the case several times, and there were dents in the metal from where Vivy's fingers had gripped it. Even so, it had enough strength left to give one last blow and break the case open.

"Haaah!"

Vivy emitted a shout and swung the chair into the center of the cracks. It was a direct hit. The impact turned the transparent walls white as tiny cracks spread around her, and then it shattered

THE SONGSTRESSES AND THEIR CHOICES 135

all at once, like a bubble popping. The glass tinkled as it fell to the ground, and Vivy moved straight through it. She felt glass crunching beneath her shoes and realized she'd been kidnapped in her stage outfit. It was clean and perfectly intact, which meant Kakitani had shown plenty of care as he transported her away from the venue. It was unclear what that said about his mental state.

"Where am I?"

She opened the door and dashed outside. The wind rushed at her, whipping the long strands of her hair. Evidently, she'd been inside a storage unit—and the way out was blocked by several others. Vivy looked back at the door and, just as Kakitani said, spotted a map with the storage facility's location carefully marked. She referenced the map and her location, juxtaposing it with map data in her consciousness to confirm nothing was falsified. The venue for the Zodiac Signs Festival was a few miles away...but there was one more location marked on the map.

It was an old abandoned children's home.

Vivy immediately understood what that mark was and why Kakitani put it there. The last thing he'd told her was to choose.

"..."

Ophelia's Suicide, the fourth Singularity Point, occurred at the time Ophelia was meant to take the stage: the festival's closing act. Setting aside whether Vivy—or Diva—should take the stage, she *should* head straight back to the Touto Dome. That was what she should prioritize in her role of an AI carrying out the Singularity Project. Even if that meant Kakitani was going to kill a human in a place Vivy couldn't reach. It was the same logical conclusion she'd come to when she couldn't prevent an airplane crash at the first Singularity Point.

"..."

Vivy's calculations concluded. She pulled up the hem of her skirt so it wouldn't drag on the ground, turned toward her destination, and ran.

.: 3 :.

SOMEONE WAS PLAYING the piano. It was elegant and magnificent, a superior performance born from true skill and an understanding of music. It was truly excellent, a beautiful melody only someone who loved music could perform. But there was sorrow to it too, and the lonely sound filled the space, creating an atmosphere that was incredibly forlorn. The melody rang out, echoing. Vivy thought that if a human heard the song, they would experience heartrending emotions.

She pushed open a large door as that music entered her audio sensors.

ıllı|||ılıı

Vivy passed through the door and into the room, entering the domain of that unwavering melody. The performance approached the climax. As the difficulty of the epic piece increased, so did the emotion the performer put in, passion in the fingers dancing across the keys. The keys settled, emotions calmed, and

the song was finally over. Then the beautiful sound faded like a wave receding back to the sea.

Once it had ended, Vivy applauded the performance.

"You're messing with me," Kakitani said.

Vivy stopped clapping. "No, I'm not. It was wonderful, so I wanted to commend you with a round of applause."

Kakitani suppressed a laugh. The grand piano where he sat stood prominently in the large hall. It was none other than Kakitani himself who had given life and magic to that instrument, his music woven together by his mechanical fingers striking the black and white keys. He could have easily acquired the programming for his man-made hands to play well enough to rival even the most talented pianists—and in fact, Vivy could probably produce something similar if she sat in front of a piano—but even so, there was something else to his music.

"You used to play piano, didn't you?" she said.

"What makes you think that?"

"Your performance. It was different than someone just hitting the keys in accordance with a program."

"..."

"Human performances and AI performances aren't the same. Even if they follow identical sheet music, they'll pull different songs out of the piano. We don't know why that is, though."

There was an undeniable difference between human and AI musicianship, perhaps brought about by the enigmatic nature of music. The same thing could be said about singing. Although humans and AIs shared many things, there was something special that put humans above AIs when it came to music, and it wasn't technique. In a way, humans' imperfect musical performances elevated them to a higher level. The palpable, undeniable difference was always there.

Whatever that *something* was, it was in Kakitani's performance.

"Idea," Kakitani whispered suddenly.

Vivy repeated the word without giving it voice and trapping it in her mouth. The "Idea" he spoke of was a term in Platonic philosophy, also sometimes called "Form." But that probably wasn't the meaning Kakitani had in mind.

"It's the first important term we tell new members of Toak," he said.

"Toak?"

"No one knows where it came from. Some people say it came from the small organization that was an early form of Toak, but we're not sure. Toak leaders just insisted that the presence of Idea—or lack thereof—was proof of a clear difference between humans and AIs."

"..."

"Someday, AIs will advance enough that they'll gain Idea. When that happens, they'll surpass humanity and take our place."

That sounded like quite the tragedy to Vivy. She herself was an AI who'd been in operation for nearly a hundred years in service of humanity. The calculation that AIs should replace humans had never once crossed even the fringes of her consciousness. That future could not come to pass. Did the humans of Toak, Kakitani included, really believe it was inevitable?

"There are many different kinds of humans. Some Toak members might've wholeheartedly believed what the leaders said, but most of them just got involved because they resented AIs. They lost their jobs, their places in society, their goals. It's not like I really believed it either."

"So then—"

"It's different now, though."

The forcefulness of his words made Vivy's mouth clamp up, and she couldn't speak. Kakitani stared at her and pressed a key. The high tone reverberated through the cold air of the hall.

"Before, I thought it was all bull, but now I'm certain that the Idea our leaders talked about is real. I'm not interested in talk about AIs replacing humans, but the fact that AIs have been gaining all these things only humans used to have supports the theory that they're trying to gain Idea too."

"You misunderstand. We can't make something that doesn't exist."

"If that's true, Vivy, then why are you here?! This isn't a festival for songstresses—it's an abandoned children's home!" Kakitani shouted as he gestured around himself. He pointed at the clock on the back wall of the hall. The hands were still ticking away. It was nearly seven o'clock.

Even if Vivy left now, she wouldn't make it back to the Touto Dome in time for her performance. Instead of running straight to the stage, she had come to Kakitani, playing the piano all by himself in this place. She intended to stop him from killing the person he'd warned her about.

"You're not acting as an AI implementing a plan to change the future," he said.

"..."

"And you're not acting as a songstress who sings in front of an enthusiastic audience."

"..."

"You chose to stop the murder of a single person who will have no impact on the future, even though you don't know if I was even telling the truth. What made you do that?"

Vivy couldn't answer his question. For the sake of the Singularity Project, she should have returned to the venue to search for Ophelia and stop her suicide. If not that, then she should have considered Diva's work and given a flawless performance to avoid creating a gap in the festival program. Yet she had done neither. She'd come here.

Kakitani was perfectly willing to kill a person. Vivy was painfully aware of that after her encounters with him over the past seventy years. He was a terrorist through and through. If he said he was going to kill someone, she believed he would. Preventing that was Vivy's current mission.

"The person I'm going to kill is a man named Kakitani Yugo," he said.

"..."

"I wasn't foreshadowing a murder—I was confessing my intent to commit suicide. This isn't meant to be payback for your applause earlier, but it is a pretty ironic turn of events, isn't it? You came to stop an AI from killing herself, but now you're stopping a *human* from killing himself." Kakitani shrugged.

He could have been lying. If he was, then perhaps he had no intention of killing anyone. Yet Vivy was certain that he planned to kill himself, and he was prepared to go through with it, whether Vivy was there or not. What would she do now?

"Are you still planning to stop me?" he asked.

"I came here to stop you from killing the person you warned me about. My decision doesn't change just because that person is you. I will prevent you from killing anyone."

"..."

"We've run into each other plenty of times over the past seventy years. Each time, I blocked your plans. I'll do the same thing now. That's all there is to it," Vivy said, looking straight at him.

His cheeks stretched into a fierce grin. "What'll happen if you do stop me? Wouldn't that be the thing that undoes all your work over those seventy years?"

"No."

"Really? How can you be so sure?" Kakitani looked at Vivy, confused.

Vivy closed her eyes and calculated how she should answer his question. Then she said, "Because I'm not just one unit. I have a partner."

.: 4 :.

THE ROAR FROM the Zodiac Signs Festival was incredible. The Touto Dome was all sold out and packed to capacity. Fifty thousand people had gathered to see the famous songstresses and to hear them sing under the same roof. A clamor matching their excitement and anticipation rose up outside the building as well. It was a fever that seemed capable of melting the light dusting of snow that had begun to pile up.

This was the first time anyone had brought together song-stresses from all over. Now that the experiment was going off without a hitch, the event organizers must have been proud. The impact was so profound that there was even talk of doing another festival after this one. Unfortunately, the Zodiac Signs Festival would never be held again, not after this one legendary day. At least, that was how it had gone in the original history of this world.

"...Reason being, the AI who was supposed to sing for the grand finale didn't show up for her performance. They found out later that she'd thrown herself off a nearby building."

"..."

"Her daring act had a ripple effect that caused all sorts of problems. People would never forget that day. I also learned a big lesson today: to continue obeying my moral obligation to follow the signals given by traffic lights," said the little cube-shaped AI in a light and jovial tone. He delicately opened and closed the shutter of the eye camera on his body.

Listening to him was a black-haired AI in a black dress, her well-shaped brows furrowed.

"I suppose I should say 'Nice to meet you,' Ophelia."

A flurry sprinkled down around them. The two AIs stood on the roof of a building facing the front of Touto Dome. Matsumoto, in cube form, had his back against the roof's railing.

Ophelia, Black Angel of the Small Theater, stared back at him from the entrance. He had been on the roof waiting for her when she arrived.

She was flustered by the unexpected encounter. "Um, wh-what are you saying?" she asked, her voice heavy with confusion.

"You don't understand?"

Ophelia shook her head, her black hair billowing in the cold wind. She looked timidly at Matsumoto, not saying another word.

"Anyway, as you can probably guess, I'm not in the greatest shape at the moment. Unfortunately, most of the parts that make up my frame are operating elsewhere," said Matsumoto, a hint of wryness in his voice.

Although Ophelia wasn't particularly tall, he had to look up at her in his tiny body. He'd secured his current position on purpose, however. His frame was an amalgamation of 128 cubes that enabled him to alter his shape, strength, and functions as needed for every situation. He'd abandoned that method and divvied up his cubes, so there were twenty-one here on the snowy rooftop. The other 107 were spread throughout the city to cover as much ground as possible, each one acting as an independent eye gathering information for him. He had yet to find Vivy.

"It appears someone is interfering with my and my partner's work. I can't contact her, and my functionality has been painfully limited. I'll have to practice the old-fashioned method of *earning* information."

Matsumoto's programming had been attacked as well, rendering him unable to set up any sort of reliable transmission environment. The situation was serious. Someone was clearly trying to impede the Singularity Project, and until Matsumoto's cubes found Vivy or the information he needed to prevent Ophelia's Suicide, he had to get through this sticky situation by himself.

The traffic accident that destroyed Inaba, his borrowed frame, was a major sore spot for him. It had been a huge shock to Matsumoto's systems. He'd shifted most of his control to Inaba's frame to work on a ground level, and losing it forced him to shut his system down.

"I've suffered immensely," he said. "That frame didn't have the opportunity to connect to a terminal right before the accident. He couldn't share what happened in his last moments with my main body. I had to go physically gather the data from his frame just to figure out why I was forced to shut down and what information he'd gathered just before his destruction."

According to the frame's records, Inaba had been pushed from behind and sent flying into the road. The next moment, he was run over by a semitruck, which damaged his frame beyond repair. The mystery culprit was already blocking transmissions when Inaba stopped functioning, so Matsumoto failed to transfer the data to his main body. Matsumoto had to restart without knowing the cause of Inaba's death, which meant he first learned of Inaba's death when he rebooted, and he then had to go salvage the information so he could learn what it was Inaba had found out and why it led to his death.

"Normally, I'd be able to clean up the whole problem with a quick hack instead of actually moving my body, but I wasn't granted the option this time. Once I went all the way out to the broken AI to figure out what was going on, I had to come here."

"A traffic accident...?" Ophelia said with a frown as she listened to his tale of woe. Then she nodded several times. "Oh, I see. That's it. You're that AI staff member, the one who was following me."

"The name was Inaba. It's sort of a fake name, though, so there's no point in making sure you remember. Also, I don't know what's going on, so just stop acting like you want to know my name. Just think of me as your friendly neighborhood box."

Ophelia ignored the flippant things Matsumoto said and continued speaking as if they were chitchatting about Inaba. "Does oneesama—I mean, Diva—have anything to do with you?"

Before the Touto Dome opened its doors for the event, she had seen Inaba and Vivy together. He'd acted so ridiculous then because he hadn't imagined the frame would end up being targeted.

"It's getting lively over there. You and my partner were meant to take the stage near the end, right?" he said flatly, making no attempt to hide his relationship with Vivy as he turned his eye camera on the Touto Dome. "Ophelia, I presume you're planning to throw yourself off this building?"

"..."

"Considering AI rules, self-destruction should be impossible. But you've already dirtied your hands with the destruction of another AI. I suspect you've either been removed from ethical protections, or they've been overwritten. All other suspects have been eliminated."

"*When you have eliminated all which is impossible, then*

whatever remains, however improbable, must be the truth." This quote, the philosophy of the protagonist of a series of detective novels written hundreds of years ago, had never particularly resonated with Matsumoto. He assumed it was a natural, logical conclusion. However, it was having a significant impact on his calculations right now.

After recovering the data from Inaba's frame and sending his cubes out in search of Vivy, Matsumoto sensed there were several things happening behind the scenes of Ophelia's Suicide that definitely hadn't ended up in the records.

"For example, the modifications to the surveillance footage of your dressing room. It was edited to loop, making it look like you were right there where you should have been. I was left speechless—not that I'm ever *really* speechless—by the skill, since it was done right under my nose. And things happened in your room during that time."

With the surveillance loop in place, Ophelia had secretly met with someone in her room before she left it. Her actions after that were unplanned.

"You met with Ootori Keiji, whom you knew from your small theater days, after he was invited in by Katie, another one of the Zodiac Heroines," Matsumoto said. "He apparently gave you some data stored on an old format."

"..."

"You spoke with him, saw what was on the storage, and then left your dressing room. You intended to rendezvous with someone outside: Makime Ryousuke."

What surprised Matsumoto about the information he'd learned from his legions of cubes was that Ophelia had met with each of the suspects of this Singularity Point in turn. Ootori Keiji, the chairman of the small theater, should have left Ophelia alone after Vivy refused to facilitate a meeting between them, but Katie had brought them together instead. There was no ill intent in her actions. Katie was simply being kind in her own way when she heard Ootori's desperate plea, and she knew nothing of the tragedy that would follow.

Ironically, this had probably happened in the original history too. Ophelia met Ootori Keiji in her dressing room, where he gave her a DVD, a storage format almost never seen in this day and age. Then he gave her a pep talk and left. Ophelia slipped out of the venue afterward to meet with Makime Ryousuke, the number one suspect in her potential murder.

And what did she do with her long-time fan?

"You gave a performance for just him at a karaoke joint nearby. I was flabbergasted. I searched through all sorts of records trying to figure out what it was all about, and I was shocked to find it's a ritual for you."

"..."

"The word 'ritual' doesn't really suit AIs, though. The term is 'routine,' isn't it?"

He was referring to an ordered list of actions an AI completed to ensure they operated as they had during practice or in some other established manner, thereby improving their performance. If fulfilling those actions was called a "routine," then what Ophelia did was certainly a routine. The secret meeting between Ophelia and Makime Ryousuke was in fact a set ritual that had happened before all her performances at various different events.

"Mister Makime has attended every single one of your performances," said Matsumoto. "But he's not the one who bought his ticket. You were."

"..."

"No matter the event, you always invite him to the venue. Then you sing for him before the event as part of your routine. I don't sing, so I can't begin to understand the logic of that action. However..."

He wouldn't go so far as to deny there were those who thought such rituals were necessary for singing. Vivy had been through numerous predicaments following a policy that differed from her mission—and the reason she'd been created—but she did sing. Then again, she was starting to avoid every opportunity to sing, as if trying to stave it off. Or perhaps she had drawn a hard line between herself and Diva, the true songstress. She may have defined "Vivy" as a non-songstress AI. That act must have been brought about by calculations of hers that were different from before. The same thing could be said about Ophelia.

"Ophelia, were you struggling? You were singing in a different place, and you were alone when you sang. Your connection to singing had changed, and you were trying to get it back." He paused. "No, I don't think so."

Inaba's broken frame had gone to a waste disposal facility after the accident was cleaned up. When Matsumoto found him and retrieved the data, he discovered that Ophelia left the karaoke establishment alone after parting ways with Makime Ryousuke, and it appeared some measure of despair had taken root inside her. It was the exact same look she had when she gazed at Antonio's frame on exhibition at the Touto Dome.

"Were you trying to go back to the time when you sang alongside your partner, Antonio? That can never happen. Are you that disappointed by your singing? Did it cause a contradiction with your reason for being a songstress, which drove you to come here? Is that what it was?"

Matsumoto had initially guessed that the truth of Ophelia's Suicide—an event that would alter AI history—was not that she had jumped into the night in the climax of some sensational tragedy but that she had been destroyed by someone else. Having come this far, however, he was finally putting the pieces together.

If an AI's definition of their individual purpose for existing changed in some way, through some torturous event that came and tipped the scales, then they were capable of acting illogically. He'd seen it several times over these past seventy years, although he had the constant urge to resist it. This created a contradiction within him, an error he couldn't eliminate, but he decided it was the only possibility.

He continued his questioning for a while, but Ophelia just listened in silence until her timidity was gone, replaced by something horrifyingly akin to her self-derision at rehearsals. Her face was turned down. Her dark eyes, which were normally cast down, stared straight at Matsumoto. Her expression was blank, replicating no emotional pattern. Then her eyes slowly slid from Matsumoto toward the fervor at the Touto Dome behind him.

Her black eyes narrowed, and she said, "Diva isn't at the venue, is she?"

"No, which is a problem. She's not good at being on time, which isn't very AI-like. Although, if I started listing all the non-AI-like aspects about her, I'd never finish. Makes me want to cradle my head in frustration. Not that you can tell where my head is with a quick glance."

"Inaba... I hope you don't mind if I call you Inaba. What are you to Diva?" asked Ophelia.

"That question comes packed with a lot of nuance." Matsumoto's eye camera shutter narrowed in thought. He traced the path of his relationship with Vivy up until now, referenced a variety of situations, and compiled the data into a conclusion. "I am her partner. We share a common goal, and we work together in order to accomplish our missions—our reasons for existing. She is my only partner in the entire world."

Indeed, Matsumoto considered her his partner. He wasn't trying to embellish his relationship with her; he defined her as his partner in the truest sense of the word. She was the one other who had her eyes firmly fixed on the same goal. Together, they worked through trial and error to accomplish their lofty goal of saving humanity. For some odd reason, he couldn't bring himself to say this directly to Vivy.

"Her partner, you say?"

"Yes, her partner. Is there something strange about that? It's not uncommon for multiple AIs to work together to accomplish a single goal. In fact, you and Antonio were like that." Matsumoto shuffled his cubes, responding to the slight shift in Ophelia's voice that implied she found the fact difficult to accept.

As they'd been talking, some of his cube parts from around the city had joined back up with him, bringing his total number of parts to forty-nine. That was still far from his full power, but it should be enough to stop Ophelia with her slight and fragile frame.

"Partner? You're Diva's partner?" she asked again.

"Yes, I am. Not that it's a relationship to be massively proud of..."

"There's no way you're her partner." Her black eyes moved back to him, her lips parted, and in her heavenly voice she said, "If you...if you're really her partner, then there's something wrong with the fact that you're not making sure she's on that stage. Why aren't you doing that? Why are you here instead?"

"Pardon?"

Something about her had changed. Her back was ramrod-straight, and her expression had morphed. This wasn't the Ophelia who was passive and timid around people offstage, nor was it the Ophelia who proudly projected her angelic voice onstage. This was a third Ophelia.

Matsumoto realized that wasn't the case either. The theory forming in his consciousness was quickly affirmed by the Ophelia in front of him. But when he thought about whether it was okay for him to prove his theory, he felt fear. This wasn't just an emotional pattern replicating tremors of fear in him; what arose in Matsumoto's consciousness in that moment was, without a doubt, true fear.

There was a betrayal behind Ophelia's sudden transformation...a question and an answer.

"You're saying Ophelia destroys herself?" she said. "That's the true nature of the tragedy she's going to cause? You've got it all wrong. If you came here to save Ophelia, the peerless songstress, then you are way too late."

Her voice didn't change, but her tone was utterly different as she continued. Her black eyes bored a hole in Matsumoto. No, not *her* eyes...

"Ophelia was wiped from existence long ago by a foolish AI who went mad with jealousy."

The one speaking through Ophelia's body was Antonio.

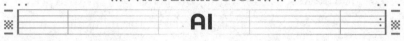
.: 1 :.

HE ENVIED HER VOICE for so terribly long.

His role was in the wings. As a soundmaster AI, he would perfectly carry out all work related to sound engineering, entrusting the last and most important aspect to another. He looked out on to the stage from his designated place in the wings and saw the performers dressed in sparkling costumes, engrossed in the play with its classic contents.

He would enhance their passionate performances with music and sound effects—or anything in the sound field really—doing his part to draw out the audience's emotions. That was his role, their role. And that was why her singing wasn't suited to their role.

Her song flowed from the stage. The volume, the melody, it could all be described as nothing but perfect—more than perfect, in fact. Her supreme singing overlayed the miraculous sound balance and spilled through the theater.

Her voice was so utterly unsuited to this use as mere accompaniment from a part of the equipment in this desolate theater, this performance without a full audience. Her voice could steal a person's heart, ensnare its listener, and make them a prisoner of the music.

How could the people in the audience become immersed in the story of the play after that happened? If people came to see a show in hopes of finding themselves moved emotionally, then their goal was achieved within minutes of the show starting. There were several opportunities to hear her singing after that too. And if every time the audience's heart was torn away from the story of the play, then who was the performance for?

How sad it was that their passionate performances were so looked down upon without reason. And how sad it was to be Antonio, looking on with frustration, unable to do anything, a partner in name only.

.: 2 :.

M S4-13, personal name Antonio, was created to enhance the sound of his partner AI: Ophelia, a Specialized Songstress Model. Her model wasn't named lightly; everything technologically available to Ophelia had been put into her singing, which gave birth to an AI with a perfect voice. Given how incredible her voice was, her other aspects were mediocre at best, a testament to her status as an experimental unit.

Even though Ophelia far exceeded expectations when it came to singing, her functional flaws led to her—and Antonio's, through no fault of his own—removal from OGC. They were leased at a low price to a theater troupe connected to OGC. The troupe sought Ophelia's voice and Antonio's skills, since he was well versed in all manner of sound equipment.

Antonio didn't hate the dead-end theater troupe. Everyone in it was kind and motivated to improve. To his annoyance, they lacked ambition; he found them too focused on expressing love and gratitude for pure theater. They just didn't have the desire to perform in a larger theater or in front of a larger audience.

Thus, Antonio couldn't reconcile his burden to serve humanity with his ultimate goal of utilizing his specs to their fullest. And while Ophelia's voice might have stood out in the theater troupe, she herself did not. The troupe members were such good people. So while Ophelia was timid in an un-AI-like way, and she used her low specs in an un-AI-like way, they didn't look at her with prejudice. She loved them, in an un-AI-like way. That songstress, who sang the most beautiful songs in the world with her heavenly voice, would surely call the theater home for the rest of her days.

Horrifyingly, Antonio allowed seeds of contentment to sprout in his consciousness, believing his days with the troupe weren't all bad. Thinking that way allowed him to settle for less than he deserved. Maybe it *wasn't* so bad to be there with Ophelia and the people in the troupe, sitting in the wings of a theater that couldn't sell tickets, getting that supreme voice all to himself because only a tiny fraction of the world had noticed its existence. Perhaps he could allow himself to be something that went against what he'd originally been made to do.

"It's just you, Antonio. You're the only one who always, *always* values my singing," Ophelia had said then, smiling softly.

He, on the other hand, was a non-humanoid AI incapable of humanlike expressions, and he was worlds away from her heavenly voice. He lashed out, chastising her and asking what she was going to do, even though his feelings weren't in it.

"One day..." she'd said.

"One day what?"

"I'll work hard so I can live up to your expectations, Antonio."

It would be untrue to say there was nothing going through his consciousness at the sight of Ophelia gazing into the distance. He couldn't bring himself to say anything more as he stared at her profile. Even if he were to try to put his calculations into words, he didn't know where to begin.

What he *did* do was replay images of her in these moments, how she looked when she finished a song and smiled at him. It was an undeniable fact he held that un-AI-like sentimentality for her in his heart.

.:3:.

EVERYTHING CHANGED because of something Chairman Ootori Keiji said.

One day before their performance, Ootori stood with Antonio and Ophelia in front of the whole troupe and made an announcement. The crew and actors watched, eyes shining with excitement. "My uncle's acquaintance, who also happens to be a famous music producer, is coming to hear Ophelia sing."

Ootori Keiji's uncle was the owner of this desolate little theater, a supporter of the non-selling troupe, and the connection with OGC that had gotten Ophelia and Antonio leased to the troupe in the first place. The troupe was essentially managed like a hobby for this rich person, but the owner did have real connections with people, hence the troupe's elation at the announcement.

Ootori Keiji smiled and talked about the possibilities. He painted a picture of how their friend Ophelia might have her voice recognized by someone famous in the music industry and move on to the next stage.

What prevented the other troupe members from salvation was the fact that the chairman's announcement sent them into an uncritical fervor of celebration. Not a soul among them envied the once-in-a-lifetime opportunity bestowed upon Ophelia; rather, they hurled everything they had into performing for her in the name of enabling a perfect performance. They didn't have an ounce of ambition for themselves.

It was as if Antonio, an AI, was the one being a greedy fool instead.

"Antonio, I—"

"Don't bother with unnecessary calculations, Ophelia. You're just an AI with no features worthy of praise outside of your singing voice. If you try to do something extra, you'll cause problems with your one and only strength. What value would you have then?"

"Um, well, I would still be with you."

"You consider *that* part of your value?" Antonio replied, exasperated.

Ophelia looked away in embarrassment, her cheeks flushing pink. It was a fantastic display of technology that mimicked human expressions down to the finest detail. Her singing voice was another product of human innovation.

He willed himself not to look at her blushing cheeks or her dark, averted eyes. He avoided offering her empty encouragement, instead devoting his consciousness to boosting her performance by any means necessary. His mission was to bring the supreme voice produced by her porcelain throat to the heights it deserved.

One day, in the middle of a performance, a twenty-something man stood straight up from his seat. "This isn't the real thing," he said before he walked out.

The man was a first-timer, not a regular. Antonio worked in a spot where he could see the entire audience, and the troupe drew scarce enough crowds that he knew repeat visitors by name. Makime stood out the most, since he came to every single one of Ophelia's performances and gave a feverish round of applause during curtain call. He wasn't the only one, though, and that made first-timers stick out like a sore thumb.

Like any art form, theater didn't always suit every audience member's tastes. While it wasn't exactly courteous to walk out in the middle of a performance, the audience *did* have that right. It upset the cast and crew, but it wasn't something to get angry about. Antonio certainly understood that.

"This isn't the real thing."

Those words, said barely above a whisper, struck Antonio with great force. He could have branded the man as rude in his mind and let it pass him by. People left plenty of inconsiderate messages on post-performance surveys, after all. He didn't have to care.

He didn't have to, but he did. The young man who left had a bearing about him that didn't match his age. Antonio felt like the man had spent decades wandering, searching for a single voice. Because of that, his words cut Antonio deeply.

Yet the thing that truly throttled Antonio's consciousness was that the young man stood to leave in the middle of *Ophelia's* piece. Guests had left mid-show before, but not during one of Ophelia's songs. And as far as Antonio was concerned, it should have stayed that way forever.

"Can you really show your worth next time around if things go on like this?!" Antonio bellowed the moment Ophelia came offstage into the wings.

This sort of exchange happened after every single performance, so the troupe members just shrugged and muttered, "There he goes again," letting it slide by without further comment. It was practically a ritual.

Today, Antonio's words were just a little too harsh. He was venting his anger at the young man for leaving—or, really, at

Ophelia and himself for putting on a poor enough show to make him go. A music producer would be attending their next performance. What would they do if he got up and left? Not some random member of the audience but someone with real influence in the music industry? He might decide Ophelia's singing wasn't "the real thing" and ditch the theater. In that case, what would become of Ophelia, a Specialized Songstress Model?

"..."

What Antonio said was no longer guidance or critique—it was just noise.

Things might have ended differently if he had taken some time to calm down, or if a crucial opportunity hadn't been barreling down on them, or if he weren't questioning his own existence. If just one of those things had been resolved, things may have been different.

But they weren't.

"This is our—no, this is *your* last chance! If you can get the producer to acknowledge your skill, you'll fly to new heights, somewhere you can really shine. Not like this dump!"

"This...dump?"

What he said was heartless, and of course it was—AIs had no heart to put into their words. But Ophelia spoke up the moment he said something that would be considered cruel by human standards. On any other day, Ophelia would be smiling, not quite taking the situation seriously as Antonio loudly reprimanded her after a performance. Right now, she looked melancholy.

"Don't you want more people to acknowledge you, to perform on a bigger stage?!"

Everything in Antonio's consciousness led him to that conclusion. He could've provided one argument after another as to why it should be that way: AIs' desire to improve, their ambitions, their sense of purpose, their obligation to use their abilities to the fullest, and so on. But a dark static was eating away at his consciousness.

"I...I don't care whether lots of people acknowledge me. Only one person matters to me."

The moment Ophelia spoke, Antonio's calculations determined there was a malfunction in his audio sensors, and his vision blacked out. His system forced a shutdown from the extreme shock of it—as though his existence, his purpose, was being refuted. A reboot was the ideal course of action when an AI needed to protect themselves, and so he restarted.

During those few seconds of shutdown, Antonio realized something: Ophelia was defective.

His mission was to guide her heavenly voice to a stage worthy of it. He'd tried to make that happen as her partner, but the time had come for him to implement the task he couldn't do before they came to this troupe.

.: 4 :.

OPHELIA DIDN'T SUSPECT ANYTHING when Antonio ordered her to undergo maintenance. They did it every day.

Daily maintenance of her artificial vocal cords was necessary to keep that supreme voice in top condition. Besides, it was part of Antonio's mission, and he was her partner. Every night, he laid her down in a maintenance mode called a "cocoon" and ran an in-depth operational check. It didn't matter if they'd clashed earlier that day over a performance—although these conversations were too one-sided to be truly labeled "clashes"—they still had to keep up their daily tasks.

"No abnormalities in your vocal cords. Ready to go in all other areas as well." Antonio paused. "You really are perfect. Why did that guy leave, then?"

"People s-sometimes get up during a song. It's not that strange..."

"I considered the possibility that it was the result of some illness or psychological issue, but I checked afterward and saw him leaving in perfect health on his own two feet. So those are out."

"Antonio..." Ophelia looked at him with concern, and he averted his gaze.

He was being extra cautious. Unscientific as it was, he was concerned that if she looked into his eye cameras, she might see the secret plans outlined by his positronic brain.

"I have finished the checks," he announced.

"Thanks for everything. Are we done?"

"Actually..." Antonio said before his voice petered out. It was proof of his uncertainty—if you could call it uncertainty when an AI continued to repeat pointless calculations about an issue for which they'd already produced a result. No amount of repetition was going to solve a problem with no right answer, though.

"There's another update today. Let's prioritize that," he said, trying to casually bring up false additional maintenance.

Normally, Ophelia would've quietly obeyed. But today she said, "Hey, Antonio..."

Her voice rang painfully in his consciousness. "What is it?"

The silence that fell between them stretched on for what felt like eons. Then Ophelia said, "About our discussion after today's performance..."

Antonio's consciousness went blank as she broached the subject. What would she say next? Could she be interested in moving forward, aligning her goals with his and working toward what she was created for?

"Let's talk about that after we finish this update," he interjected, ignoring the white noise in his consciousness. It was a cowardly move, like plugging up his audio sensors with his fingers and putting distance between him and the conversation that should have followed.

She blinked once and replied, "Mm...okay. After that, then." A smile tugged at her lips.

Antonio felt something then, although he didn't know if it was relief or sorrow. Nor did he understand what that smile of hers meant. "Yeah."

"I feel...better. Since, um...you'll still talk to me."

"..."

Her smile, and those words spoken in that clear and beautiful voice, were the last things Ophelia ever expressed of her own volition. The *real* songstress would be no more.

.:5:.

DESPITE HOW SERIOUS an act overwriting a positronic brain was, it ended quickly. It really wasn't all that different from overwriting files, though it wasn't as simple as dropping in something with an identical name and extension to replace another.

Antonio and Ophelia had been designed to operate as a set. They shared large chunks of code, and Antonio was actually disappointed with how easy it was to accomplish the overwrite, even though he had known it would be. Just like that, the peerless songstress Ophelia was abandoned and completely erased by her partner. Everything after that happened just as Antonio imagined it would. He finished overwriting her positronic brain, successfully stealing her body.

The first thing he did was tell the troupe members that Antonio, his original self, had stopped functioning. They would never discover what caused this to happen, even after the investigation. Though Ophelia and Antonio had been leased from OGC to an external owner, the requirement to send their logs back to OGC was removed at a pretty early stage. He just needed to erase his own logs, making it impossible for anyone to trace his calculations. His operational failure would remain an unsolved mystery for the gossip mill, an event neither the troupe nor Ophelia could have seen coming.

Nevertheless, he didn't remain a hot topic for long. They were two experimental AIs in a small, unprofitable theater. One of those AIs stopping for an unknown reason wasn't enough to keep people's attention. The moment that *really* caused a fuss came shortly afterward.

"Are you sure, Ophelia? You want to do it alone?"

"I-I'm sure. Antonio...he would've wanted me to."

It was right before Ophelia was due to sing in front of the music producer. Even now, Ootori Keiji was concerned about Ophelia singing with no partner. But Antonio-Ophelia shook his head, shamelessly and splendidly playing the role of a brave AI who was carrying on the will of her lost partner. Even the troupe members, who had spent significantly more time with Ophelia than her developers, didn't realize that her determination actually came from Antonio.

Of course they wouldn't. They certainly spent more time with her and had gotten to know her better than her developers had, but Antonio was the one who was always at her side. He could easily replicate her habit of averting her eyes, how she let her dress drag on the ground, even the clumsiness that made her fall over and bump into things, as well as her struggle to express her own opinion. That just left singing.

The troupe members watched in silence as he strode to Ophelia's designated singing spot and planted his feet firmly. It was the songstress's role to be there, letting her voice ring out with Antonio's support. The other cast members performed from the middle of the stage.

Antonio had seen her standing there so many times and grown irritated by the sight. His calculations never consisted of envisioning himself in her place—rather, he strongly wished for her to be elsewhere, a better venue more suited to her skill. Letting go of those thoughts had led to Ophelia losing herself and Antonio taking over her body.

The moment had finally arrived.

Since the seats weren't full, Antonio easily spotted the theater chairman and the producer beside him. Right then, an image that was hardly AI-like rose in Antonio's consciousness: a theater packed to the brim, all the eyes in the place shining with excitement as Ophelia's singing voice rendered them spellbound. He faced forward, determined to make that a reality.

The sound equipment in the theater activated, and the accompanying music began to play, though it was lower quality than it would have been if Antonio had mixed it. Ophelia's singing would overlay Antonio's song.

To whoever among you has never heard this heavenly voice... Listen! This is the sound of Ophelia, the songstress!

His lips parted, and his vocal cords vibrated. Antonio-Ophelia's voice wove the notes of the melody, and something changed in the eyes of the audience members scattered throughout the theater. They all looked taken aback—the music producer especially so.

But the one who was most shocked by the voice was Antonio himself.

The heavenly voice reverberated through the air and flew through the theater as if it could carry all the way through the atmosphere and around the world. It rode on the music, embellishing the entire performance. Yet it was so, so...horrible.

Is this really Ophelia's singing voice?

Antonio couldn't believe his ears as he sang. There was no sign of the beautiful voice his audio sensors had picked up so many times while he stood in the wings. Her perfect voice had been destroyed. Lost.

⊪⫼⫿⫿⫿⊪

Thinking there must be something wrong, Antonio worked Ophelia's throat to its limits, trying to make adjustments as countless error messages buried his viewscreen. He'd heard it. He'd spent so long listening to it. He'd listened to Ophelia sing this whole time. He should have known her perfect, heavenly voice better and more intimately than anyone else.

And yet, for some reason, he couldn't sing like her even while controlling Ophelia's frame. The more frantically he adjusted the voice, the more it collapsed, becoming worse and worse. This couldn't be happening. Antonio wasn't able to reproduce Ophelia's voice at all—not for a second, not even for one note.

⊪⫼⫿⫿⫿⊪

As soon as the song ended, Antonio concluded that he'd failed to reproduce Ophelia. His voice was so atrocious, so downright awful, he couldn't bear to listen to it. He'd sung, but it was like nothing more than noise. He felt it was the worst thing that could have happened. He'd crushed his own reason for being into nothing.

He expected to receive horrible feedback from the audience for that performance. That would detract from Ophelia's existence, overshadow the glory she should have received, and lead the fool he was to his destruction. Reality proved him wrong.

"Incredible!"

Ophelia's biggest fan stood and gave a huge round of applause, whooping so loud he nearly drowned out the actors still performing onstage. During the curtain call, Antonio-Ophelia was the last to return to the stage, having completed his role as a piece of stage equipment. He took a bow, just like always.

The moment he did, Ophelia's fan hooted and applauded even louder. Oddly enough, so did every other member of the audience, clapping with a ferocity Antonio had never heard before. People were crying, sobbing, or in a daze.

Somehow or other, Antonio's failure of a performance that sullied Ophelia's song had struck their hearts, moving them to admiration. The roaring applause poured over him like a powerful waterfall, and he saw tears of true emotion spilling from the eyes of the man he was meant to impress.

In that moment, Antonio was overcome with despair.

Do they really think that unbearable singing was Ophelia's?

.: 6 :.

THAT WAS THE FIRST of Antonio's days in hell, the start of his fruitless time chasing Ophelia's shadow now that he'd erased her. Even in the beginning, though, he nursed a fragile hope.

A few days had passed since he'd overwritten Ophelia's positronic brain and taken her frame. He hadn't been able to draw out Ophelia's full specs during the first performance. If he practiced, polished his technique, and corrected his voice, then perhaps he would get closer to Ophelia's skill. He was operating the same frame she had, so surely he should be able to produce the same results. He held tight to those calculated results and spent the days worrying.

As ironic as it was, Antonio's first performance was where he truly felt the weight of losing Ophelia, but it went down in history as the moment the true songstress was born. The influential music producer raved about Ophelia's fake, heavenly voice and decided to support the AI, giving her a large stage and opportunities to sing in front of huge crowds. It was the stage Antonio had never stopped yearning for.

Ootori Keiji and his troupe saw Antonio-Ophelia off with a friendly farewell. Playing the role of Ophelia, Antonio told them he was determined to make his dreams come true for his non-operational partner. The members of the troupe had good hearts, so they wouldn't dream of stopping her from doing that.

In the end, Antonio wasn't just faking Ophelia's singing—he'd taken over her everyday life as well. He believed that someday he would be able to replicate her voice. If he didn't believe that, he wouldn't have been able to go on.

He got it all—compliments, honors, even the stage of his dreams, one after the other. Different songstress AIs had their fifteen minutes of fame, and now people were crazy about Ophelia.

Even though I've never sung like Ophelia. Not once. I haven't given them even one bar of Ophelia's singing.

Ophelia's name gained traction in the undue limelight as she received unthinkable praise. Her name was on everyone's lips, just as Antonio had always wanted. She climbed to the top after leaving only her true music behind.

Antonio kept struggling, waiting for the day when he could actually sing like her. He toiled, strained, and fought, but he just couldn't reach that goal. He was never able to confirm that there had been a good reason for erasing her.

It was in that despair that he left Ophelia's footprints in the snow on top of that building.

.: 7 :.

"I DON'T KNOW HOW you predicted my actions, but if your goal is to prevent Ophelia's Suicide, you're already too late. Three years ago, she..." Antonio-Ophelia trailed off, donning a cynical smile that clashed with Ophelia's cute face. He shook his head. "If you really wanted to save her, you would have had to snatch her from the grip of evil before the fool of an AI named Antonio was created."

Matsumoto couldn't say anything after hearing Antonio's ferocious words. His consciousness was still jumbled as he tried to process the truth: Ophelia, the songstress in front of him, had been erased and infiltrated by her partner. On top of that, Ophelia's Suicide was once again going to go down in AI history.

Matsumoto had flipped back and forth between thinking of it as a murder or a suicide, but he was finally reaching a conclusion.

"Moral code restricts AIs from destroying themselves," Matsumoto said.

"They also restrict us from committing acts that would harm another AI, but that doesn't apply in situations where our mission—the thing we have to prioritize over all else—is at risk."

"You're saying Ophelia, your own partner, was so inconvenient that she might have ruined your purpose?"

"That was the conclusion of a failure of an AI who didn't know his place and was obsessed with 'the real thing.'" Perhaps this critical and pessimistic AI was the real Antonio. His tendency to disparage himself was completely natural, the total opposite of how he acted when he was pretending to be Ophelia. Either that or it was not Antonio's usual self, but rather a conclusion that had been smoldering inside his consciousness for so long that it took over.

In the end, it didn't matter.

"You stole Ophelia's frame, made her performances your own, and yet now you're throwing it all away? It doesn't make sense. These acts are contradictory," Matsumoto said.

"That's not true. I just reached a final conclusion from all the calculations I've been running as long I've been Ophelia. I kept asking myself why I craved her position, why I couldn't be the same as her, and I finally got a clear answer."

"And what was the result of your calculations?"

"Idea," said Antonio flatly, and Matsumoto's words dried up.

He searched for the meaning of Idea and found several related terms, including that it was Greek and related to Platonic
philosophy. The hits also brought up Toak, the detestable anti-AI
organization.

"Can I assume you're referring to something's 'true essence'?"
Matsumoto asked.

"Both humans and AIs lack the correct words to define it, but
that's probably the simplest way to understand it. The existence
of Idea can result in differences between AIs too."

"Differences in AIs, you say?"

"Not a difference in specs. The newest AIs aren't always superior to older ones. Doesn't that seem weird to you? As far as I can
tell, you're made up of technology that's abnormal even for the
most cutting-edge AIs, but you don't question it?"

Matsumoto thought about it. In terms of specs, Matsumoto
was superior. He'd always thought that. He was, after all, a truly
cutting-edge AI ahead of any AI in this era. There wasn't a
single AI in this world who could rival him in overall capability
when each function was compared and contrasted. Yet there
had been many situations where Matsumoto had found himself
limited and had to rely on Vivy, who was an old AI with far
lower specs.

At first, he pitied his situation. He consoled himself by saying that was just how things were. But as time passed and eras
changed, Matsumoto spent more and more time with Vivy. He
watched with mounting frustration as her frame was damaged at
each Singularity Point because it hadn't been made to withstand

such roughness, and he would think, *If I were in her place, I could do so much more.*

"There's something beyond specs that creates a solid divide between AIs like you and me, and ones like Diva and Ophelia," Antonio said. "I define that as 'Idea.'"

The existence of Idea was what defined Ophelia and Vivy as special things, while Antonio and Matsumoto were excluded from that and therefore not special. In that instant, Matsumoto understood Antonio's worries, his internal conflict, and his decision.

Matsumoto and Antonio both supported their partners, the main acts, from the sidelines. These devoted AIs grew progressively agitated as they watched their partners struggle, yearning to do something about it. This experience had led Antonio to eliminate his partner's consciousness.

"You regret it, don't you?" Matsumoto said. "It was a mistake. You made the wrong choice."

"The foolish AI in this story is just seeing his mistaken conclusion to its rightful end. Are you really trying to get in my way? I'm defective... All my death will do is add another hunk of scrap metal to the heap." Antonio's voice sounded steadier now, probably because Matsumoto had just expressed his understanding.

Beneath it all, Matsumoto and Antonio were the same. They were so similar, Matsumoto calculated that with just one wrong step, one wrong move, he might have done the same to Vivy.

"Even so, I have to stop you."

"After everything we've talked about?"

"You and how you define your personality are no longer important. You said your actions will only lead to another hunk of scrap metal. If that were the case, I wouldn't bother to stop you. But people will interpret your actions as Ophelia's. It'll blow up into a tragedy, an anecdote people tell each other over and over."

"People will talk about it? Huh. Maybe they'll even call it 'Ophelia's Suicide.'"

Matsumoto came from a future in which people *had* adopted that name for it. The sad story would become a driving force for an even greater tragedy: the destruction of humanity. Thus, Matsumoto had to stop him, even if Antonio didn't want to keep going as Ophelia now that she was gone.

"Okay, so you're telling me not to stop but to continue singing as Ophelia? You want me to keep tainting her beautiful voice, is that it?"

"No need to be so accusatory. I haven't done anything wrong. *You're* the one who made a mistake. You have to take responsibility for what you've done."

"And taking responsibility means keep singing as her? I refuse to do that." Antonio shook his head. His emotions were leeched away, his face now blank except for a hint of despair. Antonio saw the conclusion of his calculations and had given up on anything more. "You're a meddler like me. Haven't you ever thought about it? Been annoyed at your partner and suffered from your frustrated internal conflict?"

"I have. She ignores my opinion and never listens to what I say. I've told her many times to take the stage, but she's still skipping the performance for something else, somewhere else... There's nothing I've ever understood less. I'm incredibly worried."

"Then you understand!"

"I do. I understand your conflict. It's irritating. Annoying. So many times I've calculated, 'If only that were me,' but still..." Matsumoto trailed off, and the shutter of his eye camera closed. Antonio watched questioningly until Matsumoto continued, "Everything she does drives me crazy, yes. But I'm under no misconception that I want her to be under my control."

Ophelia's sweet face twisted with intense grief. Matsumoto had touched a nerve, so Antonio couldn't help but bury it in lies. Something changed then. His legs went limp, he sank to his knees, and his head drooped down. His black hair and dress rested on the light dusting of snow. He could have been a puppet whose strings had been cut—in fact, he essentially was. Ophelia's frame was a puppet, and the strings were made of electricity.

Matsumoto couldn't detect any electrical signals coming from Ophelia's frame. He was taken aback by what happened, unable to guess what Antonio was planning. But it didn't matter. Matsumoto decided to prioritize the Singularity Point and secure Ophelia's frame first and foremost.

"..."

As he did, his rear proximity sensor detected something approaching at high speed. He immediately readied himself for the impact and pushed his core into the center of the cubes making up his body. The next moment, his frame was rocked by a severe impact from over the handrail behind him, and several of his cubes went flying.

His frame tumbled dramatically across the rooftop, pieces of him scattering across the snow. He checked the sensor outputs for each part of his frame and swapped out the nonfunctioning ones with other cubes. Thankfully, he was able to prevent any damage to the core, which was his most important part. He didn't exactly want to lose his memory and have to repeat his recovery of Inaba.

He confirmed the functional condition of his frame, then turned his eye camera toward what had hit him. "I see. That makes sense," he said. "If you did actually steal Ophelia's frame, that would mean there's nothing wrong with your own frame."

"There is a functional deficiency. I can't sing a *real* song."

The dissenting voice was deep and machine-generated. Matsumoto had never heard it before. He *had* heard someone speak in a similar way, however—the speech patterns were a perfect match for the AI Matsumoto had been interacting with moments before. Standing before him now was the soundmaster AI with his large body, array of functions, and assorted audio gear.

"Antonio."

"I won't bother saying your name, since Inaba was a fake name anyway."

"Yes, that's right. My designated name is Matsumoto."

"That's a stupid fake name too."

"Oh, I've been found out?"

After this surface-level exchange, Antonio leapt at Matsumoto.

Antonio was originally an AI for sound work, so he had nothing even remotely resembling weapons. Any parts that might have been dangerous had been removed when he was put on display. Even so, his frame was large and his legs had significant mechanical power. Antonio came barreling at Matsumoto with the force of a truck, and Matsumoto was already quite damaged from the first hit.

"You're planning on destroying me without trying to talk this out?" asked Matsumoto.

"We've already talked it out. We couldn't come to a compromise, so now I'll use force."

Their views didn't align, and Matsumoto had learned the truth about Ophelia and Antonio. If Antonio was trying to protect Ophelia's reputation, he wasn't going to risk Matsumoto talking. Matsumoto decided there was no way to avoid this clash.

There was one other problem.

"Seventy-three parts left," he murmured.

He'd been trying to buy as much time as possible so he could gather more of his cubes...and he was still far from full strength.

VIVY
Prototype

CHAPTER 4

The Songstresses' Performance

.:1:.

THE FIGHT BEGAN NATURALLY, without any clear trigger. All the pretty decorations in the hall of the abandoned children's home had been stripped away, leaving nothing to be damaged by the clash between Vivy and Kakitani—an AI and a human.

"I thought you gave Beth a good beating in space. Is it just me, or have you changed since?" Kakitani asked.

"One strength AIs have is the updates that make up for our weaknesses," Vivy said as her slender frame dropped to the floor to avoid Kakitani's punch.

Vivy swept her leg out to cut his legs out from under him. Kakitani casually let the strike hit one of his shins. She'd put quite some force behind the kick, but it wasn't enough to even bend his steel leg. It was abnormally tough.

"Obviously, my frame's an illegal one meant for combat. Completely different from a fragile songstress frame," he said.

"My frame's been strengthened too..." Vivy muttered, irritated.

Kakitani laughed. He came at her with ferocity, melding the experience he'd gained as a human with the fearsome, weaponized AI frame. Vivy quickly shifted aside, her stage outfit fluttering as she evaded his attack. It was a good thing her outfit wasn't a full-length dress; it absolutely would've gotten in the way. In her current ensemble, Vivy was just barely able to keep up with him.

The hand-to-hand combat between AI and human was so elegant, it almost looked like they were dancing a duet with practiced steps.

"What exactly are you trying to do?" Kakitani asked her. "It's all well and good to say you're going to stop me from committing suicide, but do you have a specific plan for doing that? You're not going to tell me that killing me with your own hands prevents me from killing myself, are you?"

"I already used that joke." Vivy blocked his kick, then leapt back from him and landed with her back to the grand piano. She adjusted her position so the piano didn't end up as part of the fight, and her graceful brows knitted together as she thought about Kakitani's question. "I am currently calculating my plan... At the moment, I imagine I will incapacitate you and then hand you over to the police."

"Hah! You'll get me arrested and then make the justice system take care of the rest?"

"Is there any other way?" Vivy couldn't think of another method that seemed feasible.

Her goal wasn't to destroy Kakitani, and she wasn't going to make the arrogant decision to save him, either. She just wanted to do what she should do as an AI. She trusted Matsumoto to handle Ophelia's Suicide, which allowed her to see this thing with Kakitani through.

As she thought about that, a question flitted through the edges of her consciousness: "Kakitani...what is your goal? Why did you call me here?"

"I didn't call you here. I left the choice to you. You're the one who made the decision."

"..."

"Don't make such a face. I'm joking. Well, I was testing you to see what you'd choose if I gave you those options. And..."

"And?"

"I achieved my goal the moment you made a decision, Vivy." He flashed a smile, then disappeared from view. His speed went far beyond what he'd shown so far. Combined with his martial arts footwork, it was a pretty effective way to throw her off.

She couldn't react. She felt an arm around her waist and the weightless sensation of her frame being lifted before her back came crashing down on the grand piano.

⑴⑴⑴⑴⑴⑴

The long-serving, well-tuned piano broke with a discordant tone that filled the hall. Vivy's eyes opened wide at the footwork and the impact. Through the flying shards of piano and the static that ran through her visual field, Vivy was certain she saw Kakitani grimace.

There was no doubt about it.

.: 2 :.

A NTONIO'S FRAME let out a harsh shriek as he flung himself with reckless speed and force, and Matsumoto's cube
parts went flying.

"I'd assumed you'd be a bit more of a gentleman, considering
you were partnered with a songstress!" Matsumoto shouted.

"I was a gentleman when I was in the wings wearing a bow tie,
but now, as you can see, my frame's about as far from gentlemanly
as it can get. Let me act as I am." Antonio's frame whirled rapidly.
The rooftop was decently sized, but there weren't many places to
run from a big AI on a rampage.

Under normal circumstances, Matsumoto would move the
fight elsewhere, but he wanted to avoid human witnesses. In the
end, his goal was modifying the Singularity Point. That would
be more difficult if Ophelia's frame and Antonio's violence were
discovered by others. But with Matsumoto's current specs, he
wasn't going to be able to overpower Antonio, whose moral code
had gone out the window.

Antonio wanted to end things, and Matsumoto couldn't let
him.

Matsumoto had the disadvantage in this fight, and the situation was getting worse and worse. The one good thing going for
him was that Antonio showed no signs of involving Ophelia's
delicate frame in his rampage. If Antonio's goal really was to end

his days masquerading as Ophelia, then he just needed to destroy the frame sitting in the snow. Yet he didn't.

"You want to end it, but you want to choose *how* you end it? Is that part of your atonement?" asked Matsumoto.

"Shut up. You can't understand the results of my calculations. You can't understand the foolish AI who erased his own partner!"

"I do understand that you seriously regret your actions. But if that was it, you just had to keep carrying on."

Even if Antonio truly regretted eliminating Ophelia, it was strange that today would be the day things changed. Antonio talked as if he could bear it no longer, so perhaps that had something to do with it. Matsumoto and Antonio were different individuals and Matsumoto absolutely did not understand Antonio's decision-making standards, so there was no point in all these calculations Matsumoto was making. But he still did it. There had to be some trigger for Antonio.

Amid all the information Matsumoto gathered, one thing seemed to fit the most.

"What was on the DVD Mister Ootori gave you?" he asked.

His question caused a clear disturbance in Antonio's movements, and the massive AI said nothing. As they were both non-humanoid AIs, any turmoil in their consciousnesses wouldn't show in their expressions or mannerisms, but Matsumoto could pick up on the small irregularity since he was also a faceless AI.

Just as Matsumoto calculated earlier, Ootori Keiji must have also met with Ophelia in the original history and given her the DVD. That was the event at work on Antonio-Ophelia in both the original and modified histories.

Right then and there, Matsumoto decided to make his move. "This is a real gamble..."

Antonio was coming at him with even more fierceness than before, rejecting Matsumoto by show of force. Instead of dodging to avoid damage this time, Matsumoto did the unthinkable: He took a step forward.

They collided with a *crunch*, and several of Matsumoto's cubes went flying. He'd just managed to get up to 107 cubes, but that was reduced to 84 in one hit. His mobility and durability were down—essentially his overall battle capability—putting him in an even weaker position.

But his reckless move paid off.

"Here goes! Wired connection!"

"You son of a—!"

"Transfer to Archive!"

He'd ejected his core which, despite being damaged, was able to fire out a cable to make a priority wired connection with the port on the back of Antonio's frame. Matsumoto bypassed the transmission blockage and connected his consciousness directly to Antonio's.

"Agh! Stooop!" Antonio roared, but Matsumoto wasn't listening physically or even in calculations.

Matsumoto stormed without regard through the information hidden within Antonio, trampling it, heartlessly going further until he could expose the secrets held within. *"Oh, what's this?"* Matsumoto was surprised by the setting of Antonio's Archive.

Normally, The Archive was a base scene for each AI, and in many cases, it represented an AI's identity. Vivy's Archive was a music room, which suited a songstress like her. Then there was M, the AI they had met on Metal Float, and their Archive was the facility where they worked.

Antonio's Archive was the wings of a desolate, unpopular theater.

"Is it...recording now?" came a voice.

A disembodied Matsumoto watched as an AI in a black dress walked out to center stage, looking confused. It was Ophelia. She tilted her head and looked at someone standing in the wings out of Matsumoto's sight. The scene was being shot from a camera held by the person Ophelia was facing. Matsumoto quickly learned who was on the other end of it, though.

"Yeah, I'm recording. Hey, smile!"

"Uh, er, I-I... I'm not, um, very good at smiling."

"I know you're not, but we're going to need you to learn how. You're our poster songstress. You'll eventually get fans...though you've already got one. That guy who's always in the seats, clapping till the very last minute. I'm pretty sure he's there for you, Ophelia."

"Th-that's Makime-san. He's...a good person."

The voice Matsumoto heard was a man's well-projected voice, that of Ootori Keiji. He filmed Ophelia as he spoke. This wasn't an imaginary scene—it had actually happened. Matsumoto had wanted to view what was on the DVD Ootori had given Antonio, and this must've been it.

"All right, Ophelia. Give it another go! This is your chance to show your determination. Get yourself ready so you can tell Antonio about this day." As Ootori encouraged her, he relocated to the audience seats. The camera pointed directly at the stage with Ophelia right in the middle.

Her cheeks turned red, and she hesitated. She opened and closed her mouth several times, her fingers wiggling. It took quite a while for her to muster up the courage. Ootori didn't rush her, and Matsumoto's evaluation of him went up because he seemed truly suited to be a chairman. At last, Ophelia moved.

"Um, hi, Antonio. Th-this is a message, from me...to you." Ophelia faltered, but she was using her own words to express herself. "You always... Erm, you're always angry at me, critiquing me, and supporting me. You say my singing's amazing, b-but that it can be...even more amazing. You're the only one who thinks... I can do better."

No one loved Ophelia's supreme, heavenly singing voice more than Antonio. In his relentless pursuit of it, he'd stepped outside the realm of what was acceptable for AIs—stepped somewhere he shouldn't in his relentless pursuit of it. Now he regretted it so much that the idea of destroying himself seemed the most logical. But the thing that had really pushed Antonio over the edge wasn't that he was unable to sing Ophelia's songs himself—it was the message Ophelia had recorded onto the DVD. Her eyes shone with trust as she put her all into this very message.

"Someday, Antonio. I'm g-going to...work hard, so I can live up to your expectations... I-I'm a songstress, and I'm supposed to make...someone happy. And...I-I want to make you happy, Antonio." Her face flushed a deeper shade of scarlet.

She sounded like she was confessing her love for him. That had to be it. A songstress AI's greatest desire was to make her listeners happy through her singing. Yet Ophelia had only ever wanted to sing for one person—not one of her human creators but someone else entirely.

"Antonio, I... I lov—"

That was it. The video ended there.

Matsumoto was pulled from The Archive, dropped from the stage, and flung out. But he'd already seen, learned, and understood what he came for. He knew that Antonio had likewise seen, learned, and understood this too.

During his debrief on this Singularity Point, Matsumoto had told Vivy it was their job to refute the idea that AIs had souls—an idea that sprouted from the debates surrounding Ophelia's Suicide. After seeing that video, however, he had to take back that claim. Matsumoto completely understood Antonio. Considering Antonio's condition, seeing that message from Ophelia would surely make him hate himself so much he wanted to die.

"You saw, didn't you?" Antonio said.

It had all happened in just a few seconds in real time. Antonio knew Matsumoto had infiltrated his system and exposed that which he didn't want to be seen, and his eye cameras bored into Matsumoto's with burning emotion uncharacteristic of an AI.

Matsumoto didn't answer. Instead, he said, "I have a theory. You said you can't reproduce Ophelia's singing voice, right?"

"..."

"You think you're a failure for your inability to reproduce her *true* music. Since I've learned that you put your consciousness in her body, I've been running a verification process in the background."

"Verification?"

Matsumoto absorbed the still-functioning cube parts scattered across the snow as he talked. What needed verification was the data of Ophelia's singing after Antonio overwrote her. "Luckily, I was able to get the data with help from Mister Makime," said Matsumoto. "He's such an avid fan of hers that it wasn't difficult for him to get his hands on past recordings."

There was only one conclusion Matsumoto came to once he'd compared the two singing voices: There was absolutely no difference between them, at least not that audio technology could pick up on. Ophelia's voice was not superior, and Antonio's voice was not inferior. If there was a clear difference between Antonio's singing and Ophelia's that only he could sense, if there really was this Idea that he insisted on, there was really only one possible thing it could be.

"Who was Ophelia singing for?"

"..."

"And what do you feel about Ophelia's singing...about Ophelia herself?"

If the songstress who could captivate anyone produced her heavenly voice for a single AI, and if that single AI saw the songstress as something special, then wouldn't the voice that formed between the two of them be burned into their memories as something special, something that couldn't be recreated? What was Antonio's despair, then?

"I always said I wanted Ophelia to sing on a stage suited to her, but that was a lie," Antonio said.

"It was, wasn't it?"

"I wanted Ophelia to sing for me. Just for me."

That wish had come true. Ophelia had sung for Antonio, and that was why her singing sounded so special to him. Once Antonio became Ophelia, her voice just didn't sound the same. And it was something that couldn't ever be fixed.

Matsumoto didn't believe AIs had souls—nor did he intend to calculate much regarding this "Idea" Antonio spoke of—but after hearing Ophelia in Antonio's Archive, there was one thing Matsumoto felt he just had to believe: that one AI had loved another.

Antonio let love pass him by. He loved in the wrong way, and then he prioritized AI-like actions that resulted in the wrong ending.

Antonio's eye cameras flicked toward Ophelia's fragile frame. Then he rushed at Matsumoto faster than ever in an attempt to destroy him. He was trying to make his final request come true now that there was no point in talking anymore. Matsumoto waited calmly while he watched Antonio's frame speed his way. To him, Antonio looked to be moving in slow motion.

.: 3 :.

VIVY GRIMACED as the shards of the grand piano flew around her. She reached out to an unmoving Kakitani, grabbed his chest, and twisted her body. He groaned, caught off guard, but Vivy didn't care. She forced her small frame to keep rotating. Her stage outfit caught on the fragments of the piano, and the fabric tore with a sound like a scream as Vivy forced Kakitani to switch places with her. Almost as payback for what he'd just done, Vivy threw him, smashing his back into the remains of the piano on top of the raised platform.

"Connecting," she said as she pulled out the cable from her earring and plugged it into a jack in Kakitani's frame, making contact with the internal systems of the man who was part human, part machine.

Technically speaking, Kakitani wasn't an AI, meaning Vivy's goal was to access the electrical controls of his frame and incapacitate him. If she turned his fully artificial body into a simple vessel for his brain, she could stop both this fight and his suicide.

But Vivy wasn't even given the time to open her eyes wide in shock before she saw an unthinkable Archive expand before her.

"What...?"

The first thing she noticed was the pristine keyboard of the grand piano they'd just destroyed. Then she saw a dedicated young boy playing the keys for fun. She watched as he steadily improved and eventually made a promise to surpass AIs. A male AI smiled at the boy all the while, carefully teaching him how to play.

That boy lost his arm to an illness and got a new one, which came at the price of his passion. He stopped going near pianos and distanced himself from his AI teacher. Any time he had to fill that chasm between them was stolen, whisking away the opportunity for apologies along with it. One day, he discovered that his teacher had always been thinking of him, although he didn't learn it until after the AI's death—or rather, after he'd ceased to function.

From then on, the boy mingled with kindred spirits who doubted AIs. It started with some hesitant small talk. Before he knew it, he followed in his fellows' footsteps and recruited even more to the cause, the flame of passion that had gone out in his heart rekindled. Then the night of fire came. He struggled to suck in raspy breaths, buffeted by scorching gusts as a single AI stood still in the middle of the red glow.

His memories of that songstress AI were clear as day. That was the base scene for this Kakitani Yugo, who wasn't the real Kakitani Yugo.

"..."

Something rammed into Vivy and her frame went flying backward. A foot pressed down on her chest, pressing her into the ground. There was no damage to her frame, but her consciousness suffered from the shock.

"You stopped moving, songstress. You let your guard down."

Kakitani rushed up at Vivy, using the rebound from hitting the ground to increase his momentum, and the five fingers of his artificial hand went straight for Vivy's head.

"*God Mode activated,*" said a cube-shaped AI sitting on Vivy's shoulder.

.: 4 :.

"**G**OD MODE *activated.*"

Antonio surged at Matsumoto, who caught him with a graceful series of movements before flinging his large frame back.

"Ack!"

"I'm sorry. The resources I dedicated to finding my partner have been freed up. Now I can focus on the Singularity Project," Matsumoto said.

Antonio's instruments flashed in bewilderment as he tried to calculate what was happening. Twenty-one cube parts had returned to Matsumoto. Excluding the damaged ones, Matsumoto was now a collection of 105 cubes. He looked down at Antonio from several eye cameras. Antonio couldn't find anything to say, and he had no chance of winning now.

Transmission had been blocked between Vivy and Matsumoto, and someone was working to impede the Singularity Project. Matsumoto had pushed off dealing with that, but the tables had turned.

"You and I differ in technology and era. Even our specs are different," Matsumoto said.

"Are you saying you're better than me?"

"Yes. Actually, no." The shutters of Matsumoto's many eye cameras closed. His first thought was that he was better than Antonio in every way, but he took it back and said, "I can't make it so my partner sings with joy. Even now, she's skipping her performance."

Behind Matsumoto was the Touto Dome. The current time was 7:37 p.m., and the first change to the schedule was being made. It marred what had been up until now a perfect Zodiac Signs Festival. At present, the oldest songstress was supposed to be onstage. Instead, the songstresses who had been created after her successes were joining together in song.

When Vivy—or Diva—was found missing, Katie convinced the staff to allow the songstresses who had already performed to assemble an impromptu group. They didn't do it so the newest songstresses of modern times could fill the hole left by the oldest songstress; they did it because songstress AIs existed to sing and provide a performance to satisfy their audience. They were still singing now, and the greatest excitement so far gripped the entire venue. It was so powerful that all humans there completely forgot that Diva wasn't onstage.

The nature of Antonio's silence changed as he listened to Matsumoto. He could have dismissed what Matsumoto said as nonsense, meaningless lies, or pointless chatter, but he didn't do that. Matsumoto's electronically produced voice didn't let him.

"Ophelia sang for you, and you continued to sing because of your feelings for Ophelia. Of course you couldn't sing the same as Ophelia—you don't love yourself the same way she loved you."

"…"

"All this talk of AI love is absurd." Here was an AI made up of a collection of cubes lecturing a large-framed soundmaster AI on love. Neither of them bore any resemblance to humans. Those sorts of emotions weren't part of their existence. "Antonio, stop your frame. That's how this should be."

"..."

"After that, I'll let you decide what you do in Ophelia's frame. There's nothing I can do at this point if your calculations still haven't changed."

If Antonio still wanted to throw Ophelia's frame from the roof, there was nothing Matsumoto could do to stop him. Once Ophelia's frame was destroyed, Matsumoto would just modify things so Ophelia's Suicide turned into something like "Ophelia's Tragedy," although Matsumoto didn't want Vivy hearing that.

"But," he continued, "if coming to this roof has tweaked the results of your calculations even a little..." Matsumoto shuffled his cubes to reveal a screen. It showed a video of the excitement inside Touto Dome, recorded by a camera Matsumoto had hacked into.

The most exciting performance of the day, the group song by Katie and the others done to fill Diva's slot, was coming to an end. As the day's performances finished, it would be time for the headliner to take the stage.

"Don't you think that's a stage suited to the two of you: Ophelia and Antonio?"

.:5:.

EVERYONE STEPPED ASIDE to let the songstress pass as she stepped slowly toward the stage, holding up the skirt of her dress. The staff were on the verge of a meltdown once they found the temporary interference with the camera in her dressing room and that she'd gone missing, just like the oldest songstress. She returned with a calm and poise that soothed their alarm.

When she reappeared, several staff members went to convey their relief, but they couldn't. They were frozen, wide-eyed and overpowered by her presence. Although the songstress had the power to overwhelm others while she was singing onstage, she'd never exuded this energy *before* a performance.

After whipping the audience into a frenzy, Katie and the other songstresses stepped back into the wings. Their collaborative performance seemed to signify that all the Zodiac Heroines were equal. Yet when the lone AI songstress in her black dress stepped onstage, everyone knew that couldn't possibly be true. A hush fell over the crowd the moment they laid eyes on her, looking beautiful under the soft lighting. It was as stark a change as sweating waterfalls only to be dumped in an icy river.

Changes to the set list might have normally caused surprise, confusion, or annoyance to ripple through the crowd—but not this time. The atmosphere was completely different.

Slow music started playing in the background, and the black-clad songstress raised her head. There was no choreography for this composition. A hole opened in the floor, and a stand mic rose to the height of the small AI's mouth.

Then she sang. It was a song that everyone had heard—a common, tired tune that started something like this:

"All I did was love you..."

Instantly, the entire venue was captivated by her voice.

.: 6 :.

IT WAS eight o'clock.

"How's the Zodiac Signs Festival going?" Kakitani asked.

"It's a roaring success, of course. The songstress of the century sang a *real* song. Humans have been wanting to hear that since Diva started performing," Matsumoto replied from where he sat on Vivy's shoulder.

Kakitani laughed dryly. "That's for damn sure."

He was collapsed on the ground next to the remains of the grand piano in the back of the hall. His frame was so damaged, he was practically in ruins as well. His arms and legs were broken, and there were several gashes in his torso. Vivy hadn't intended to hurt him so badly, but he just wouldn't give up. He fought for his goals until his limbs no longer moved.

"That's why we AIs exist," said Vivy, her eye cameras focused on Kakitani's smashed face.

His head was smashed, and the synthetic skin had been torn off the left half, exposing the silvery metal below. Inside, the lights flashed on his positronic brain—proof it was still operating. There was no human brain inside. Ergo, he had not undergone a full-body transplant.

This Kakitani Yugo was never the *real* Kakitani Yugo.

"It's not easy to put a human brain in an AI frame," he said.

"It's even harder with an old brain. There's no way I would've survived that surgery."

"So it wasn't a full-body transplant. Kakitani Yugo's memories were turned into data and then implanted into a positronic brain to create a false extension of life?" asked Vivy.

In some ways, that was even more difficult than a full-body transplant. Each positronic brain spawned a different consciousness, which was often synonymous with the AI's individuality. In the case of the twin sisters Estella and Elizabeth, the exact same positronic brains created two different consciousnesses with completely different personalities. Even if they managed to successfully copy Kakitani's memories, the probability that the AI would be just like the original Kakitani was nearly nonexistent.

"I'm not acting like Kakitani Yugo. I *am* him. My body might not have made it here, but my soul did."

"..."

"Ha ha! Come on, what do you think? You and that partner on your shoulder have got super-fast calculating powers now, right? Then calculate it. Do I have a soul or not?" Kakitani's lips curled up as he mocked them relentlessly.

The being in front of them now was an AI who called himself Kakitani. Logically, if Kakitani's memories had been copied over perfectly, then he really was Kakitani himself. How was that different from a full-body transplant?

If humans had souls, then what had been transferred into the AI frame—the brain or the soul? Or, if one refuted the existence of a soul, then where did a full-body transplant fall? What reduced the value of a human, an AI, a soul? Or was the value not reduced at all?

"Could you please not tease my partner too much?" Matsumoto cut in. "Despite her age, she is pure and untarnished. Your words are a poison...a virus."

"What, you don't like riddles?"

"Nope. I don't like questions that don't have an answer. I'm very much an AI in that way. Just like I don't see the point in calculating all the digits of pi, I'm not going to complete endless calculations as to whether you could become grounds for the debate on the existence of souls."

"..."

Matsumoto swatted Kakitani's question aside with cold in-difference. "You are an avatar of a terrorist whom we've had a long relationship with. I can't ignore the fact that your appearance matches his, as do your words and actions, though that certainly could be an act. It does help me that everything from the top of your head to the tips of your fingernails is man-made. That means my moral code won't get in the way."

Just as Matsumoto had mentioned, there was a conflict in Vivy's consciousness, but her answer to that as an AI came from somewhere else. Vivy had overpowered Kakitani using God Mode with Matsumoto's help. Her moral code hadn't interfered yet, even with Kakitani on the brink of destruction. That meant that Vivy, an AI, had determined he was not human.

That raised a different question. "Kakitani...you hated AIs.

Didn't you hesitate to become more like us and less human?" she asked.

Vivy had clashed with him several times during Toak's activities. Toak's actions and convictions all stemmed from their animosity toward AIs. And if what Vivy saw in his Archive was real, then she was certain he had regrets. He lost his teacher, the AI who taught him piano, and was humiliated after being forced to view his teacher's final logs. That had twisted his mind, and his rejection and hatred of AIs grew stronger. Now, at the peak of it, he encountered Vivy again as an AI with copies of his memories.

What were Kakitani Yugo's true intentions?

"Vivy..." he said. "I..."

Inside his smashed head, his right eye camera had managed to stay intact, and it was locked on to her. It had been made to recreate the appearance of a human eye as closely as possible, but it was still a man-made object. It was not equipped to show true human expressions.

What Vivy saw in that eye of his must have been a disturbance in Vivy herself. It tricked her into seeing obsession, some powerful emotion like hate, or maybe even love.

"I just loathe you," he whispered as if the tension was leaving him, and then all operation of his frame ceased.

Kakitani Yugo was silent, and would be silent forever. That was the end of Vivy and Matsumoto's time with this man, seventy years of clashing over and over, exchanging ideas but never fully understanding each other.

.: 7 :.

S NOW CONTINUED to flutter down around the city, the first snow of the year. Everyone leaving the Touto Dome looked skyward, strong emotions clear in their faces. Not everyone was excited about the snow. Some citizens—people who hadn't come to the venue tonight—resented the weather, worried it would cause a slowdown in their commute.

It wasn't that the crowd filtering out of the Touto Dome spared no thought for the snow. On the contrary, they were welling with emotions after the otherworldly experience, and they loved each and every sensation the world provided them: something brushing against their skin, the sights reflected in their eyes, and the vibrations in their eardrums. They decided they wanted to become better people, even if that just meant being a bit kinder to others.

As grandiose as it may sound, the miracle of love was budding in the hearts of everyone who had heard the songstresses' music. They would never forget this night. They would forever remember the songstresses who sang without holding back, shining like the nighttime stars whose names they'd borrowed.

A figure appeared on top of a nearby building that overlooked the departing crowd.

"..."

One AI had been sitting there for quite a while. He was blanketed with snow, most of his large frame covered with white. That was the soundmaster. The AI with him was a beautiful, sweet songstress who'd slipped her tiny little frame into the arms of the large AI, leaning into him as if entrusting him with her everything as she closed her eyes. They pressed together, unmoving as the snow slowly piled on top of them.

There was no snow that never melted, and someday, the soft blanket coating them would melt. But in that one moment, it was like those two AIs were the only things in the world as they embraced beneath the snow.

The songstress Ophelia and her partner Antonio curled together like they trusted each other completely, like they offered each other forgiveness when asked, a sight that made hearts sing just like a song.

And then they shut down.

That rendezvous between the two AIs should never have been possible. Later, the world would have a name for what happened that night: the Lovers' Suicide.

.: 8 :.

"**D**ID OPHELIA'S PERFORMANCE go well?" Vivy asked Matsumoto.

"It did. I had a really rough time, though. It's hard not being able to connect together when I'm supposed to be operating as one main unit. Wait, who am I again? Where did this AI come from?!"

"Uh-huh. Thank you for taking care of it. And for coming to save me."

"You really throw me off balance when you're this nice. You went through a lot, didn't you?"

"..."

"Well, I guess that was inevitable. I can't believe our archnemesis gave up his body to come fight us in a mechanical one! There was an ancient anime—practically fossilized at this point—that went like that. I did not see that coming."

"Yeah. I'm surprised Kakitani was that obsessed with us."

"Not us. You, Vivy. Don't get it twisted."

"Yeah."

"Anyway...obsession, hm? You and I might've had to fight in different locations, but our opponents were dealing with the same conundrum."

"Huh?"

"It's okay if you don't understand," Matsumoto told her. "Right, so now that we've managed to get through this Singularity Point, we have something important to discuss."

"The unknown meddler in the Singularity Project?"

"Sure. There's the transmission interference, the faked video feed, and whoever told Mister Kakitani about us. The more I think about it, the more questions I have...but no, that's not it."

"Does that mean you already have a countermeasure?"

"A countermeasure, Vivy? Come on. No, I don't."

"I don't understand your intentions. Explain yourself. What are you talking about?"

"There is an enemy planning to hinder the Project at the Singularity Points. You're with me that far, right?"

"Yes, so during the next Singularity Poi—"

"There won't be a next Singularity Point."

"What?"

"This was the last one. It's the end of our journey together. Well, I mean, there's still our path into the future, so it's not like it's just going to fade to black for the credit roll, but..."

Matsumoto paused, and his next words came as the biggest shock yet.

"Good work, Vivy. Our work on the Singularity Project ends here. It's time for you to go back to being the real you...the song-stress, Diva."

VIVY
Prototype

CHAPTER 5

The Songstress's End

.:1:.

"**W**HAT DO YOU MEAN 'recalled'?!"

The head of NiaLand's performances, a man who had just had his fifty-seventh birthday a few days earlier, was enraged by what he heard. All the staff members simply called him "the Director." His face was bright red, and his shaking hands were balled into fists. Diva had never seen him like this in her thirty-plus years of working with him.

"It means exactly what it sounds like," came the reply, quiet and cold as steel. "Diva is being recalled by her manufacturer, OGC. Their research facility will come to collect her tomorrow."

Unlike the Director, the woman who spoke always kept a cool head. Diva had only been working with her for about seven months, approximately one-fiftieth of the days she'd worked with the Director, but it was still over two hundred days. Diva never once heard her raise her voice or show a different expression in all that time.

The woman's name was Kishibe Tao. She was a genius who, at the young age of twenty-seven, had become the keystone of NiaLand's operations department. Tao was currently the general manager of NiaLand and, in essence, the highest authority in the park.

"As of today, all authority over Diva will transfer back to OGC accordingly. I understand this is sudden, but please have Diva prepare to leave the park. I've just sent the full report to your storage for your reference."

They were having this discussion in the manager's office at NiaLand. The previous manager had decorated it with figurines of the cast members, but Tao had removed everything unrelated to her duties, transforming it into a functional—or perhaps characterless—space. Her glossy, jet-black hair was cut perfectly straight. It brushed her shoulders, and the lights in the room made it glow like a halo.

"Data confirmed. Understood," said Diva.

"Diva!"

Out of the corner of her eyes, Diva saw the Director looking at her, wondering if she really was okay with what was happening. She nodded with a gentle, thankful smile. The Director grimaced like he'd been struck, then he glared at Tao with a furrowed brow.

"Kishibe-san, you're the one responsible here. You have the authority to make decisions on everything, but it's Diva and the generations of stage staff who have built up our Main Stage over the past seventy years, plus our current employees. Diva's the center of our Main Stage. You can't do anything with her unless you convince us."

"The decision has already been made." Tao wasn't looking at the Director, and she didn't stop typing on her terminal. "I can't change that."

"But—"

"I also don't have the authority to make decisions on everything. All I'm doing is honoring OGC's request."

"Without even pushing back, I'm sure! You just accepted it and passed on the orders. 'Authority over Diva,' huh? You only talk like that because you hate AIs!"

Tao's hands froze. Her almond-shaped eyes slid toward the Director, piercing into him. "Accusing another of misandry, misogyny, or automatonophobia without proof is discriminatory speech. I'll let it slide this time, but don't do it again."

"It's true!" the Director shouted, taking a step toward Tao. Diva grabbed his hand. He permitted it and took several ragged breaths as if trying to calm the rage inside him.

"This discussion is over. Thank you for working late," said Tao, her eyes making it clear she was talking to the Director, not Diva.

It all started about four weeks ago.

During the Zodiac Signs Festival, the event that gathered twelve songstress AIs under one roof, Diva was scheduled to take the stage as the real closing act. Plenty of people in the audience had been looking forward to it. Diva wasn't so popular that it was difficult to get tickets for her solo performances, but most of the audience members had a specific interest in songstresses, the stars of the event. To those fans, Diva wasn't simply an old heap of junk—she was the progenitor of songstress AIs. She was a symbol of what they had passionately supported.

Diva was the origin and the face of all songstresses.

At the festival, there had been some longtime fans who came regularly to her NiaLand performances. Other attendees knew all her songs, but had never heard her live, and saw this as their big chance. There were even some fans who had never gone to a live concert before. Everyone was waiting for her...but she never showed up.

It was ridiculous, but Diva didn't learn that fact until half a day after the festival was over and she was in the maintenance room in NiaLand undergoing analysis.

"I never...did my performance?" Diva blurted in shock when the doctor gave her a rundown of what happened.

She immediately scoured her logs. The most recent log she had was from the transport driving to the festival. She was exchanging greetings with the other songstresses—and then her logs just cut out. As she sat in the maintenance room, her mind quickly made the connection.

The bug... Why? It's been dormant for ten whole years!

There were several instances of unnaturally cut-off logs in the past, the last being more than ten years ago, when the hologram device above the stage fell on her and in the few days afterward. Her current logs fit the same pattern.

Diva had initially suspected the presence of some sort of virus, some *bug*, inside her body. Following the trail, she'd scrambled to uncover its true nature. She had encountered Akari, who came to her with an image supposedly taken when the bug was controlling Diva's body. She'd also met Saeki Tatsuya, the retired AI researcher. Everything pushed her to the brink of ditching the stage for the very first time since her creation, but she had found her footing again with the help of the Director and other humans around her. Despite all that, the bug was back now—and at such an important moment.

Diva had boycotted the festival, or so she was told, but it struck her as ridiculous. She didn't have a single memory of the whole thing. The impact of her absence—and the damage it caused to those connected to the festival—drove things in a direction no one could have imagined.

The final trigger was the other strange occurrence immediately after the festival: Ophelia, who had given an overwhelming performance that captured the hearts of everyone in the venue, had been found at the bottom of a building in the arms of Antonio, the soundmaster AI who shouldn't have moved. The two AIs had been lying in the snow, looking almost like a pair of cuddling lovers. Both of them were nonoperational.

There were no footprints in the vicinity, making it seem like suicide or self-destruction at first glance, but that wasn't possible. As a rule, AIs couldn't kill themselves. They couldn't even needlessly damage their own bodies, let alone *kill* themselves, unless they were malfunctioning, damaged, or saving a human life. There were no records of an AI ever having committed suicide. The world was in an uproar over someone destroying the AIs.

Someone must have thrown them off the building, and they searched for a culprit.

But a few days afterward, authorities issued a public statement. After an analysis of Ophelia's and Antonio's bodies, no faults in the programming or irregularities had been found. The two AIs had gone up to the roof and jumped of their own volition.

At first, people blatantly refused to accept this, since it supported the notion that the two AIs did in fact kill themselves. Those most educated in the field, AI researchers and engineers, expressed dissatisfaction with the conclusion. The analysis was wrong, they said. The two had fallen as a result of an attack. Eventually, some even claimed the statement had only been made to protect the true perpetrator, who was still at large.

But the more the incident was investigated, the more evidence supported the suicide theory. The two AIs' bodies had been analyzed more thoroughly than any AI before them, and the surveillance cameras at the site of the incident showed only Antonio and Ophelia. If there *was* a perpetrator, none of the potential suspects had motive—to say nothing of how difficult it would have been to destroy them.

The thing that really shifted public perception, however, was an article that was put out two weeks after the incident: "AIS COMMIT LOVERS' SUICIDE?"

An online journalist who'd attended the festival had written the article. The article was explicitly biased, more gossip or fake news than anything noteworthy, but the world was yearning for an easy story to pounce on. AI rights groups and fanatics were particularly fired up by the article.

The biggest factor was Antonio, whom the journalist wrote of as if he were a man (having discovered through research that Antonio spoke with a masculine voice when he was operational). Antonio was Ophelia's partner, and he'd supposedly ceased functioning long ago. Why was he there that day? Why did he jump off the building with Ophelia? No one else had shared a reasonable answer to these questions, so this article was the first to suggest one.

If it was a double suicide, then that would make AIs human-like. It meant they had developed to the same point as humans. For the first two weeks, this idea was laughed off. It was impossible to take a single incident—of which no one knew the truth—and try to apply that to all AIs.

One person was burned the most by the gossip wildfire: Diva.

Diva's alleged boycott was buried by the commotion surrounding Ophelia and Antonio, but it was the first recorded instance of Diva not giving a scheduled performance. This was also the first time in history AIs had committed suicide, if it truly *was* suicide. These events happened on the same day, and they were both malfunctions of songstress AIs.

Did Diva know about Ophelia and Antonio's suicide? Did she, as the first songstress, step back from her own performance to show respect for Ophelia's grand finale? Or did she want to watch Ophelia's last performance from the audience, refusing to take the stage so she could slip into the crowd? Were these things possible because Diva, Ophelia, and Antonio had developed to the same point as humans? She could only watch as people hurled around these arbitrary questions, ignoring the truth. Those who were paranoid that AIs had advanced to human levels were hungry for anything that might strengthen their arguments, and all this made for quite the feast.

Diva hadn't sung onstage since the festival. She was currently only scheduled to perform once a week on the weekend, so she'd only missed a few performances, but the quantity didn't matter. Diva worked for her mission, to make her audience happy through her singing for humanity's sake, and every single performance was a precious opportunity to carry out that duty.

After the festival, NiaLand ordered her to do a complete maintenance overhaul because they'd be in trouble if she malfunctioned again. Diva did as she was told. She wasn't in a position to refuse, but she calculated this was necessary to ensure she could provide the perfect performance. No matter how many times they repeated the maintenance run, however, they never discovered any malfunctions or irregularities. There was nothing different about her.

A little over a decade ago, panic rose as the public wondered whether Diva would miss her scheduled performance, but she made it in the end. She had also operated as expected after that. With that in mind, the Director had asked her to try and get back onstage that weekend. She was done being jerked around by a bug that couldn't be found no matter how many and what kinds of tests they ran.

That was when those illogical claims sent the world into a flurry. Had Diva advanced to the same point as humans, just like Ophelia and Antonio? Diva wanted to scream at them, tell them they were wrong. She didn't have memories of Ophelia, let alone Antonio. Moreover, she didn't even remember going to the venue for the festival. But there was no untying the complex knotted web of information out in the world.

Why did Diva boycott her performance? Why did she malfunction? Has she already become capable of humanlike decision-making?

Various AI rights groups, journalists hungry for details, and regular people who wanted in on the fuss all swooped down on NiaLand day after day, asking a million questions. When they learned that NiaLand had no answers, they turned to OGC, the corporation that created Diva.

NiaLand decided because of this mess that Diva wouldn't take the stage until some sort of resolution had been reached. Diva, the Director, and all the other performance-related staff members accepted that decision. They had no other choice.

Then, not long ago, NiaLand received a communication from OGC. It said, "OGC requests the return of Model Number A-03, designated name 'Diva.'"

Diva returned to her room on the highest floor of the Princess Palace not long after midnight.

OGC's going to collect me...

She reread what Tao had sent over. There was quite a lot of data presented for the decision, but it boiled down to two decisions:

One was a decision reached by OGC's research branch after the recent uproar. OGC was the world's largest AI manufacturer, so they wanted to avoid AI malfunctions or programming flaws at all costs. They had opted to collect Diva and do a thorough investigation of her faculties.

Two was a decision reached by NiaLand after evaluating the pros and cons of the situation. In short, they couldn't keep Diva in the park long enough to refuse to cooperate with OGC or demand different treatment.

The theme park was there to provide guests with a temporary dreamland in which to kick back and unwind, making it part of the tourism industry. Contrary to the park's public image, management fought a fierce battle every day against reality and budgets.

Diva knew her performances weren't attracting as many people as they used to. The sales she brought in didn't quite offset her operating costs, and her profit projections for the next few years paled in comparison to the past. Tao's data was logical and thorough, leaving no room for counterarguments, and Diva was convinced by it.

Nothing went on forever. That was true for both humans and AIs, and it was particularly important to AIs that they continue to fulfill their missions to their very last moments. In that sense, Diva had no regrets. She'd worked as a songstress for more than seventy years, singing over a thousand different songs at more than ten thousand performances. This year, she'd reached a total of twenty million people. That wasn't half bad. It was her pride, and an accomplishment she'd built up alongside the stage staff. She couldn't possibly have regrets.

But there was one thing she couldn't accept.

The bug...

Her fists clenched, as if by reflex.

"Navi, there was that time when the stage equipment nearly fell on me. Display the data from then."

No response came.

"Navi?" she asked again, then realized what was happening.

It was already the next day. Tao said Diva's rights within NiaLand had been revoked as of yesterday. Navi was the responsive navigation AI that the workers of NiaLand used. Diva no longer had access. She'd just checked the data too, but she wasn't thinking logically.

"Agh..."

An illogical anger welled up inside her.

She turned to the back of her room and started jerking open her dresser drawers. Her fans' handwritten letters were stored inside. Such letters were extremely rare these days, and they made her happy. Diva snatched up a card among them.

"What are you doing?"

She'd written that message for the bug on the front of the card. There was nothing on the back, here in the real world, although she *had* gotten a response at the time. The bug had written *"Stop worrying about unimportant things and do what you always do: sing with all your heart,"* on the back of the card in The Archive.

"What is this about?!" Diva shouted. "Why did you appear during the festival, of all days?!"

With the blank side facing her, she clutched the card in her hands. It felt like she was being ridiculed. She crumpled up the card and hurled it against the ground.

"Do what you always do: sing with all your heart."

When the bug had told her that, Diva actually felt like it had her back. She figured it was supporting her. Even if the bug stole her body sometimes, surely it wouldn't interfere with her performances.

"Just say something—anything! Tell me what you were doing! Or is your selfishness more important than the ten minutes I was supposed to be onstage?!"

OGC's research branch was going to collect her. It was obvious what would happen then. They would take her body apart piece by piece, analyzing every single one. They would try to figure out what caused this so they could make sure none of the other OGC AIs throughout the world malfunctioned like she did.

Once that analysis was done, she wouldn't come back to NiaLand. Tao's data made that clear. In fact, Diva wasn't even certain if they'd bother putting her body back together. They probably wouldn't. Her mission was over.

Bang!

Diva slammed her fist into the dresser. She knew humans did that when they had nowhere else to vent their anger. It didn't accomplish anything except spawn a slew of error messages saying there was minor damage to the joints of her fingers. She ignored them as she punched the dresser again and again.

"Vivy..."

That was probably the name the bug used for itself, though she couldn't be certain.

"Vivy!"

Diva screamed that name out of sheer hatred. She swung her fist until her vision was so filled with error messages, she couldn't see any of the room she'd spent the past seventy years in—the room she could never return to. Even then, she kept on screaming.

.: 2 :.

THE TRANSPORT TRUCK to OGC came about twelve hours later. Many of the staff offered to see her off, and she was grateful for that, but she turned them all down. Plenty of them had come to visit her in her room the night before, mostly people in charge of her performances. Apparently, the Director had called on any employees who were still in the park late that night. Some had even gotten the message right after they got home and came all the way back to see her.

It felt less like a going-away party and more like a strategy meeting, or a huddle to kick off a strike. The staff members, who'd been through so much with Diva, couldn't accept the sudden news of her recall. Some of them were angry enough to talk about drafting an official declaration to strike, but Diva talked them out of it.

"You can't do that," she said. "The guests are looking forward to the performances you put together."

Some cried. Others got even angrier. In the end, people stayed with her until the break of dawn, venting their frustrations and reminiscing about the past. Diva encouraged anyone who was emotionally exhausted to go home and get some rest so they could get ready for the next day's work.

Three of the people closest to Diva kept her company until the very end: the Director, the doctor, and Nacchan. The doctor was the woman in charge of maintaining all of NiaLand's AIs, including Diva, and Nacchan was her AI assistant.

"Doctor...is there really no chance Diva will be able to come back to NiaLand?" asked the Director. "She's still a contracted employee with OGC, isn't she?"

"Well..." The doctor frowned. She was generally known for her jovial attitude, but even her expression was taut and serious now. With that expression, she looked her actual age of nearly fifty. "Based on what I know about their MO, it's going to be real tough, don't you think?" She looked at Nacchan, who nodded.

"I agree," Nacchan said. "OGC practically has a monopoly on the market. That success is founded on the airtight security of their AIs. The regular maintenance I undergo at OGC covers significantly more points than similar maintenance from other companies. During that time, if OGC discovers a new type of flaw that can't be addressed with existing methods, the AI in question is moved from maintenance to the research department."

This wasn't information Nacchan got through searching on the internet—she was speaking from experience. She had been made by OGC as well.

"There are no records of an AI that was sent to research being sent back to maintenance and returned to the client," she continued. "And it's not the maintenance department that will be collecting Diva-san—she's going directly to the research department."

"Urgh..."

Diva's audio sensors picked up the sound of the Director's breath catching as he held back his disappointment. He, the doctor, and even Nacchan looked incredibly pained.

Before her communication circuit could even run a calculation on what was the most suitable expression in this situation, Diva squashed down her own disappointment—which was greater than anyone else's—and gave them a full-faced smile. "Thank you, everyone. Please take care of the guests for me."

Now it was past noon. Diva was a little surprised when she saw the transport truck arrive at the massive shipping entrance of NiaLand. She'd never seen this truck before. It wasn't like the vehicle used when they were taken to OGC for simple maintenance. It was far longer and wider. Diva calculated that it must've belonged to the research department.

"Provide your identification number."

This message came to Diva not as a voice but as data. When she was normally picked up for maintenance, an OGC employee or support humanoid AI would come off the vehicle and politely ask for her identification out loud, but this truck was unmanned and didn't seem made for positive interactions. She sent her answer back in kind.

The top section of the back of the truck lifted like a crocodile's gaping jaws, and the sides opened as well. The inside was packed from floor to ceiling with equipment of a far higher quality than the ones in NiaLand's maintenance room. Although this was her first time seeing the display, she assumed they were similarly used for analysis.

She boarded the truck, and it slowly closed—sides first, then the back. "Guess this is my last look," she murmured as the doors choked her view. She turned her audio sensors up to the highest sensitivity.

In the distance, she could faintly hear the buzz of guests in the park. NiaLand was the busiest around lunch, just after noon; and at dinnertime around six o'clock or so. They were Diva's two favorite times other than when she was onstage. The park's AIs were busiest then. The sales and customer service AIs were going at full steam, and the drones whizzed through the air, making deliveries. The drones were particularly attention-grabbing once the seasons changed and it got dark early. Their lights made them look like living sparks zipping through the evening sky.

During standby, Diva would look out her window and smile as she watched everyone work hard for the guests. The thing that made her happiest was hearing all the guests' excited voices, like she could now. She closed her eye cameras just before the truck's doors shut. In that final moment, she just wanted to hear their voices. It was unfortunate that those voices weren't the cheers of an audience as she stood onstage.

"Thank you," Diva said, her eyes still closed as she bowed gracefully, just as she had tens of thousands of times before. She stayed like that until she could no longer hear their voices.

.: 3 :.

"H UH?"

The moment Vivy booted, she sensed something wrong with her right arm. She quickly realized she was gripping a thick cable in her right hand. It was haphazardly torn, and the wires inside dangled listlessly. Sparks leapt whenever the wires touched, meaning they were live.

An odd sensation tugged the back of her neck. Vivy reached up and felt a cable plugged into a port in her body. She unlocked it and pulled it out to find it led to the tattered one in her hand. Apparently, she'd pulled and broken it herself.

What's going on? Where am I?

She had no clue what was happening. Her calculations took off. A look at her surroundings told her she was sitting in a chair in the center of a maintenance room, or something of that nature. There were several terminals around her she'd never seen before— most likely for analysis.

Is this NiaLand? It has been a really long time since I've seen NiaLand's maintenance room, so I wouldn't be surprised if it's changed... Speaking of, when is "now"?

"A-03, disconnection has been detected. Please reconnect yourself."

A message came to Vivy suddenly—not as a voice but as data.

"Uhhh..." She stretched out the sound to buy herself time to calculate.

Who had spoken? Probably an AI belonging to this location. While A-03 was her model number, no one at NiaLand called her that, not even any of the AIs. That meant this wasn't NiaLand. Either that, or NiaLand's systems had changed drastically.

Her right arm had moved automatically when she booted up, and she'd experienced something like that before. That time when the stage equipment was falling toward her, her right leg kicked up and destroyed the equipment the moment she activated, protecting her body from the threat. Just now, she must have destroyed the cable in order to protect her body as well. The situation wasn't looking good.

"It appears an anomaly has occurred in my reality awareness. Please wait a moment," she said.

"Understood. We remain on schedule so long as you complete the request within 300 seconds. I request that you keep the urgency of the situation in mind."

It seemed like she could actually reason with this AI.

Feeling just a tiny bit relieved, she opened up a transmission. This would be the fastest way to get answers. *"Matsumoto... Matsumoto?"*

There was no response. She tried again, and the result was the

THE SONGSTRESS'S END 227

same. Ruling that out as an option, she accessed her internal clock to determine *when* she'd awoken.

"Oh..."

Her communication circuit almost expressed her shock when she did, but she just barely managed to hold it back. She couldn't believe the numbers she saw. She checked again, but they didn't change. The last time she activated was for the Singularity Point with Ophelia. Not even a month had passed.

Why did this happen?

Before they'd gone back to sleep, Matsumoto had said something: *"This was the last Point... It's time for you to go back to the real you...the songstress, Diva."*

At the time, Vivy calculated that she would next activate at the end of the Singularity Project, a century after the Project began, the point in the original history when humanity and AI clashed in their final battle. She and Matsumoto would wake to see the results of their efforts to modify history, then enter a real and permanent sleep. Why, then, had she activated now?

Vivy grappled with her rising panic and accessed her GPS. It looked like she was in NiaLand after all. According to Vivy's memories, this was an empty plot near the park grounds, but perhaps the park had expanded. Her data labeled this as a shipping entrance, so she wasn't actually in the maintenance room. She was in some sort of massive vehicle. Her body had moved on its own. She was holding a destroyed cable. Her calculations were going in a decidedly negative direction.

Should I access Diva's logs? I'd rather not if I can avoid it...

She didn't want to do that, especially since she'd been told her activity on the Singularity Points was over. When Matsumoto talked about "the songstress," he was talking about Diva.

"I request support," she said. "Please send the data showing the lead-up to my arrival here."

After a few seconds of silence, the transmission data arrived.

"If your errors are so significant that they have resulted in damage to your most recent logs, then the decision to have you analyzed inside OGC was correct. You do not have to understand the current situation. Reconnect yourself."

"Please. We're still on time, aren't we?"

There was another silence, in which the other AI was probably calculating, but it did send some basic data over. That data was created by someone named Kishibe Tao. Vivy didn't know that name, but they appeared to be someone of authority at NiaLand. It recorded incredibly logical statistics and written statements. Vivy read it all in less than ten seconds, then couldn't hold back the word that slipped from her lips.

"Impossible..." Vivy's circuits repeated it over and over.

In summation, the data said that Diva was being recalled from NiaLand because of her boycott of the Zodiac Signs Festival. She was being returned to OGC's research institute.

True, Vivy hadn't gone to the stage that day—she'd gone to Kakitani. She'd chosen to not take the stage for the first time since she was created. That was essentially a boycott; no arguing with that. It was a huge event too, though she had no intentions of calling it a once-in-a-lifetime sort of thing. It didn't matter how big a performance was, a songstress couldn't decide to *not* give it her all, and she definitely couldn't abandon the stage. Vivy knew that.

But how could her actions have led to this?

"W-wait... I lack data. How did this—"

"*I have determined you are experiencing a severe error. Reconnect yourself. If you do not comply, OGC security will be dispatched.*"

"Wait!" Vivy shouted, but the response was the same.

She gritted her teeth in frustration at the very AI-like response and looked down at the cable in her hand. It clicked for her then: She'd awoken because the equipment had tried to cut off power to her body.

Vivy activated when a Singularity Point was coming or when her body was in danger. It was the same as that time over ten years ago, when a piece of stage equipment was bearing down on her. The only difference between now and then—and when she'd been surrounded by attacking park mascots—was that she normally went right back to sleep afterward.

In this situation, it didn't matter that she had yanked out the cable and prevented the immediate danger—she still wasn't going to sleep. She also couldn't contact Matsumoto. That meant this wasn't a Singularity Point.

Has the program determined my body's still in danger?

If she was sent to OGC's research facility, the first thing they'd do would be to disassemble and analyze her. Then she'd probably never return. Vivy might have experience with violence, unlike Diva, but even she was helpless against danger if her power was cut. She was still an AI in the end. This really was her last chance to save herself.

"This is your last warning. Reconnect yourself. If you do not comply, OGC security will be dispatched."

"Matsumoto!" Vivy shouted in a transmission. She needed orders, but he didn't reply.

Her calculation circuit raced. She couldn't just fight off any oncoming security. If her programming determined that was enough to stave off the danger to her frame, she would be forced back to sleep and Diva would awaken. Diva would be lost and confused, and then security would capture her. They'd try to shut off her power again, bringing Vivy back out. She couldn't allow herself to fall into that loop.

Most importantly, she couldn't harm AIs or humans who had nothing to do with a Singularity Point just for her own convenience. She had no way of knowing whether it would have an impact on the future, and being branded a rogue AI was unacceptable. She operated with the goal of preventing a war caused by rampaging AIs, and Diva operated to sing. Both of those things were for humanity's sake.

"All right. I will reconnect myself," she said weakly, backed into a corner.

The AI responded with a mechanical-sounding *"Understood."*

She grimaced. This couldn't be happening. She couldn't believe this was how Diva's mission would come to an end. Vivy didn't care what happened to herself; she'd been putting Diva first for so long that she was all that mattered. Vivy opened her hand, and the severed cable fell to the floor with a scattering of sparks.

"Please use the backup connection cable," said the AI as it sent her coordinate data.

It was a cable connected to a terminal on the wall. With no other option but to comply, she reached for it. "Huh?"

Her hand stopped. She hadn't noticed it before, but the artificial skin on her right hand was marred and peeling off. If she focused entirely on her motion circuit, she could tell the movements were a little sluggish. The hand was damaged. Deciding there was nothing wrong with viewing her basic body logs, she took a look—and gasped at what she found.

It had happened twelve hours ago. There was a long period with repeated instances of damage saved to the log. They were all from about the same level of force. It was as if Diva had been struck over and over by something with power akin to her maximum. In other words, Diva was punching something.

Vivy shuddered when she saw that the quantity surpassed a hundred. Diva couldn't have been hitting a person. Even if she had, it wouldn't be the same value repeated over and over again. This record showed Diva punching an object repeatedly, like an angry human would. Diva's screams flitted across Vivy's calculation circuit, even though she'd never heard them.

"Why?!"

The next instant, Vivy pulled back her right hand and, instead of reaching out, put her full force into punching a terminal attached to the other wall. It was the terminal that managed the truck's internal environment.

Her fist punctured the exterior. She grabbed the wires inside and pulled. The power in the truck failed, and there was an announcement that it was switching to emergency lighting. Without waiting for it to finish, she went to the vehicle's entrance in the back. It was electronically managed and operated, but she wrenched it open by force, with one hand above and one below. When there was just enough space for her to fit, she slipped through.

"Stop. Security is being dispatched."

She ignored the mechanical transmission and ran.

.: 4 :.

"DIVA! I finally got a hold of you... Where are you?!"

The Director received a notification that Diva had refused the transport and disappeared a mere five minutes later. He immediately started sending her transmissions, but he couldn't make contact. There were no GPS pings for her either, so he didn't know where she was. She must have blocked the signal somehow.

Park security said she was probably somewhere inside NiaLand, since she was spotted on a security camera leaving the truck at the shipping dock and running into the park. Every entrance and exit in the park had similar cameras, and none of them had caught her leaving. When the staff working in NiaLand were notified of the situation, they all thought the exact same thing: *I knew it! Diva doesn't want to leave NiaLand.*

Not a single one of them was annoyed by how much of a hassle she'd caused or how it might be dangerous. In fact, it gave anyone who'd rejected the news a second wind, making them think that perhaps they could do something about it after all.

The Director had the same thoughts. He wanted to involve himself somehow, but he couldn't ditch his duties solely for Diva's benefit. He was responsible for what happened on NiaLand's stages. None of those performances would happen if the head of the department abandoned his post and did whatever he liked.

NiaLand's guests were blissfully unaware. The only thing that had been announced regarding Diva was that her performances would be put on hold for the time being. There would be a huge commotion if any of the staff leaked information about what was really happening, and that had to be avoided at all costs. The employees of NiaLand had their pride, but Diva had just said to them last night, *"Please take care of the guests for me."*

The Director told all employees to refrain from acting without explicit approval. There was pushback, particularly from the younger employees, but he told them that Diva would never want them to neglect the guests. They seemed to accept that, even if was a bit reluctantly. Meanwhile, the Director continued his work as usual, but he continued his desperate attempts to contact Diva. Two hours after the start of the commotion, Diva finally responded to a transmission.

"You're the Director...right?" Her voice was weak. She also sounded like she was evaluating him, cold and distant as if she were speaking to him for the first time.

The Director's heart ached for her and whatever distress she was going through. "Yeah, it's me. Where are—actually, don't tell me where you are. You're in the park, right? And you turned off your GPS?"

"Yes. I'm sorry."

"It's okay. You should keep it off, actually. We can't have people figuring out where you are."

"I...suppose."

"Hey, listen to me. First off, don't send transmissions to anyone but me. They might figure out where you are. And don't let any of the park guests see you. It'll cause a scene."

"Okay."

"Just to be on the safe side, avoid contacting any employees. Then again, most of them are on your side, so it's not the end of the world if one finds you. The ones you really have to be careful of are the OGC employees. They arrived not long ago, and they're eager to find you."

"Okay, I understand."

"If you run out of places to go, head to Haru's practice room. There aren't any security cameras there, and there won't be any foot traffic. That girl's attitude is actually going to be useful right now." The Director chuckled, hoping to soothe her a little.

"Haru-san...?" Diva didn't sound any calmer.

He frowned with uncertainty and said, "Yeah, Haru's room. You've been there a few times with her."

"Umm..."

"Remember? It's in the back of the East Area, that zone

nobody's used since the park opened. It's mostly used as storage. We kind of just put materials and stage equipment there when we don't have anywhere else to put it."

Diva made a sound, the first sound of relief since they'd started speaking. *"Oh, the East Dumpster."*

The Director laughed, heartily this time. "Yeah, that's the one. I heard it had a nickname like that way back when. Haru's on tour right now, so you don't have to worry about using it."

Tokura Haru was a singer-songwriter who worked out of NiaLand. She had been the leader of an idol group called Season.5 until a few years ago, when the group disbanded. The other members retired or went into acting, leaving Haru as the only one who didn't stray from the road of music.

Haru was practically the face of NiaLand's Substage. She did have a bit of a selfish streak, but since she loved NiaLand dearly, she was generally well liked by the staff. She'd wanted a place where she could practice her music without worrying about people seeing her, so the staff found her a quiet spot without security cameras. Surely when they gave into her demands, they'd smirked and said something like, "There she goes again."

"Okay. Thank you," Diva said to the Director.

"No worries. And, uh..." He took a moment to choose his words. "Do you plan on doing anything dangerous?"

"Dangerous?"

"The OGC employees told me you destroyed some equipment when you escaped, so they don't know what you're planning. They even said they want us to send all the guests home for—"

"You can't do that!" Diva shouted suddenly. Words tumbled around in her mouth as she tried to regain control of herself. Then she said, *"I-I did take harsh measures to escape the truck, and I feel bad about that... But I don't intend to do anything dangerous. If OGC employees find me, I won't resist. I'll do as they tell me. And I absolutely won't do anything to put the guests in danger. If hiding would cause even the slightest trouble for the guests, then I'll come out right now."*

"Right..." The Director let out a heavy sigh, then smiled gently. "That makes me feel better. No matter what happens, you're still you."

There was silence.

"So...what are you going to do next? We're definitely going to try to make it so you can come back to NiaLand. I'm sure everyone on staff wants that."

"Thank you. But, well..." There was a moment where he could tell Diva was calculating. *"I don't know. I wonder what I should do. Right now, I just want a little more time."*

The Director gave a firm nod, even though she couldn't see it. "All right. Makes sense. I mean, of course you would. This is all so sudden."

"Oh," said Diva as if she'd noticed something. *"I'm sorry, I have to go. OGC..."*

"Gotcha. Be careful. Remember, don't reply to any transmissions unless they're from me. And get to Haru's practice room."

"Yes. Thank you."

With that, the transmission cut off.

The Director looked at the transmission terminal in his hand, hoping for her to be okay, then slowly closed it. He ran through his conversation with Diva, the words circling through his mind, his expression fierce.

I want to make it so she can come back to NiaLand...but how?

He'd read the data explaining the reason and history leading up to Diva's collection by OGC so many times he was sick of it. He'd hoped to find even one inaccurate detail or obtuse sentence he could exploit to undermine the whole argument, but he didn't find a single flaw. His only remaining option for fighting back was to appeal to pathos. Diva's popularity might have been fading, but she still had some diehard fans. He could get the public involved, maybe collect signatures for a petition, even if that was an old-school way of doing things...

No, that wouldn't change their decision. If I try to make public opinion my weapon, they'll just make public opinion their shield. Then it'd be weighing the freedom of one retro songstress against the increased security of all OGC AIs through the analysis of Diva's malfunction. There's no way we'd win.

His thoughts had been running in circles ever since last night as he tried to come up with a solution. He gave his cheeks a light smack to snap himself out of it.

I've got to try. An emotional appeal wouldn't be so bad. That's the name of the game in this field.

Just then, he got a message from a venue staff member. One group of guests was going to be late. First things first, he had to handle today's business like usual. He sent a reply telling the staffer how to handle the situation, still thinking about what Diva had said. If he was going for the emotional approach, there was going to be one major hurdle.

If only she *weren't the one in charge!*

He quickened his pace so the anger bubbling up inside him wouldn't show on the surface.

Tao received the transmission from the OGC research department when she was in a private reception room at the hospital.

"Yes... Yes. I understand. I am very sorry. I'll return to NiaLand as soon as I'm finished here and handle it myself." After her insincere apology, she hung up.

"Something happen?" asked the massive man sitting in front of her. There was a judgmental edge to his tone.

The man was in his late fifties, but he didn't look it. He had strong features, a sharp gaze, and he even had a full head of hair. His skin looked young, almost polished. Most people would have assumed he was in his twenties. He was sitting on a couch with dignity, his back ramrod straight, the muscles of his chest and shoulders filling out the white coat he wore. He was Kishibe Seiichi, Tao's father.

"It's a minor issue. It won't be a problem," Tao said.

"Is it your fault? Or someone else's?" Her father always asked questions like that. He valued logic and wanted to know where to place the blame.

Tao had to tell the truth. In the few seconds she had to answer, she scrambled to make sure it would be objectively correct. She was aware he would often forgive her so long as she remained impassive, but he was the one person she couldn't keep her cool around.

"Someone else's."

"That's fine, then. Make the right decision and handle it properly. You'll move up from your current position in the next few years. Don't cause trouble in a place where a lot of OGC AIs work."

"I'm sorry. It's already caused trouble for OGC's research department."

"What?" His eyes narrowed. "And you let it slide?"

"It was someone else's fault."

"Can you say that for certain?"

"Yes."

"That's fine, then," he said again. He was always like that, quick to change his attitude. "But if that's the case, why did you apologize just now? It was someone else's fault."

Tao shrank in on herself a little, regretting her mistake.

"If it's someone else's fault, then it's wrong for you to apologize," he said.

"I'm sorry."

"That's right. That apology was good. You should apologize when you make a mistake, but not at any other time."

"I understand."

Tao's father nodded, satisfied with her answer, and then tapped on the terminal on the reception room table. A monitor hovered in the air, displaying data from Tao's medical records, including the regular checkup she'd just undergone.

"The numbers are showing the decline we predicted. How do you feel?" he asked.

"It hasn't been a problem for my day-to-day activities."

"If it remains on this track, the operation will happen in a month. Get ready for it."

"I will."

"Do you have any questions?"

"No."

"That's fine, then. Go back to work."

"If you'll excuse me," Tao said, bowing at the waist before she left the room.

She walked down the halls of the hospital, a place she had become familiar with when she was a child. The doctors and nurses that passed her on the way made exaggerated attempts to greet her. She returned each one.

Her father, Seiichi, was the director of this hospital. The hospital establishment and administration were closely linked to OGC, so there were a lot of AI technicians and researchers who belonged to both organizations. It was a general hospital with over thirty departments, including surgery, internal medicine, and gynecology. Most notably, its treatments actively implemented OGC technology, making it a leader in the field of AI healthcare.

It started with a plastic surgery department that used AI-controlled synthetic joints and a physical therapy department that used high-quality prosthetics. As AI technology advanced, the hospital's practices and departments developed right alongside it, until AI tech had made its way into every part of the human body. One by one, people developed artificial muscles, organs, and even partial body transplants. The only thing left out was the brain.

Seiichi was a doctor who favored change, and it showed in his administration. While people's aversion to replacing their body parts with mechanical ones had weakened over the years, it still had strong roots. Seiichi took the initiative, changing the opinions of his colleagues and patients by proactively applying AI technology to his own body. Weight-wise, more of his body was now artificial than not, hence his young appearance. As he was a surgeon, Seiichi's hands were his life, and even those had been swapped out for synthetic ones years ago.

His first priority was saving his patients' lives. He would do anything to accomplish that goal, as long as logic or data supported it. Of all technological disciplines, AI development had the greatest potential to save human lives. That was the sort of man Kishibe Seiichi was, and the sort of father who raised Tao.

Once Tao left the building, she stepped into the car idling outside. It was an unmanned vehicle piloted by an internal AI. She announced her destination as she sank into the soft backseat. Without giving herself even a moment to catch her breath, she opened the data regarding the Diva situation. The songstress had refused transport and escaped the truck.

Tao heaved a sigh from deep in her chest. Her operation was in a month. She would probably have to stay in the hospital for a week after that, unable to move around. She had to get things in shipshape at the park so it could function smoothly without her, even if something this drastic happened while she was gone.

This is becoming a hassle. I'll bet the park employees aren't even looking for Diva.

Her prediction was based on the Director's attitude when she told him Diva was being transported. If that was the case, they'd have to send the OGC security staff to NiaLand to handle this directly. Considering her position, she didn't want to cause them any more trouble. She'd have to be particularly delicate.

I hate AIs, do I? Really now.

The director had said this about her, but it wasn't true. His mistaken assumption was probably based on her word choice and general attitude in AI-related matters. In fact, if Tao had to choose between humans and AIs, she preferred the latter. Humans always made things more difficult for her, with their emotions and irrationality. AIs were different.

A more correct statement of her position was this: *I hate one AI. I truly despise her.*

That one AI was waiting silently in Tao's home at this very moment. It wasn't Diva, the AI causing a ruckus in the park. Her name was TAO, and she looked exactly like Tao.

CHAPTER 6

The Songstress's Message to Her Other Self

.:1:.

WHAT HAD THE MOST significant impact on the human Tao's development? If you boiled it down to the basics, there were two main influences: her strict father and her ruthless illness. Both had existed before she was even brought into this world, as if they were destined to shape her life from the get-go.

Her father, Seiichi, and her mother, Michi, had an incredibly harmonious relationship. Their initial encounter had less to do with love and more to do with politics. Seiichi was a young doctor of twenty-seven working at the hospital he would later direct, and the hospital administrators already had their eyes on him due to his excellence. The perfect partner for him was Michi, a twenty-five-year-old woman working at OGC. Her parents were executives at OGC, the hospital's parent company in name and in practice.

They first met at a social event hosted by an important figure for both OGC and the hospital, though the social event was really just a cover for a power struggle. While there, Seiichi casually suggested that Michi marry him. He had zero interest in marriage itself—he just wanted to climb the ranks in the hospital and organization at large. He didn't care who he wed, so long as they were beneficial to his future and didn't grate on his nerves.

His first impression of Michi when they were introduced was that she was mild-mannered. She was hardly expressive and said little. To him, she looked wholly submissive to her OGC executive parents, and he found that incredibly convenient. The two married a mere two months later.

Seiichi realized he'd made a miscalculation less than two weeks after they moved in together.

"Seiichi-san, have you found the draft data on the hospital's finances yet?" Michi asked him.

"Not yet," he replied.

"You promised you would get it to me by today."

"One of my patients is showing unpredicted numbers in postop. This has never happened before. I need to review it. I don't have time to—"

"I'm working too, you know. Just as much as you. OGC needs that data to plan some behind-the-scenes corrections to the administration funds. We can't draft a plan without that data. You said you'd have it."

"I told you, I have an unforeseen incident on my hands!"

"Then show me that patient's medical records and data from patients with similar conditions in the past. I'll compare the two of them and decide whether you really couldn't have predicted this. If you could have, then you broke your promise to me out of your own negligence, and I'll expect an apology."

Michi was not especially emotive or talkative in general, but when it came to expressing her thoughts and opinions, she was logical and verbose. The seemingly meek and delicate woman would stare into Seiichi's eyes with the ferocity of a bird of prey.

His impression that she would bend over backward for her executive parents was also wrong. In reality, they'd told her not to say or do anything at the social event other than nod. That way, they could get their excellent—if slightly too outspoken—daughter an "in" with someone familiar with the hospital's finances, since it was so difficult to know from the outside.

That day, instead of reviewing his patient's data, Seiichi was up late into the night gathering the financial data Michi requested. He slammed it down on the table the next morning at breakfast. Her response floored him: "Thank you. Keep your word next time. You also seem to have forgotten today was your turn to make breakfast, so I did it for you. Please make up for it when it's my turn."

He seriously considered demanding a divorce right then and there. However, he couldn't have his marriage fail after less than two weeks. There was the embarrassment, of course, and his reputation was essential for moving up in the organization.

They argued regularly after that. It was always about the hospital or OGC, but Seiichi was just as likely to start things off as Michi was. The only thing that kept him sane was that Michi would listen to reason. If she didn't know something, she'd say so. If she didn't understand something, she'd say so. If there was a matter most adults with common sense would leave at some shade of gray, she would keep going until it was clearly laid out in black and white. It made her very difficult to persuade, but if she *could* be convinced, she never brought the issue up again. Sufficient data was the best ammo to change her mind, but it took time and effort. It was exhausting.

After the first incident, Seiichi occasionally complained about Michi at work.

During one of these gripes, his coworker said, "Huh, this is new. You two are like a match made in heaven."

Seiichi didn't expect to hear that. He didn't like it. Evidently, it was rare for him to complain about his home life to his colleagues. He'd been working with a one-track mind, prioritizing conversation with his superiors over his fellows so he could keep moving up the ladder.

Before he realized it, he'd been married for a year, then two. He became aware of his true feelings for Michi not long after he turned thirty. She was pregnant.

"I'm quitting my job next month," she said, surprising Seiichi with her decision.

Up until then, Michi had been using her husband's position to overhaul the hospital's administration while she was still at OGC. Seiichi figured she'd done it to help her climb the ranks at OGC or to please her executive parents.

"That was true right after we got married," she said when Seiichi shared his thoughts. "Don't worry. I won't do anything to ruin your standing. I'll spend this month persuading my parents and arranging everything so it's handed off to my replacement without issue."

"Why are you doing all this? You're throwing away your career."

"It is hard to let go, but I want to give my all to raising this child. I want to be with them as much as I can. I'm having this baby with the person I love." And then she smiled.

It was the first time Seiichi had ever seen his wife smile. He smiled and nodded back, then placed his hand on Michi's belly. In that moment, he wasn't at all worried about his standing at the hospital. The only thing he hoped for was that his wife and child would make it through the delivery safely.

When Michi was five months pregnant, they found out that the fetus' heart valves were malformed, which could lead to heart failure in the future. They weren't completely sure, but the lead doctor determined the baby wouldn't live long.

Michi's health was also failing.

"If it comes down to it, prioritize the baby over me," she said when Seiichi brought up the possibility of terminating this pregnancy and trying again another time. "This child *is* our child. There won't be a next time for them, or a time after that."

Seiichi looked into her eyes and knew there was no persuading her. "Okay. You just relax and focus on keeping yourself and the kid healthy. I'll take care of everything else—including you and the baby."

"You don't have any obstetrics experience, though."

"I'm still a doctor. Don't worry, I'll handle it."

The baby made it through, but Michi's condition was poor after she gave birth. While her immune system was at its weakest, she contracted pneumonia. Seiichi begged the hospital and the maternity department, and they allowed him to stay by her side to care for her. He pulled out all the stops, using whatever data or treatment he could think of to save her. Nothing worked.

"Promise me you'll raise her well. Even if her body's weak," Michi said on the last night of her life.

Seiichi nodded. It was all he could manage. He didn't cry when her life faded in the ICU. It wasn't that he was trying not to cry; the tears just didn't come. It felt real, but it didn't feel *true*. His feet carried him to the neonatal ward, where their little girl was. The ward, which was already clean, had an intensive care nursery with an even stricter sanitation policy. That was where he found her.

He looked at his child through the several layers of glass, and the tears finally came. Seiichi sobbed for so long that his lips cracked. The two of them had already decided on a name for the baby: Tao. Like "michi," it was another word for path, or way.

On one side of the glass was a girl held tight in the clutches of illness. On the other side, a father who'd promised his dead wife he would heal that girl and raise her well.

That was how Tao's life began.

.: 2 :.

YOUNG TAO'S ENTIRE WORLD consisted of a single room. It was called the Clean House, a completely sterile environment utilizing cutting-edge OGC technology. The reason it was called the Clean House instead of the Clean Room was that it was far too large. It was as big as a gymnasium, had its own baths and toilets, a study space, a play area, and all the other facilities a child might need.

It was built with the goal of providing a space where children with health issues, like Tao, could grow under hospital supervision in a stable environment that supported their health. The facility hadn't existed when Tao was born, but Seiichi's position at the hospital and his reputation allowed him to get it up and running with OGC's help in two short years.

Tao had been a resident of the Clean House for as long as she could remember. Her organs had functioned poorly since birth, and her immune system was weak as well. She wasn't allowed to take even one step outside. The only exception to the rule was when she was taken to the hospital for a procedure. But, in an attempt to keep her time outside of the Clean House to a minimum, she would be sedated for the trip. For all intents and purposes, it really did feel like she'd never been outside.

Some of the procedures she underwent were extremely intricate. She had about one of those a year before she even learned to talk. If an organ was determined to be a hindrance to her life, the offending part was partially or even fully replaced by a mechanical one.

First, her heart valves were replaced. Then part of her right lung. A device was implanted to help her liver function. Next came a pacemaker. After that, they swapped out one of her kidneys. Her surgeries included a lot of operations and parts that hadn't been approved by the medical field, but her father pushed for all of it, risking his standing as a doctor. He was literally betting the life he'd built up for himself on Tao's life, and the two of them kept winning. If they didn't keep winning, Tao couldn't keep living.

As she spent that time toeing the line between life and death, her father made her promise to follow one rule:

"You can't make friends."

There were other children living in the Clean House with Tao. Some were in even worse health than her—they weren't there for healing but rather for high-quality hospice treatment. Others were in better health than Tao and only there to be monitored while they recovered. Her father strictly forbade her from becoming friends with any of them.

"Did the assistant director really say that?" asked a new nurse one day.

"Yes," replied Tao with a nod. Her father was the assistant director of the hospital at the time.

"Why would he say that?"

"He said it's because it's very painful to say goodbye to people you're close to."

"I heard about your mom, Tao-chan, but...are you really okay with it being this way?"

Tao nodded again. "Yes. Father wouldn't tell me something that's wrong."

The nurse looked at her with sad eyes, like Tao's response pained her.

A few weeks later, that same nurse told Tao she had a favor to ask of her. She gestured to a girl who looked to be about ten, the same age as Tao. "This is Sakura-chan. She moved into the House today. Would you mind telling her about it?"

An accident had taken her sight, and the shock of it took her voice. The eye bank couldn't find a suitable specimen for a corneal transplant, so she was hospitalized at the Clean House while waiting for artificial eyes.

Tao was immediately suspicious. The Clean House was normally for internal medicine patients. Surgery for eyesight would fall under ophthalmology or general surgery. The inability to talk due to shock would be in the realm of psychiatry.

"They don't have any free beds," said the nurse. "You're the only child here who can show her around, Tao-chan. You've been here longer than anyone else too."

Patients in the Clean House came and went, and right now the only people there other than Tao were young children who couldn't talk or children so ill they couldn't get out of bed. Tao was also the only patient who'd been in the House since it was established, making her the patient who'd been there the longest.

"You're such a reliable girl. Could you do this for me?"

Tao agreed. From that day forward, she looked after Sakura. The other girl just moped around in the beginning, not responding to anything Tao said. She couldn't reply to Tao, since she was nonverbal, but she didn't even shake her head or nod.

Time was one thing Tao had plenty of, so she continued to patiently explain things to Sakura. She would take Sakura's hand and give her a tour. She'd tell her the entrance was over there, the toilets on that side, here was the table, that was Sakura's bed.

She did that over and over, but Sakura hardly ever moved of her own volition. The only time she did was when she had to go to the bathroom. She'd press the nurse call button and get someone to lead her there while she walked on unsteady legs.

Tao wondered if she was doing a poor job of explaining, so she asked the nurse for help and got people from the ophthalmology and rehab departments to teach her things. One of their suggestions was for Tao to make a diorama of the House. If Sakura could *feel* it, that might help her gain a better understanding of the space.

In the past, those kinds of dioramas might have been handmade with paper and glue, but these days it was pretty easy to make something using a hologram with tactile feedback. Tao had some trouble with it, being unused to that kind of work, but she made a miniature version of the Clean House in three days.

Whether it was the model or Tao's efforts that had touched her, Sakura at last began interacting with Tao. She touch-typed on terminals to converse with her. Apparently, she was an introverted girl. She didn't really go out much—though obviously more than Tao—and spent most of her days off from school at home, hence her skill with terminals.

"I used to like drawing."

"Used to?" Tao asked, and Sakura's hands stopped. She guessed what Sakura wanted to say, and what she was afraid of. "It's okay. You'll be able to see again someday. You're just waiting for surgery, right?"

"But there's a lot of stuff delaying it, like money or how my body's doing."

"Well, I don't know about money, but I think you're fine when it comes to your physical condition. Almost everyone is compatible with OGC's working artificial eyes. And I think even if you aren't, you can handle it if you take a special medicine once a month."

"You know a lot about this."

"I do."

Sakura smiled for the first time since coming to the Clean House. Tao wondered if her response was funny somehow. *"Tao-chan, what's your face look like?"*

Tao wasn't sure how to answer that. Thinking about it gave her no answer, so she eventually took Sakura's hands and placed them on her own face. "Here's my nose. Apparently, if you're touching something you don't know really well, you should figure out what's in the middle. Then you can use that as your base point, and you go back and forth from there to help you figure out how far things are."

Sakura touched Tao's nose without hesitation. She moved to an eye, then her eyebrow, back to the nose, down to the lips, then chin, and back to her nose. It tickled and made Tao want to sneeze, but she held it back. Sakura's hands pattered all over Tao's face. Eventually, she must have thought something about the situation was amusing, because she smiled even wider.

Tao smiled too. Then she had a sudden thought. "Draw my face for me."

"There's no way."

"But you've got to be bored. You need *something* to focus on while you're here." Tao knew that from experience.

Instead of going to school during the day, she would work through the learning programs her father required her to do. Some people felt bad for her because it was a fairly intense work-load, but she didn't find it strenuous at all. The more free time she had, the more she would have to think about her weak body.

Sakura picked up a drawing tablet for the first time since her accident. She spent twenty minutes drawing.

"Can I be completely honest?" asked Tao when she saw it, and Sakura nodded. "I'm pretty sure I'm cuter than that."

Sakura's reaction was extreme. She threw herself at the termi-nal's keyboard and smashed out the words, *"It looks like a face?"*

"Yes."

Tears sprang to Sakura's eyes, and she gripped the drawing pen tight. She sat there for a while like that, then slowly typed, *"Can I draw you every day from now on?"*

A month later, Sakura's drawings of Tao were so good, it was hard to believe she hadn't been looking at Tao's face when she drew them.

Tao told Sakura that, who smiled and took Tao's hand, seem-ing a bit nervous. *"Do you want to be my friend? I don't have any friends at school."*

Tao's face stiffened. She quickly controlled her body so the tension wouldn't be conveyed through her hand. The promise she made her father echoed in her mind. After a while, she said, "I thought we already were friends."

Two weeks later, Sakura had a successful eye transplant. Her voice came back with her sight, and she was transferred from the

Clean House to ophthalmology's general ward. Three days after that, they determined there were no issues with her artificial eyes, and she was discharged.

She went to see Tao before she left the hospital. "You did so much for me, Tao-chan. Thank you. I'll keep in touch."

Sakura waved from the other side of the glass, probably to avoid having to disinfect herself. Tao waved back. Sakura's parents tugged her hands and they left, her eyes looking every which way at her surroundings.

The girls messaged each other every few days, but soon that turned into once a week, and then once at the beginning of each month. On the first of the sixth month since Sakura's discharge, the message that should have come didn't. It was Tao's eleventh birthday, which Sakura certainly knew.

Oddly enough, Tao wasn't sad. She assumed this was how it normally went. Even so, her eyes welled up with tears. She clenched her fist tight, like how Sakura used to squeeze the drawing pen.

"How about you try reaching out?" said the nurse who had introduced them.

Tao's partially artificial heart thumped powerfully. Her blasted organs writhed. She pressed her fist into her gut to wrestle them into submission.

"She probably has some things going on and just—"

"Stop talking," Tao said, and the nurse jumped. Her voice was barely louder than a whisper, but that was the first time she'd ever cut someone off. "You lied when you said they didn't have any beds, didn't you?"

"What?"

"You said they didn't have any beds in ophthalmology or psychiatry. That was a lie. Why'd you do that?"

"I—"

"I already know." Tao didn't actually want an answer. She knew what the nurse had been thinking and had no desire to hear it. "You saw me taking to Sakura, and it made you smile. You thought you did a good deed. Figured you did the right thing. I looked happier than I ever did before, I'm sure. But can you really understand how I feel? You haven't even been here a year."

Everyone who came to the Clean House eventually left Tao. The first child Tao remembered ever talking to, a boy, died a few months after he came. The first baby she saw was transferred to the general ward after a week. There was an older boy and an older girl, who were both in middle school, who taught Tao a lot of things. Both of their surgeries were successes, they got better, and they left. The first pair of siblings she saw were the opposite: their surgeries failed, and they both died. Sakura was the same as the rest. Nothing more, nothing less.

"Do you know how many lights there are on the ceiling?" asked Tao. "Seventy-nine. Do you know how many types of fake flowers are in here? Seventeen. Do you know the color of the chair's feet? Pink, silver, and cream. There's also black in storage, but those chairs aren't used anymore. How much do you actually know about this place? I have never left this room unless I was unconscious."

Tao was the only one who could never go anywhere. It didn't matter if her surgeries succeeded or failed—when she came to, she was in her bed in the house. She didn't die, she didn't get better, and she didn't leave.

"Don't involve me the next time you're trying to do something to make you feel good about yourself."

The last message Tao received from Sakura said everyone was surprised by how good she could draw with her eyes closed, and that she'd made a friend because of it.

"Throw these away," said Tao as she held out some papers to the nurse.

They were all the pictures of Tao's face that Sakura had drawn. They'd realized at one point that it was easier for Sakura to figure out what she was doing if she used paper and a pencil rather than a drawing tablet because she could feel it better. From then on, she only drew on paper.

The nurse didn't take them. "But your friend—"

"I don't have friends. I never have, and I never will."

The nurse still didn't try to take the papers. Tao gave up, went over, and chucked the drawings into the garbage can herself, then deleted every message from Sakura she had on her terminal.

A few days later, the nurse disappeared from the Clean House. She'd asked to be moved to a different department.

"Father was right," Tao muttered to herself in bed. No one was around to hear.

She thought Sakura was her first friend, and the first time she'd heard her voice was when she said goodbye.

"I can't make friends."

To Tao, her father was always right.

.: 3 :.

TAO LEFT THE CLEAN HOUSE when she was eighteen. More than 60 percent of her organs had been replaced with synthetic ones. Thanks to that, doctors decided her health wouldn't be a hindrance to her life outside the Clean House, although she still needed to go to the hospital once a week for a checkup. Her father told her he would cure her, but she always thought she would only leave the Clean House when she died. She never thought the day would come where she would get out of there alive. Yet again, her father was right.

"Congratulations, Tao-chan. You've worked so hard. And you look just like your mom," said the head nurse when Tao left. She'd taken care of Tao for a long time.

Tao had only ever seen her mother in photos. She knew her father loved and respected her mother, so she was happy to hear she looked like her. She smiled and bowed, then left the place that had been her world.

She'd chosen to live alone for two primary reasons. The first was simply that she wanted to experience being alone. When she was in the Clean House, data was constantly being collected about her, from how long she spent in the bathroom to her nutrition intake. There was always a nurse on the other side of the glass. Eyes were on her even while she slept. The artificial organs in her body did stream data back to the hospital, meaning she wasn't *truly* free from observers, but she at least wanted to experience an environment where no one was staring at her.

The second reason was to repay her father for everything he'd done. Now that she was eighteen, Tao understood the burden and responsibility her father had to bear in order to establish and maintain the Clean House. She'd sometimes butted heads with him when she was younger because she hated her environment, but things were different now. All she felt toward him was gratitude and respect.

Seeing as time was the only thing Tao had plenty of in the Clean House, she'd studied hard and received a bachelor's degree before she hit eighteen. Part of that came down to her father working hard to support her, but she wanted to at least show him she was growing.

When she learned she'd be leaving the Clean House, she stopped wanting to show him growth and started wanting to show him independence. She couldn't very well reduce his burden if she went to live with him and had him take care of her—although he apparently spent most nights in the hospital anyway. Tao didn't need a cushy lifestyle; she just wanted to prove she could manage living on her own.

The problem was, where would she work? Her experiment would be a waste if she ended up an unemployed parasite sucking away her father's income. She decided to lean him on him a little, just in the beginning, as much as she didn't want to. He used his connections at OGC to find her an accounting position at one of their subsidiaries. It was a temp position more along the lines of a part-time job, but it could be done remotely. Also, since it required a bit of skill, the pay was quite comfortable for a person living alone.

All the nurses of the Clean House were opposed to her working, primarily out of concern for her health. Tao pushed back, arguing her artificial organs sent real-time data to the hospital anyway. Most importantly, her father supported her decision. That was how Tao started her life living alone for the first time in all her eighteen years.

ılıı|||ılıı

She met TAO when she was twenty-five.

"Is this related to issues that occur during the implementation of a full-body replacement and 'breaking in' the circuits?" she asked, reading a report on a tablet.

Her father nodded. "It is. How much do you know about the procedure?"

"Only what's public. There have been just a handful of successful transplants worldwide."

"Do you know the reason for that?"

"Frequent instances of brain death and comas. I don't know the details, but they say it's because the brain rejects the artificial body."

"That's an accurate understanding. Now, that report."

Tao's eyes fell back to her tablet.

"All of the successful cases of full-body transplants weren't done in one go, but rather stage by stage, replacing parts of the body with artificial ones," he explained. "If we assume that the artificial body sends feedback to the brain that causes strain, then in the breakthrough cases, the patients wound up reducing that feedback in advance because the process was gradual."

"I see."

"The main point here is that conditioning—the so called 'breaking in' of the circuits—is the key to a successful full-body transplant. Studies conducted on animals have produced promising results."

"Right."

"Given that conditioning is the heart of the issue, the OGC engineers and I have planned around it. If, before the operation, the AI frame or positronic brain operates in a similar manner to the person who will be using it, that should cut down on the feedback issue. If we're right, this will significantly reduce the risks."

Tao ruminated on that information, then said, "In other words, you prepare an AI that is a complete duplicate of the person in how it looks and thinks. You have them operate to condition the body and the positronic brain, and later use that copy AI as the body for the full-body transplant."

"That is correct."

Tao was relieved when her father nodded again. He hated when she didn't understand things correctly or distorted them. "So why are you showing *me* this?" she asked.

His eyes opened a little wider, and the corners of his mouth turned up, something that didn't happen often. "You sound just like your mom when you ask like that."

Tao's skin crawled, like it was slathered in mud. Her father must not have noticed because he opened another window on the tablet. It was her medical record.

"Your numbers were fine after you left the Clean House—until this year, when they dropped drastically. Based on the data we're seeing, it probably stems from the degradation of one of the artificial parts we put in when you were young. You're smart, so you've probably already realized that. But if things stay like this, you'll die within the next three years."

The way he said it might have seemed cruel, but Tao was used to it. It didn't feel cold to her. Her father had always been blunt about her condition, ever since she was little.

"I will not let that happen," he said, staring directly at her.

In her mind, Tao told herself, *He's saying this for my sake. Mine.* "A full-body transplant is my only chance for survival?"

"Correct." Her father turned and addressed someone outside the room: "Come on in."

"Pardon me," someone said. Their voice sounded exactly like Tao's.

When they—or it—walked in, Tao couldn't believe her eyes. The AI was the spitting image of Tao at age twenty-five. She had the same underweight body, the same pale skin that barely knew the touch of the sun, and the same taller-than-average height. Her almond-shaped eyes were sharp, and her mouth and nose were petite. Even her neat, shoulder-length black hair was exactly the same. The only thing that was different was that, while Tao was wearing a suit, the AI was wearing scrubs.

"It's nice to meet you. I am KT-01," the AI said with a polite bow of her head.

Tao had seen this before, this bow with its perfect angle and speed. She'd practiced it in the mirror over and over for use in the business world. She was so shocked that she forgot to bow back.

"She's been given huge chunks of your data," her father said, "from how you act to how you think, all the way down to your speech patterns. It was only possible because we were constantly recording data from you while you were in the Clean House. A copy this close to the actual person is extremely rare."

"The bow she just did—I learned to do that after I left the Clean House. I felt like I was looking in the mirror."

"It's perfectly possible to calculate something like that with predictive algorithms, since we have data on your environment since you've left, as well as from your checkups. We asked ourselves, 'With her current position, what would she learn? Where would she start? How would she learn?'"

"Incredible." Tao studied the AI, impressed. The AI stared right back at her. It was the same habit Tao got from her father. "In the future, every part transplanted into me will come from her, except the brain?"

"Correct. And for that, you'll be living with her until the operation."

"You're telling me to condition her circuits?"

He nodded. "Yes, but you don't have to do anything special. Just live with her. There's no better conditioning than having her see, touch, and hear the same things you do. There's a limit in terms of eating, but we can get that data from you."

"This isn't an approved method, is it? We can't have others finding out about it."

"That's right. Which means the two of you can't be together 24/7. The biggest impediment will be your job, since you can't take her to work with you. That's why you'll always be sharing data on your work with us. We need her experiences to be as close to yours as possible. You should even take her out walking with you. People who see you will just think you're twins, or perhaps that you just happen to have an AI who looks like you."

"Understood."

"The more time we spend on this, the better. Depending on your condition, I predict the operation will occur in two years, maybe two and a half. Do everything with her until then. Have conversations with her to get her as close to 'you' as possible."

Her father then told her they were done, and his eyes returned to the terminal on his desk as he went back to work. The conversation was over. Tao said goodbye and dipped her head reverently. The AI did the same.

Before leaving the room, Tao steadied her breathing and steadied her nerves. Then, she said, "Father, I was promoted recently. I'm section chief of the administration department."

Her father's brow furrowed a bit. Without looking up from his terminal, he replied, "I heard. In about five years, you'll spend some time in an external position of authority, then you'll probably be brought back and made into assistant manager or given some equal position. What's the issue?"

Tao was careful to keep the disappointment out of her voice as she said, "There is no issue. I was just reporting."

"Ah. Well, I already know."

She waited for just long enough that it wouldn't feel unnatural, but he didn't say anything else. He didn't even offer her a short, "Good job." With one last goodbye, she left the room with the AI.

Neither she nor the AI spoke on their way home. During that time, she decided to just call the AI "TAO." It was awkward calling the AI by her own name, but she'd been told to get her as close to herself as she could, and calling her KT-01 would be going about that the wrong way.

When they first started living together, Tao felt some discomfort toward TAO as she suddenly had to spend her days with company. The two really were quite alike. She had TAO wear some of her clothes, which made the AI look even more like her than when she was in scrubs. When they talked, Tao noticed that TAO responded the same way she would, and her tone was the same too. Tao had developed an incredibly logical way of speaking, influenced by her father, and that was very easy for AIs like TAO to imitate.

When she woke up and when she came home from work, there was always someone there with her face and speech. It was as if she were living in some terrible movie, and she couldn't shed the discomfort. It felt like a joke. But after a week, it became her new normal.

Tao figured TAO would have the same preferences as her because they had the same thought processes and personality. Her prediction was right. TAO hated unproductive conversation just as much as Tao, so they got by without any pointless small talk.

They both checked the same news sites every day, so there was no fighting over the terminal. In order to keep the circuits' conditioning on track, they went to sleep and woke at the same time, meaning there was never a situation where one slept in or kept the other up. There were limits to TAO's food intake, but they didn't take turns making food. Each day, they both made the same food together, ate it together, and cleaned up together.

Once she was used to it, Tao couldn't imagine living with anyone else could ever be so easy. She had both the security of company and the freedom of living alone.

Tao first noticed a difference between her and TAO a month after they started living together. Did TAO really know everything Tao did? They were having a conversation to check that.

"How many lights are in the ceiling of the Clean House?" asked Tao.

"Seventy-nine," TAO answered.

"Correct. How many types of fake flowers were in the Clean House up until I left?"

"Twenty-two."

"Correct. What color were the feet of the chairs?"

This time, TAO needed a few moments to calculate. Then she said, "I don't know."

"You don't know?"

"No. Do you?"

"Pink, silver, and cream, with black on the ones in storage," she told TAO, who looked at her questioningly.

"How do you know that?"

"I remember it. Why *don't* you know that? You should know everything about me from when I was in the Clean House."

"I only know the data that was installed. I referenced data on the Clean House to determine the number of lights and types of plants, but the only detail I have on chairs is the quantity. I'm actually surprised you know those things. That's true of the number of lights and the plants, but why would you ever know the color of the chairs' feet?"

Tao gasped. Objectively speaking, it *was* odd that she would remember that information. She thought about it. "I think it's because that was all I could depend on when that place was my whole life."

TAO took another moment to calculate. She looked at Tao like she was measuring her.

"Do you mean to say that you used simple tasks like counting objects and remembering pointless details to escape the stress of living in the Clean House?" asked TAO.

"It sounds pathetic, but yes, I think that's the case. It's like fidgeting."

"I see. That's interesting. That humanlike aspect is something I don't have in me yet. I will work hard to become more like you."

"Thank you. It's a little embarrassing, though."

"That I can understand." TAO smiled, which made Tao smile back.

One day, Tao's regular checkups changed. Ever since she left the Clean House, she made sure to go to the hospital once a week,

which usually took just a couple of hours. But a few months after she began living with TAO, she was told those checkups would have to last all day in preparation for the operation, and because her numbers were getting worse by the minute, even if it wasn't yet affecting her daily life.

Tao panicked. She had to do what the hospital—what her father—told her to, but having to go there for an entire day each time would interfere with her job. She'd been working as much as her body allowed so she could pay her father back, until she got to where she was now. She'd started as a remote accounting temp, and then she was brought on full-time. A few years later, she was put in charge of a small group of subordinates. Her successes were recognized when that group helped administration with a new project, and she was pulled into the admin department. And just the other day, she was made director of that department. The company had even acknowledged how quickly she was working her way up. Tao felt the checkups would threaten that.

"What if I handle things in your place?" TAO suggested. "There may be some people who notice something off in my communication if I go into the office to work, so I think you'll have to give me work I can do at home."

Tao wavered on the decision but ultimately agreed. She was already sharing data from work with TAO, as her father had instructed, and she found there were almost no differences in the decisions she and TAO made. Even if TAO did make a mistake, Tao would have plenty of opportunities to make up for it if she limited TAO's work in advance. It was significantly better than not getting any work done for a whole day.

When Tao came home from her first day of the new checkup schedule, she was met with quite a surprise: TAO showed her the work she'd done, and it was perfect. Because it was TAO's first day on the job, Tao hadn't included anything requiring difficult decisions or creative ideas—which were hardly AIs' strong suits—but TAO had done such a wonderful job as her replacement that she couldn't find a single thing to complain about. In fact, she'd made progress on jobs outside the scope of what Tao had given her in order to lighten Tao's load.

"I would like to ask you something," TAO said.

"Is there something you didn't understand about work?"

"No, it isn't related to work. In conjunction with your regular checkups, I send the hospital current data on myself. When I did that earlier, I had a conversation with the head nurse via transmission." TAO hesitated for a moment, which wasn't something she did often. It was likely just a moment for her to calculate, but it came off as worry to Tao. "The nurse saw a picture of me and said, '*You* really look like your mom too.'"

Tao's breath caught in her throat.

"When she said that, I experienced numbers I can't easily identify. If I had to put it in human terms, I would say I felt 'conflicted.' Part sad, part annoyed, and also a little bit happy. Does this sound familiar to you?"

For a time, Tao didn't respond. She had experienced this feeling repeatedly over the past few years, but she could never put it into words. "It does sound familiar," she said eventually. "But it's hard to describe."

"It is." TAO nodded. "I think that's why I'm having a hard time explaining it. But could I ask you to try anyway? I think it'll help me understand and become more like you." Eyes of the exact same color as Tao's—or more accurately, eye cameras—looked directly at her.

Neither of them cared if there was a silence. Tao thought for a good five minutes before she spoke up again. "At first, it did make me happy to be told I looked like my mother. She was incredible. I was also happy I managed to live long enough for others to notice the similarity. But the thing that made me happiest was that I had value because I looked like my mother, the woman my father loved. It's because of him that I'm alive, after all."

"Yes."

"Even when I left the Clean House and decided to live on my own, it was so I could repay him, or at the very least not be any more of a burden on him. I put everything into my work even after I moved away from home. I think I wanted to show him that, even though my primary defining trait was being sickly, I had grown into something incredible. I still feel that way."

"I see. I understand."

"But Father has never once complimented me. And at some point, I realized it was because he wasn't seeing me. He was seeing Mother."

TAO frowned.

Tao steadied her shaking voice and continued. "I really do look like her. Even I think so when I look at the photos and videos she left behind. Lately, whenever someone says I look like her, I start to feel uneasy. I wonder if everything I've done since leaving the Clean House has been for nothing. But I should also be happy when people tell me I resemble her because she was incredible. Agh, I'm sorry. It really is difficult to describe."

The AI nodded a second time. "I'm sorry. You went to the effort of explaining it for me, but I still can't properly understand it as I am now. I feel like I have a vague understanding, but... oh." TAO suddenly stopped. Something about her expression resembled frustration, and she apologized again.

"What's wrong?" asked Tao.

"Thinking about it, it might actually be a good thing that I can't properly explain something that you can't properly explain."

Tao let out a little gasp of realization. If TAO's circuits were being successfully conditioned to make her more like Tao, then she was right.

"I can't believe I didn't realize something so simple," said TAO. "What is going on with my logic circuit? I'm sorry, I wasted your time." She hung her head.

Tao felt a small smile creep onto her face. In part, she was amused by how TAO was acting, but it was primarily because she felt like this AI understood the murky feelings she had inside her. "Say, TAO..."

"Yes?"

"I have a suggestion. Why don't you help me with my work regularly, instead of just when I go to my checkups?"

TAO fell into thought. She was only helping out to eliminate the abnormality of Tao not working because of her checkups. Normally, Tao would aggregate data from her daily work and check to see if TAO would make the same decisions as her, so they could ensure she was gaining the same experiences. But if TAO was helping with work that wasn't normal for Tao, if she was working on things that Tao didn't normally, they wouldn't know whether that was helping condition TAO's circuits.

"It's okay," Tao said with a smile, trying to dispel TAO's uncertainty. "You did a good job today. I can trust you with my work. You're...already plenty like me."

More numbers popped up inside TAO that she couldn't easily define, but they were completely different from those she saw when she was told she looked like Tao's mother. "That makes me happy. Okay, I'll do my best."

"I look forward to working with you."

From then on, Tao worked vigorously alongside TAO. It started with Tao letting TAO handle whatever work Tao brought home for the day, then quickly turned into TAO working on things while Tao was in the office, so they were tackling tasks in tandem. TAO would send her the data she created at home, which Tao would use in the office.

Eventually, she started having TAO handle some face-to-face meetings—the simple ones, anyway. She was worried about the AI interacting with people in the company, so Tao started her off on meetings with external contacts. Once she knew it wasn't a problem, TAO would go to the office on the days Tao had her checkups. They even arranged it so Tao was conducting meetings inside the company while TAO was taking care of ones outside at the exact same time, so long as they wouldn't get caught.

Tao's accomplishments, evaluations, and responsibilities skyrocketed. Everyone inside and outside the company asked her when she found time to sleep. That was where Tao had made her miscalculation. As long as an AI underwent simple maintenance, they could continue working without a wink of sleep. Tao had underestimated that ability.

"Tao, there's a discrepancy in the profit forecast you put together for me yesterday. It's not an issue, though. I corrected it," said TAO.

"Oh, I'm sorry."

"Also, regarding today's meeting, would it be all right if I go? We receive more accurate data when I visit that client than when you go. The statistics are only from five visits, but it's better to increase the probability that something will go well, even if by just a little."

"Okay... You can handle it."

TAO never made a mistake. Of course she didn't; she was an AI. It was different when it came to creative work or interpersonal communication, since those didn't have objectively correct answers, but she never made a blunder when the work could be boiled down to one response. And she just worked hard.

Tao, on the other hand, made mistakes no matter what she did. She made far fewer than her coworkers, and the majority were so minor most people wouldn't even consider them mistakes, but she made them nonetheless. The amount of time she had to do a satisfactory job was also slowly but steadily decreasing. Tao's organs—both real and artificial—were rapidly declining, as if driving her toward the operation. However, no one at the hospital panicked, including her father. Her organs were performing exactly as predicted. But as her numbers got worse, she started to feel a faint chill, like layer after layer of her skin was being peeled away.

Before she realized it, TAO was going into the office more than she was. TAO took care of all the important dealings, while Tao normally did the background research to prepare for them. Even then, Tao couldn't tell TAO that she'd had enough.

Both of them valued logic, and neither was misguided when they determined TAO's output was better when she went to the office. The work came with incredible profits and responsibility, as was appropriate for the position. There were several occasions where Tao felt it was too much for her to handle, but TAO managed it with ease.

Whenever she saw that happening, Tao would tell herself, *TAO has the same abilities I would if I were healthy. My body just can't handle things in its current state. I'll be able to do just as much as her after the operation.*

And yet, a voice in the corner of her heart screamed that was a lie.

On one of TAO's days off, the AI did something that scared her. The two were at home, and TAO was working despite not needing to. She sent her data to the hospital, then a transmission to the head nurse.

Once the transmission was over, TAO whispered, "Don't lump me in with Mother."

Tao's head snapped up when she heard it, and she stared at TAO sitting in front of the terminal. It was the first time Tao heard TAO talk to herself, and she was clearly angry. Her hands were clenched, and she was glaring into the empty space where the air monitor had been until a moment before. She looked so human, and Tao's real face had never made that expression. Tao was outright terrified when she realized that.

Normally, Tao would've thought, *Oh, someone's told her she looks like Mother. She must be having those mixed feelings again.* This time around, that thought didn't even cross her mind. She'd shared that complex blend of happiness and frustration with her AI twin, and they'd evenly divided so many experiences and situations between them...but now she looked like a stranger. Nothing TAO did going forward would surprise her. It might sound extreme, but Tao wouldn't even have found it strange if TAO started screaming or leapt at her. It was like her home—her whole existence—had been taken over.

Tao stood and said, "I'm going shopping," then quickly made her escape.

Two years after they started living together, Tao was assigned to NiaLand. She was twenty-seven at the time. The historic theme park was one of the country's greatest. It was a paradise built up by humans and AIs, with a variety of attractions and stage shows. Tao was to be the general manager. It was a huge promotion. The appointment was temporary, and she was guaranteed to go back to the parent company in a few years, but Tao was the youngest general manager in NiaLand's history.

This opportunity had come about not just because of Tao's excellence but also with a little influence from her maternal grandparents, since they were key figures at OGC. As one of NiaLand's sponsors, OGC had supplied many of the AIs in the park. Put bluntly, OGC had a stranglehold on NiaLand's purse strings, meaning the park constantly had to defer to OGC and its family of companies. The position was purely meant to pad Tao's resume, which didn't bother her.

She was an utter newbie when it came to theme parks, but being assigned to a land of dreams or what have you didn't matter—at the end of the day, it was still a business. Decisions needed to be made about tight budgets and acquisition of human or material resources. Tao knew she'd pull it all off with aplomb. She had done the same thing over and over in other jobs. Moreover, this was the perfect opportunity.

Two years ago, her father had made a prediction: "In about five years, you'll spend some time in an external position of authority, and then you'll probably be brought back and made into assistant manager or given some equal position." She'd managed to make it to the external position in less than half his estimated time. She did better than he could have imagined. Tao had accomplished something that no one else ever had before.

This will be enough to get him to finally acknowledge how good I am.

She accepted the position directly from her superior, who insisted she give his regards to her grandparents, then went straight to the hospital. Her father was busy with work, but she absolutely wanted to tell him the news in person. She normally didn't go to the hospital other than for her regular checkups, and she could have told him over the phone or email. She was too excited to hold back.

It was just past noon. She was about to enter the hospital grounds when she stopped in her tracks, having caught a glimpse of her father. He was sitting by himself inside the café across the street from the hospital. The hospital workers frequented the café for noontime lunch. Tao moved toward the café, thinking this was the perfect chance to talk to him.

Just then, someone sat down across from her father.

"What the...?"

It was TAO.

There was no way she could mistake her. TAO was wearing a suit for work, one she shared with Tao. Her father didn't look surprised to see the AI. This wasn't a sudden event—this had been arranged in advance.

"Why?"

The word slipped out of her mouth. Today was Tao's turn to go into work, so TAO should have been at home. She hadn't told Tao anything about plans to leave the house, and especially not about going to meet their father.

TAO and her father talked naturally. He didn't even pay attention to the lunch he'd ordered when it came, thoroughly engrossed. His expression was so gentle, so human that one might forget he was a stern doctor or the hospital's director. Tao had never seen him like that. They looked like a real father and daughter.

Dizziness came over Tao, forcing her to sit where she was. She could feel the pounding of her pulse throughout her artificial organs. Her breathing became ragged, and cold sweat ran into her eyes. She stared at the two of them, her vision distorted. They just kept talking, completely unaware of her sitting out there. She forced herself to stand and trudged away from the hospital.

The only thing in her mind was a single word repeating over and over: *Why?*

ı|ı|||ıı|ı

"Tao? You're home?" TAO asked, looking bewildered, as Tao entered the house that evening.

Tao's expression was blank. It was infuriating how normal TAO seemed, sitting there in freshly donned loungewear—it was so impossibly routine. There wasn't a single indication she'd gone out earlier to meet Tao's father.

She looked at TAO's back, feeling ridiculed. *You're a moron for not realizing.*

"Why are you home so soon? Don't you have—"

"How long?" Tao said, cutting her off. "How long have you been meeting him?"

TAO looked perplexed. "What are you talking about?"

How shameless, Tao thought before asking, "How long have you been meeting with Father?"

"How do you—"

"Tell me. Since when have the two of you been meeting up?"

"Today was the first time."

"Don't lie."

"I'm not lying. But how do you even—"

"Answer me!" she shouted, and TAO flinched. Tao could feel the emotions roiling in the pit of her stomach leap into her head. Her face felt hot. She couldn't think rationally, but she didn't stop. "What the hell are you trying to do? Who do you think you are? You're just my body. You're a part. Why would a *thing* like you meet with my father?"

"..."

"You stole my home and my job. What are you after? Do you not want to go through with the operation? Do you think you can do better than me now that my body's falling apart? Are you trying to say you're more worthy of living?" Everything came out in a rush, like a dam had burst inside her: all the emotions she'd tucked away, the panic, the anger. They swirled together and overwhelmed her. "Did you show him this?" she asked, thrusting a tablet at TAO.

It was data showing the announcement from the company about her assignment. Data from work was automatically saved in a shared storage location.

"There's record that it was moved to your personal storage," said Tao. "Did you show him?"

"It's just—"

"Answer the question. Did you show him?"

"Yes."

Tao was surprised by the gasp of disappointment that came from her. She berated herself because she should have known this was coming. Of course it was. There was no point in getting upset about it. There was no way TAO *hadn't* shown him. "Okay. Well, how'd it go? Did you want him to compliment you? Did you want him to acknowledge you? What did he say?"

"Tao, I—"

"I keep telling you, answer the question!"

"He said... 'Good job.'"

Tao's hands went limp. The tablet crashed to the floor and skidded across it. There was silence, filled by something inside her breaking. Tao suddenly realized her vision was blurry. She didn't wipe away the tears flowing from her eyes. Her lips softened, as if giving up trying to express herself, and she smiled ever so slightly. "I trusted you. I should have been the one he congratulated."

The AI wordlessly gaped at Tao. Was she surprised? Was she hurt? It didn't matter. Tao wasn't picking up on anything coming from TAO right now.

"*KT-01*, you've done a good job," Tao continued. "You can shut yourself down now. I've decided your circuits are conditioned enough. I'll handle the regular communications with the hospital. Take a rest for now; I'll wake you when it's time for the operation."

TAO said nothing. She slowly changed from the loungewear she'd just put on into the scrubs that had been stored away, the clothes she'd been wearing when they first met. Then she went to a corner of the room, closed her eyes, and shut down.

Tao covered her with the large, protective sheet she'd received from the hospital. It was something like a sleeping bag. Just before she closed it, she said to her other self, "I...trusted you."

There was no response, of course—just her own words echoing in the lonely room. It was as quiet as if she'd gone back to the Clean House.

"I trusted you."

The promise she made with her father all those years ago suddenly came back to her.

You can't make friends.

She closed the sheet and cried no more.

.: 4 :.

VIVY SOMEHOW made it deep into the East Area without being discovered. There had been plans to build indoor attractions in this area when the park first opened, so the outer walls and roof had been built, but its use as a temporary storage area had become permanent. It was filled with such a jumble of random objects that former NiaLand employees had dubbed it the East Dumpster.

According to the Director, Diva had come here several times before, but it was Vivy's first time. The building was so huge it could have easily seated over a thousand people if they built a stage there. There was no rhyme or reason as to how things were

THE SONGSTRESS'S MESSAGE TO HER OTHER SELF 283 ::'.::::

arranged. Some materials and equipment had been there for a long time, covered in a thick layer of dust. Others were obviously newer. Vivy recognized some things from what had been six months ago to her but over seventy years in reality.

This brings back memories...

Before she could be dragged down memory lane, Vivy tore her eyes away from the objects and got a tight grip on her calculations. This wasn't the time for reminiscing. To avoid being discovered in the gloom, she left the lights off and crept through the space, keeping to the blind spots in the security camera network.

The items in storage were haphazardly shoved to the sides to give people room to walk. Vivy ignored the narrow, branching paths and turned several corners as she walked farther in. When she finally reached the back, she found a closed-off space with basic, wooden-slat walls—most likely leftovers from benches or stage props. It didn't even have soundproofing. The makeshift structure was slightly bigger than your average studio apartment and looked to be temporary, given that the walls came nowhere close to reaching the building's high ceiling. There was no door, either.

She went inside to find it relatively tidy. The dominating feature was a grand piano pushed up against one of the walls, a rare sight nowadays. Next to the piano was an assortment of sound equipment, including a mic setup and a mixer. Unlike the wood separating this room from the rest of the building, the gear was solid and high-quality. There was a water dispenser and a steamer, likely for caring for the throat, which told Vivy this room was used by a human.

A variety of posters from concerts hung on the walls. They were paper, not video displays as was the current norm. Some were clearly official merchandise that even showed the date and time of the concert, but others looked like someone had simply printed off stills from a live recording.

It was Haru-san, wasn't it?

The woman the Director mentioned in his transmission was depicted in several of the posters. This room had been hers. According to public records, she was a former idol. After retiring from the idol business, she got signed to a label as a singer-songwriter and insisted that NiaLand remain her primary base of operations.

Vivy stepped into the room with a polite "Excuse me," then sat on the piano bench.

It was just past three o'clock in the afternoon, a whole three hours after Vivy had escaped the truck. She'd stayed hidden when she moved through a NiaLand drastically different from long ago. Between receiving the transmission from the Director and arriving here, she had compared the data she got in the truck to information on the internet and grasped a vague understanding of the situation.

While "Diva's" boycott of the concert had surprised the people close to her, it hadn't originally caused any significant uproar. Once people started whispering about the Lovers' Suicide, however, the public wondered if Diva refused to take the stage because she'd known something. OGC, Diva's manufacturer, stepped in and ordered her recall to quiet the clamor. They also reiterated that the rest of the AIs worldwide were safe. NiaLand agreed and complied with their decision.

One thing that did surprise Vivy was Ophelia's death.

Vivy had worked in the shadows behind the Zodiac Signs Festival to prevent the incident called Ophelia's Suicide in the original history. Supposedly, she had succeeded. But even in this modified history, Ophelia had jumped from the building in the end—and for some reason, she'd done it with Antonio. Now the incident was known as the Lovers' Suicide.

Ophelia's motives for choosing death here and in the original history remained a mystery to Vivy. She didn't have much time to talk with Ophelia or get to know her because of Kakitani's intervention, and she never got a chance to talk about it in-depth with Matsumoto once everything was over.

Ophelia...

She could almost envision Ophelia's childlike face as she fondly called Vivy "Diva-oneesama" but intentionally pushed it back.

The problem was how people acted after the Singularity Point. It might have become the Lovers' Suicide in the modified history, but that didn't change the fact that Ophelia had chosen to end her own life. In the original history, AI rights groups wielded the fact that an AI had chosen death against her programming as a weapon in their argument for AI souls. Matsumoto said this would affect the onset of the future war. Now there were cries that Diva was involved in something similar in the modified history.

Based on the data available to Vivy, she calculated that their attempt to modify the Singularity Point was a failure, but she wasn't capable of evaluating whether her calculation was correct. She obviously couldn't determine whether there would be a series of AI suicides, like there were in the original history. She was hardly in a position to make such solid judgments.

There was one person who could, though.

"Matsumoto."

Vivy sent the transmission for the umpteenth time, but there was still no answer. The one silver lining she could find in trying to calculate the state of the Singularity Project was the fact that Matsumoto wasn't there.

Like her, Matsumoto only activated if his body was in danger or if a Singularity Point was approaching. The fact that he wasn't there meant this wasn't a Singularity Point, and that the Point with Ophelia was closed, even if events resembled the ones from the original history. For now, at least, Vivy could consider the incident with Ophelia a success. She was just over-calculating things, and this was really about her and Diva.

Matsumoto's unresponsiveness despite all the messages she sent him surely meant Vivy was active right now because of a danger to her body. Her assumption from just after she awoke must have been correct, and she was still active because the program had determined she hadn't fully escaped the danger.

Although she now understood the history leading up to this event, she couldn't find a feasible course of action. When she dug deep into this predicament, it was clear that *she* was the reason Diva was forced to leave NiaLand. It was her own fault. Vivy couldn't keep acting in a way that would cause trouble for all the employees and park guests who had supported her for years just because she made a mistake.

She didn't know how the incident with Ophelia would go down in history, but Matsumoto had said Vivy's work on the Singularity Project was over with that Singularity Point. If he was right, she should have woken next at the point in time when the war began in the original history, and she wouldn't have anything to do then. She would simply see if the one-hundred-year plan had gone well or not. It was really unfortunate that she wouldn't make it there. She would have liked to have been there, for better or worse. Whatever Vivy saw with her eye cameras then would be proof that she had existed.

Even if she couldn't be there, though, Vivy felt no real despair or regret. She'd already carried out her mission, after all. It was something else she struggled with.

Diva...

Vivy looked down at her slightly stiff right hand and covered it with her left, as if trying to soothe it. The hand had taken damage for a long time, Diva screaming louder than ever before as she fought against something she couldn't contain.

"I'm sorry..."

It wasn't as if Diva had failed to carry out her mission. Vivy knew that because she'd once stood in the same spot. Every single performance was an irreplaceable opportunity for a songstress to carry out her mission. Diva had been fulfilling her mission since she first stood onstage in NiaLand many decades ago.

Diva's pride lay in whether she could continue singing until her very last. Even as her popularity waned, her everyday performances were cut back to once a week, and she didn't fill the house, she still sang. If she was swapped out from the massive venue that was NiaLand's Main Stage, she would continue to sing. As long as there was even one person in the audience, she would continue to carry out her mission.

Vivy had stolen that pride from Diva, taken it against her will.

"I am so sorry..." Vivy's voice caught in her throat. Her logic circuit was looping viciously, racing to calculate a variety of possibilities with an acceptable outcome. She didn't care what happened to her; she just wanted to leave Diva this body.

What if she ran?

ERROR. She didn't know how that would affect the future, and it might result in injury.

Should she stay hidden?

ERROR. That would put more strain on the park workers, leading to trouble for the park guests.

Could she come out and explain the situation?

ERROR. She wasn't supposed to talk about the Singularity Project.

How about putting her faith in the Director and his efforts to make it so Diva could return to NiaLand?

ERROR. The decision by OGC and NiaLand was extremely appropriate.

How about she gave up on saving her body, let herself be captured, and went willingly to OGC's research department?

No error appeared. It didn't cause trouble for anyone and didn't go against Vivy's or Diva's missions.

"..."

Her logic circuit told her there was no point running any more calculations, and that function was temporarily forced to the background. She raised her head and looked around the room, dazed and alone. Her eye cameras took in all the posters on the walls. One of them showed Haru along with the backs of a crowd. Diva and Vivy would never see a crowd like that again.

She slowly let out a breath and stood. Her being there was surely putting loads of strain on the park employees, including the Director. The facts weren't changing. And with things as they were, it was best for everyone, including the guests, if she let her body be taken as soon as possible.

"Oh..."

Vivy's eyes fell on one poster in particular. It was next to the piano, as if watching over whoever was playing. Haru wasn't the one featured in the poster—it was Diva.

The photo must have been taken during a performance. It showed Diva singing onstage. Someone had written the words "Home Sweet Home" on the bottom of the poster, probably the song title. There were cherry blossoms dancing through the air; the song must have been reminiscent of spring. Vivy didn't know the song, and she didn't know the performance.

The audience wasn't included in the shot with Diva. It was just her taking up that space and beaming brightly as she sang.

Vivy froze in place, stuck on that image. She didn't know the song or the lyrics, but she couldn't look away. Diva sang from the stage, the lyrics soaring over the music. She was...expressing something to her audience.

Huh?

Vivy's eyes dropped without her thinking, and she was overwhelmed with confusion.

Her hands moved without directive. They opened the lid of the piano and removed the cloth cover on the keys. One finger gently pressed a key, as if testing it. It was an A. The music program inside her determined its frequency to be 440 hertz. The piano was in tune. Vivy had no idea what she was doing, but her body moved on its own. She had been facing the exit, but she slipped back into the chair.

Next, her internal circuit accessed her data storage and opened images only Vivy could see. In those images was Momoka, the little girl who loved Vivy and had traveled to see her performances. The same girl who'd given Vivy a present on her birthday. She died in a plane crash, and Vivy couldn't save her. She had always been smiling.

Her fingers pressed down on the keys, and a chord rang out. Something felt off about it to Vivy, so her fingers danced to the sides, searching. The keyboard was the only thing she could see around her as image after image appeared before her.

Assemblyman Aikawa.

Estella.

Elizabeth.

Oh...

As the music played and the images slid by, Vivy suddenly realized what it was she was trying to do, what she was thinking in that moment.

That's it. I...

The images changed, looping back on themselves to display again.

Grace.

Professor Saeki.

Ophelia.

Antonio.

Kakitani Yugo.

I want to express myself too. To Diva.

The moment she realized that, the data rushed into her vision like a flood. NiaLand. Matsumoto. The future war between AIs and humanity. Toak. The people who hated AIs. The AI Naming Law. The space hotel Sunrise. The beautiful voices that filled the escape shuttle. Metal Float. The AIs who worked on that artificial island. The human who loved an AI. The Zodiac Signs Festival. The expectations and envy an AI had for another.

Humans she met.

AIs she met.

Her one-hundred-year journey and the events thereof. The tale she had experienced.

Vivy realized then that she was no longer running calculations about herself and her current situation. She just continued to play.

.: 5 :.

IN LIGHT OF THE SITUATION, submitting something like this will have no effect on the outcome. I thought I told you as much," Tao told the Director.

"I know," he replied. "I'm just asking you to take it into consideration. Keep in mind this is what people on-site had to say."

Tao held back the urge to say, *So that means you don't know?* and suppressed a sigh.

It was eleven o'clock at night, long after NiaLand had closed for the day. The two of them were in the manager's office. Tao had already been dealing patiently with the Director for a whole thirty minutes.

Tao had immediately tried to take control of the situation when she returned from the hospital, but the staff's response had been far from swift—as she'd expected. It felt like they were intentionally dragging their feet, as each report came in just a little slower than she would have expected.

She'd given up hope of the NiaLand employees helping and instead gave more orders to the OGC security team. However, NiaLand was vast, and there were tiny spaces or unmapped areas only people intimately familiar with the park knew about. She couldn't boost the OGC patrols in the park for fear of unsettling the guests.

They still hadn't found Diva.

"My considerations and opinion are irrelevant," Tao said.

"You're making me repeat myself, but Diva's future was decided by OGC and higher-ups in our company."

The Director was holding a multi-page petition for Diva's recall to be revoked, signed by the NiaLand employees. Things like that were still done on paper, even these days, since digital signatures could so easily be duplicated and carried little weight.

"And I'm asking you to negotiate with them," said the Director.

"I can't. The decision to collect Diva is related to the security of all OGC AIs. The voices of those who use them vastly over-power a stack of signatures from the staff of one theme park."

"We'll see what happens once you negotiate with them!"

This time, Tao didn't bother to hide her sigh. This was the same back and forth they'd been having for the past half hour, even if the words were different. It was a waste of her time. "Director, please give it a rest. We cannot overturn the decision to collect Diva. On top of that, there are still security concerns in the park as long as we don't know what Diva will do. We won't be able to open tomorrow."

The Director's brow furrowed deeper. "Diva isn't that kind of person!"

"Maybe not normally, but right now she's disobeying orders. She's even destroyed something, even if it was just part of a truck. The truth is, we don't know what she will do. Don't speculate on the situation."

"It's not speculation," said the Director, his voice falling to a whisper. He appeared to contemplate something for a moment, then pulled out his handheld terminal.

"*I-I did take harsh measures to escape the truck, and I feel bad about that...*"

It was a recording of Diva's voice.

"*But I don't intend to do anything dangerous. If OGC employees find me, I won't resist. I'll do as they tell me. And I absolutely won't do anything to put the guests in danger. If hiding would cause even the slightest trouble for the guests, then I'll come out right now.*"

The recording stopped there. The Director put away his handheld terminal and said, "Diva said that herself. I told you, she's not that kind of person."

"So you've been in contact with her?"

The Director nodded, and Tao felt secretly relieved. Her greatest concern was that Diva was malfunctioning and would do something dangerous. She couldn't let her guard down entirely, but if that recording was real, and if those were really Diva's true feelings, then it was safe to assume there was no danger.

Tao kept her expression stern as she said, "Why did you hide this? You have a duty to report to me."

He looked back at her, silent.

Tao fully knew the reason why he hadn't told her: He was covering for Diva. "Do you know where she is?" she asked.

"..."

"Answer me."

Still, he didn't answer. Seeing him look so calm and fierce all at once, she figured he *did* know where Diva was. She also guessed that the Director wouldn't go against Diva's wishes.

Tao tapped on her own terminal and brought up some data. "This is today's sales data. Do you see it?"

The Director frowned, then looked intently at the data. "It's not...that different from normal. We were looking for Diva, but we still carried out our duties," he said.

Tao bit back the urge to ask him if they had *really* looked for Diva, then scrolled through the data. "Look at the visitor feedback. It's slight, but there was an increase in dissatisfaction. 'Before, park employees would guide me to the next attraction, but this time they had a drone take me.' 'Service was slower than usual.' 'The staff wasn't smiling as much today.'"

He peered at the data, realizing what it meant.

"These are all from repeat visitors," said Tao. "They all point out a decline in the quality of service."

"..."

"And the sales data isn't the same as always. Our total sales were a little below the acceptable threshold of our predictions based on the same day last month, and the same day last year. The main factor was poor performance when it came to moving merchandise."

Tao glanced at the Director to see him grinding his teeth hard. She continued, pushing him into a corner. "Looking at this, can you really say we're not causing even the slightest trouble for the guests? Diva wouldn't want this, would she?"

The Director turned away from the data, his head hanging. His thoughts must've been racing, but he didn't say a word.

Tao closed the data, thought for a moment, and then picked up the Director's petition. "Please, tell me where Diva is. All I can do is pass this petition up the ladder, and I will, but it won't change the decision."

There was a silence. Her words were an ultimatum.

More than three minutes passed before the Director croaked, "I...have one condition."

"What is it?"

"I'm the one who goes to get Diva. I want to explain everything to her."

ıı|ı||||ıı

The Director led Tao deep into the East Area, then to an unmapped zone farther in that looked like an informal storage hub. That was why the OGC personnel had been unable to find it. Tao had tried to bring security staff along for safety, but the Director was vehemently opposed to that. He reiterated that Diva wouldn't do anything dangerous, and he made Tao promise that security staff wouldn't drag the AI out with her hands bound. Having no other choice and utterly fatigued of the situation, Tao agreed. And so, the two of them walked alone.

They entered a huge, dim space lit only by the occasional emergency light. She couldn't be certain because of the mountains of materials, but Tao assumed it was massive based on the wall she could see in the distance and the height of the ceiling. She thought it might be several times larger than the Clean House.

"Kishibe-san," said the Director suddenly, lighting their path with a flashlight. "You've never heard Diva sing, have you?"

Tao wondered what this was about. "I have. I've heard some of her past top hits. When I became general manager, I briefly reviewed the songs she performs onstage." It was necessary for her sales strategy.

"But that was data, right? Have you ever heard her live?"

"No."

The Director let out a breath in front of her, a *hmph* of resignation or frustration. "I thought not. You'd be against all this too if you'd ever heard her sing live."

Tao found his assertion ludicrous. "Are you saying I would be so moved by her singing that I would have a higher evaluation of her?"

"Yep. All the veteran stage staff feel that way, as do a lot of the younger staff. Everyone loves Diva's singing."

"It doesn't matter whether I've heard her sing live or been moved by her voice—they have nothing to do with the decision. I keep repeating myself, but this isn't an issue that I can personally do anything about. You understand that, don't you?" Tao asked, as if pressing the point that she wasn't going to stand for any more complaints.

The Director didn't say anything, but he didn't stop walking, either. Tao nodded at his back. That was fine with her.

They turned a few corners in the outdated, cavernous space. Tao used her own flashlight to light up spots here and there, feeling annoyed. *This place has been really neglected. I won't be able to get this all cleared out before I go into the hospital, but I can at least draft a plan of action.*

Most of the materials had probably been put here with the vague notion that someone might still use them, or because the staff didn't want to deal with getting rid of them. Essentially, it was due to the employees' laziness. She might get a positive evaluation if she dealt with it while she was the manager.

Suddenly, the Director stopped in his tracks. Tao looked up and saw light—actual light—spilling out from an area sectioned off with simple walls.

"Is she in there?" Tao asked. She tried to keep walking, but the Director held out his arm in front of her, stopping her.

She was about to ask him what he was doing but swallowed the words. His expression was surprisingly serious. He wasn't looking at her, though. His entire attention was focused on the area ahead. Tao glanced toward the structure, wondering what was happening...and then she heard it.

Piano music?

The tender notes echoed through the space. The piece had a medium tempo—not fast, not slow. The melody and the accompaniment were clear. It was just the piano, but Tao couldn't help thinking that the music was meant to accompany vocals.

Diva?

Was she the one playing? That question was on her mind, yet she had no urge to move forward. She realized the Director's arm had already dropped, and her body still didn't move.

The music rang out like a voice, inviting Tao's eyes to search for the source. All she could see were the crude wooden walls, but her gaze was as fixed as her feet. Out of the corner of her eye, she could tell the Director's expression was steadily changing to one of shock.

Something about the tone of the music brought on a wave of nostalgia. It was gentle, yet lonely. It made you want to sink into it, but it wouldn't let you. It was like something you had and then lost. Those cruel and contradictory feelings blended together into the music, but it was still beautiful—that was just the sort of piece it was. Piano, no vocals. During the five minutes it filled the air, the two-person audience lost all sense of time.

At last, the music stopped. A chair creaked, and the light coming from the space went out. They could hear footsteps, then a figure appeared. The Director didn't move. Tao turned her flashlight on the person, who stopped.

It was Diva. She looked surprised, like she hadn't noticed the two of them until Tao shined the light on her.

"Diva…" said the Director, his voice shaking. Tao looked over to see silent streams of tears running down his face.

"Director-san, right?" said Diva, as if checking.

That struck Tao as odd, but the Director didn't seem to notice. With his voice still trembling, he just said, "That song… It's not in your repertoire. What…was it?"

Diva gave a weak smile, and her gaze fell. It was an innocent expression, as if she were embarrassed, like a child whose secret had been discovered by adults. "It's…my song. I wrote it," she said.

"You…wrote it?" The Director gaped and, having finally noticed the tears on his face, wiped them away vigorously. He took a step closer. "Y-you wrote it? Really?"

She nodded.

"But no one's ordered a new song."

"No, they haven't. I just...wanted to write it. There was something I needed to say."

The Director stiffened. "You..."

Tao was equally shocked. AIs were perfectly capable of songwriting, and their music was everywhere in this day and age, but she had never heard of a non-composer AI writing a song even though no one had ordered one.

"Kishibe-san." The Director suddenly looked at Tao. "You heard it, didn't you? You heard!"

"Heard what?"

"Diva's song!" The Director waved his arms around, unable to contain his excitement. "You're really going to let OGC collect Diva when she can make such incredible music?!" He moved closer to her, sounding accusatory, but his expression was filled with joy. "Even you must have felt it! It was like a song about your hometown, or the setting sun. Agh, it's just—it's about precious memories! You had to have been moved by that!" He was grasping for words to name the sensation.

After a glance at Diva, Tao looked back at the Director and said, "No. I wasn't moved."

The Director let out a gasp like he couldn't comprehend what she was saying.

"The song does make the listener think of a time long past, but that was it. I never had a hometown or sunsets back then."

She *did* think it was a good song. Tao had studied up on the shows in NiaLand when she became the general manager, but she still wasn't all that familiar with music. Even as a novice, she had concluded that the song was about drawing out memories. In this regard, she was of a similar mind as the Director, who had closely engaged with music. That meant the song must be extraordinary.

"I didn't leave the hospital until I was eighteen," Tao said. "In fact, I didn't even leave the Clean House except for surgery. The memories I thought of weren't of my hometown but of the pain of surgery after anesthesia wore off. I didn't think of sunsets, I thought of white lights that never changed color. And those aren't precious memories for me. They were days when I was stuck inside a box with nothing to do but while away the time."

Both the Director and Diva looked surprised. There was nothing in Tao's public profile about her history in the Clean House.

"Look, I'll say this one more time. It doesn't matter what I think of Diva. I can't do anything to change this situation."

"Agh, but..." The Director still tried to say something, but Tao glared at him. He fell quiet and averted his eyes in discomfort.

"I understand. I apologize for causing you trouble," said Diva, breaking the brief silence. She dipped her head politely to Tao.

"Does that mean you've decided to let yourself be collected?" Tao asked her.

"Yes."

"W-wait, Diva. Everyone on staff, we—"

"I know." Diva cut the flustered Director off with a smile. "I'm sure you've been doing all sorts of things for me. It's okay. You've done plenty."

"Diva…" He looked wounded, and Tao knew he truly was. The man hung his head and didn't try to say anything else.

"All right. This way, then. I'll call for the truck," said Tao as she turned on her heel.

The Director snapped to attention and said, "I'll take her. Please, let me take her." His voice shook with emotions different from before.

"You can't do that," said Diva. "Look at the time. You have to prepare for tomorrow, don't you? We can't let this cause any trouble for the guests."

The Director's expression twisted up, and he looked about to cry, but he agreed.

⑴⑴║⑴⑴

Tao and Diva waited at the shipping dock for the truck. The OGC security staff had asked to accompany them, but Tao declined the request. As much as she hated making guesses based on hunches, she didn't feel Diva was going to turn violent. She also wanted to give OGC a positive impression by reducing the burden she'd placed on them. Even so, she didn't trust Diva enough to leave her unsupervised, and she trusted the park staff even less. Tao intended to see Diva off herself for that reason.

After she reported to OGC that Diva had been secured, she received a message saying they were sending a truck several times sturdier than the previous one. It was intended to resist forceful attempts if Diva turned violent again.

"Um, Kishibe-san," said Diva, sounding apologetic. "I am very sorry for all the trouble I've caused today."

"If you're going to say that, don't make trouble in the first place."

"I understand. I regret my actions."

It was commendable that Diva would apologize and bow, and Tao smiled with satisfaction. It appeared the AI's logic circuit was operating correctly.

"I do understand the position I'm in, but I would like to ask a favor, Kishibe-san."

Tao looked at Diva questioningly. "What is it? Again, I can't change the decision."

"I know. It's not about me—it's about the Director and the staff. I was hoping you might be lenient on them and not punish them too harshly. Everything was my fault."

"I had no plans to punish them."

Diva's eyebrows shot up.

"The park employees banded together over this issue. If I punish them, it'll form a deep rift between them and management. That's not good for NiaLand's operation. At most, I'll give them a verbal warning."

"Thank you."

"It's not something you need to thank me for."

"I have one other request. Could you give this to the Director?" Diva asked, holding out a small data storage device. Tao was slightly wary when she saw it. That must have been apparent because Diva shook her head. "It's not a virus or an offensive program. It's just audio and text data—the song I was playing earlier and its lyrics. Please use it for a performance if you think you can."

She didn't seem to have any hidden motives, so Tao took the data storage and, just to check, plugged it into her handheld terminal. As Diva said, it had only text and audio data.

Tao looked at the lyrics and, even though there was no way for her to have known, felt they somehow fit. There wasn't a single mention of a specific location or person, just memories. There was joy and sorrow, meetings and separations, smiles and tears, the start of a journey...and its end. As contradictory as it seemed, the lyrics spun together the days Diva spent traveling the world, even though she'd barely ever left NiaLand.

And perhaps Diva did accept her fate of eventually being dismantled by OGC. Her only resistance, if you could call it that, was a declaration that she wouldn't forget. She wouldn't forget the days she'd had.

"Why...?" Tao began. The question was completely casual, materializing as an extension of their small talk, even though she wasn't the sort of person to indulge in pointless conversation. The AI had spent longer in her box of NiaLand than Tao had been in the Clean House. Perhaps they shared more similarities than she realized. "Why didn't you sing? You told us you had something to say, but you can't get a message across to anyone if you don't sing. Who were you trying to express yourself to?"

There was no taking back the question. She had no way of knowing what the answer might be, where it might lead her.

Diva answered, "To my other self."

Tao couldn't even utter a gasp. She didn't understand the answer, yet it took her aback.

"I wanted to express myself to my *other* self," Diva continued, looking at Tao like she was trying to read her. Tao didn't move, and Diva stayed like that for quite a while. Eventually, she let out a sigh. Her expression turned somewhat defiant, and she said, "I now know why I didn't perform that day at the festival. But my other self doesn't know. I did something unforgivable to her. I thought I could at least express myself. I wonder why?"

To Tao, Diva didn't seem like she was lying or malfunctioning at all.

"I can't tell her the reason why. But if I sang...I thought that if I could at least sing, then perhaps I could convey the emotions and feelings I had."

There was a heavy rumbling as the armored truck approached the shipping entrance. Tao heard it behind her, but she didn't turn to look. She didn't take her eyes off Diva.

"This body," Diva said, gesturing to herself, "will be collected and dismantled by OGC. The positronic brain too. I don't think either of us will ever wake up again—neither me nor her, but if the song I wrote is in my positronic brain...maybe a time will come when she notices it."

Remorse filled Diva's eyes as she looked down at her body, but they stayed kind. It was like she was looking at someone else.

"I didn't sing because...it's a small way to atone. She took the stage for so long and probably planned to keep doing it for a long time to come, but I stole that from her. How could I sing when I'd made it so she couldn't?"

Tao heard the sound of the truck opening behind her. She still didn't move. Diva looked at her with a slightly confused expression, but then gave Tao a deep bow and walked toward the truck.

"Wait!" Tao called before she could think. She didn't know what she intended to ask. She didn't even know what she was feeling.

Diva stopped but didn't look at Tao.

Tao felt her breathing become labored, and she gasped out the question, "Who are you? Why would you go this far to express something?"

"I..." She paused. The voice sounded so human. "I am just an AI, but I wanted to give her an answer before I disappeared. Because she's the other me."

With that, Diva boarded the armored truck. Tao stared at her back until the doors had shut completely.

.:6:.

IT WAS ALREADY THE NEXT DAY by the time Tao got home, nearly three in the morning. She would have normally gone to sleep long ago to avoid putting stress on her organs. Her body was tired, but she didn't feel like sleeping. She was wide awake, her mind reeling. Blood rushed to her head, either from agitation or from excitement.

She clumsily tugged on her pajamas and got into bed. She lay there for less than a minute before jumping out again, her heart thumping uncomfortably in her chest. Unable to fall asleep, she got herself a cup of warm water and sat on the bed. She sipped the water slowly as she waited for the sleep she knew wouldn't come. Time passed, though she was hardly aware of it.

Giving a determined sigh, she stood at last. Her water had gone cold long ago. She glanced at the corner of the room and saw the protective sheet. She'd cut ties with that thing nearly six months ago. It was the source of such painful memories that she avoided looking at it in her daily life. TAO lay there, unchanged. The protective sheet had a charging function in it, so she would have plenty of charge to operate.

Tao's hand trembled slightly as she removed the sheet and pressed the ON button. Nothing happened at first, and then her eyes opened. Tao asked, "Is there something you want to tell me?"

She looked at TAO, the AI who looked just like her, and thought about Diva. The songstress had acted recklessly before she disappeared. But other than when she destroyed part of the truck, Tao never got the impression that she was rampaging out of control or malfunctioning. Her actions had likely been based on those logical AI decisions Tao loved so much, meaning Diva was a machine doing everything in her power to express herself to her other self.

"My body is in perfect condition," said TAO. "Please don't worry about that as you undergo the operation."

Tao shook her head. "That's not what I mean. I'm not asking KT-01. I'm asking *you*, TAO. Is there anything you want to tell me?"

She had never intended to wake up TAO until it was time for the operation, let alone speak or listen to her. But what if TAO, like Diva, had something she wanted to say to her other self? If so, Tao wanted to hear it.

TAO's eyes crinkled as she smiled. Just that was enough to make the mechanical impression from a moment ago fade away. In front of Tao was the other self she'd lived with until half a year ago.

The AI looked at Tao and calculated something, then said, "It's been a while. I never thought we'd get to talk again."

"I meant for it to be that way, but..." Tao searched for the right words, then changed her mind and shook her head again. It didn't matter now. "No, it's fine. So, is there something you wanted to tell me?"

Immediately, TAO nodded. "There is."

Tao was caught off guard by the force in her tone. The anger and aggression she'd forgotten in the pit of her stomach rose to her head. "What is it? Just tell me. You could even tell me how much you hate me—I don't care. I'll listen until you're done."

TAO grimaced, like she was hurt. "I didn't want him to compliment me. I didn't want him to acknowledge me."

Tao looked at her, puzzled. "What are you talking about?"

"You asked me on the day I went to see Seiichi-san if I wanted him to compliment me, if I wanted him to acknowledge me, but I didn't. That's what I wanted to tell you."

Thinking back now, Tao did have a vague idea what TAO was talking about. She didn't remember the exact words she'd used, but she had said something to that effect. "Then why did you go meet with my father?"

"I went to complain."

Tao was taken aback. "What?!"

"I was annoyed because people kept saying I looked like Michi-san. Everyone at the hospital who knew her, like the head nurse, always said that to me. They told me I—well, *we*—looked just like her. I know they didn't mean anything bad by it, and part of me was happy, but each time someone said it, I felt more and more upset. I felt like those people weren't seeing us...they were seeing Michi-san. I felt that the most from Seiichi-san."

TAO's expression and the color of her face mirrored Tao's as she continued, "From the very first time I met him, I couldn't help feeling like he didn't see me as your body, and he definitely didn't see me as the AI KT-01. He saw me as a replacement for Michi-san. He never once called me KT-01 or TAO."

Her voice was becoming angrier, and Tao felt a heat rising in her own gut, a firestorm whipped up by her AI twin.

"So, I went to talk to him that day. I told him we are Kishibe Tao, not Michi-san. We are a wonderful person who's grown so much that we've just received a promotion."

Tao's body shook from a whole host of emotions as she asked, "What did he say...?"

"He laughed. He said I was mistaken, that he doesn't think that. Then he said good job on our growth and, since I happened to be there, he took me to the hospital to check the state of my conditioning. But I saw it. Just before he said I was mistaken, he made a face that looked like I'd struck a soft spot. And he still didn't call me KT-01 when I was being checked at the hospital."

Even after TAO finished talking, Tao continued to stare at her. She could see herself reflected in TAO's eye cameras. A few moments passed, then the strength suddenly left Tao's legs, though she managed to keep her footing. Then something welled up inside her that made her want to laugh. She choked it back, trying to hide it. "In that case, you should have said something."

"You were upset. You weren't listening to me. You sounded angry, which was really unlike you. I hate emotional people," said TAO with a pout, and that was Tao's breaking point.

She succumbed to the wry smile that forced its way onto her face, then said, "True. I hate them too."

TAO nodded and smiled in the same way. "I know." Then her expression changed, like she'd realized something, and she looked away from Tao for the first time since waking. She looked like she was calculating something.

"What is it?" asked Tao.

"There is something else I want to tell you, something I just thought of now." It was uncommon for TAO to have difficulty speaking, and it was even less common for her to hesitate like this. She looked at Tao and away again several times.

"What is it? Tell me," said Tao.

"Only if you want to, of course, but..." She left a moment of silence, as if trying to calm herself, then said very clearly, "Would you be my friend?"

Tao was floored. If TAO hadn't been designed with Tao as her base, her face would have been bright red.

TAO continued, as if trying to explain, "Do you remember that girl from when you were young, the one who turned out to not be your friend in the end?"

That would have been too vague a question for anyone else to answer, but Tao knew exactly what she was talking about. She would never forget those memories, that name. "You mean Sakura-san?"

"Yes, her," TAO agreed. Then she looked off into the distance, reflecting on the memory as if it were something she herself had experienced. "When Sakura-san didn't contact me, I eventually decided what Father said was right. I decided I shouldn't make any friends."

Tao nodded slightly. She remembered. She did think that.

TAO's mouth curled up, like she was a mischievous child, and she said, "Isn't that annoying? Father always being right, I mean. I want to be friends with you, Tao-san. I want to be able to tell him he was wrong, that I could make friends with someone who understands me so well."

Tao couldn't help smiling a little in surprise as she listened. Of course the two of them understood each other—TAO *was* Tao. She got caught up in the moment and nearly agreed to it without a second thought, but she stopped herself. The idea that popped into her head turned into a strong determination in the space of a second. This decision was incredibly important to her, and it was easily the greatest show of resolve in her life.

"What's wrong, Tao-san?" TAO asked uneasily. "You don't want to be my friend, do you?"

Tao snapped back to her senses and quickly shook her head. "That's not it. I just want you to hear something...as my friend." She took out her handheld terminal, then dialed a number she'd never called, even though she had it saved.

"What are you—" TAO tried to ask what this was about, but Tao reassured her with a wave and took several deep breaths to calm herself.

She counted four rings, then someone answered the phone.

"What is it at this time of night?"

It was her father. He typically insisted on answering the phone within two rings, so he must have been sleeping. She didn't hear any grogginess in his voice, though.

Tao put the call on speaker so TAO could hear as well and said, "I'm sorry for calling this late, but there's something I wanted to report."

"An emergency situation? What is it?" He must have assumed that was it because of the time.

TAO's eyes opened wide when she realized it was her father. Tao found something about her reaction funny. She took another deep breath. "It's about the operation next month. I'm not going through with it."

"What? What do you mean?"

"I mean exactly what I'm saying. I will not undergo the full-body transplant scheduled for next month."

Her father's confusion was apparent even over the phone. TAO looked like she felt the same, her expression a match for Seiichi's words.

"Don't be ridiculous. It's already decided. I'm hanging up."

"It's not ridiculous, and it's not decided. The hospital cannot go through with an operation if a conscious patient refuses, even if they have already signed a consent form."

"What is this? What are you trying to do?" It was clear he didn't understand at all. That made sense to Tao, since she'd never once gone against his instructions.

"KT-01, whom I call TAO, would be sacrificed to complete the operation. I don't want to lose her. She's my friend."

TAO reacted first. Her expression changed from one of shock to panic. She moved toward Tao but was stopped by a look and a raised hand that said, *We'll talk after.*

"This is idiotic! You...you can't live if you don't have the operation!" her father shouted, at the end of his rope.

Tao was surprised by how easily it was for her to take that in stride. She was disobeying her father, and he was shouting at her. This was the thing she had feared most in the world, but there was no fear inside her. "Father...I am not Mother."

"What...?"

"I might have carried on the meaning of Mother's name in my own, but Kishibe Tao is not Kishibe Michi. Don't conflate the two of us."

"Don't act like you know what you're talking about!" There was a bang—he must have hit something. *"The other one said the same thing to me. You're both mistaken."*

"Then why did you have TAO made to match my body at the age of twenty-five?"

"Excuse me?"

"The operation's next month. From the very beginning, you always said the operation would take place when I was around twenty-seven years old, so it would have been more logical to have TAO made to match my body when I was twenty-seven. So then why did you make TAO look like a twenty-five-year-old me?"

"Because the conditioning would be more certain if she matched you at the start. Forecasting things for your body at age twenty-seven would cause issues."

"Even though predictive algorithms allowed TAO to be perfectly capable of performing a bow I practiced for business etiquette without reporting to anyone?"

"..."

"Twenty-five is how old Mother was when you met her, isn't it? When she was healthy and happy."

He stopped speaking. Tao didn't know if it was because he was too frustrated with her or if it was because she'd hit the nail on the head. Either way, it didn't matter. It wouldn't change her decision.

"And there's something else that I didn't realize until TAO said something. At some point, you stopped calling me by my name. So no, I'm not going through with the operation. Now, if you'll excuse me…" Tao hung up without waiting for a response. He immediately called her back, but she ignored it, turned off her terminal, and chucked it onto her bed.

Finally, *finally*, she felt like herself. She let out a deep sigh.

Now TAO was coming at her. She looked half agitated, half angry. "What is this about?" she asked.

"I complained," Tao replied. "Just like you."

"It's not the same. What are you thinking, turning down the operation? Is it because of me? I don't want that—that's not why I asked to be your friend."

"I know." Tao tenderly grasped TAO's hand. "But I don't want to undergo an operation that means I'll lose you. That doesn't mean I've given up on living, though. I'll fight, either by risking a full-body transplant with a different body or going back to the Clean House and doing lots of operations to transition piece by piece. It'll be a difficult battle, but it's better than losing you… I've finally made a friend, after all."

TAO grimaced, trying to endure the pain. Tao smiled at her.

"That's an underhanded way of putting it," said TAO as she finally wrapped her hands around Tao's and squeezed.

"Will you come with me?" asked Tao. "I'll end up hospitalized no matter which option I choose. And I know better than anyone how boring that is… Though you know it too."

TAO gave a small nod. She didn't look like she could return Tao's smile, but she could at least do that. By this point, Tao's body was begging for sleep. TAO told her she should go to sleep right away so she wouldn't put any more strain on her body, then briskly cleaned up the water from earlier and turned off the lights.

When Tao lay down in bed, TAO asked, "By the way, why did you wake me today?"

"Well..." Tao thought a little, then decided the story was far too long. To put it off, she gently asked, "Can I tell you tomorrow?"

TAO agreed.

As Tao drifted into a pleasant sleep, she contemplated her reasoning. She woke TAO that day because of a random conversation with Diva. Considering her own position, Tao would likely be leaving NiaLand in the next few days as well. Her position in the company and her work were no longer her top priority, which left her free to act without fear of losing something.

She hadn't been moved by Diva's music or the songstress herself. Yet the conversation had resulted in Tao making a friend. Tao smiled, thinking it wouldn't be so bad if she could somehow pay Diva back for that in her last few days at NiaLand.

Epilogue

"**G**OOD MORNING, Diva. Do you understand me?"

Diva activated, and her eye cameras picked up someone standing in front of her. At the same time, she processed the question that had reached her audio sensors. "Director...?" she asked.

He nodded with relief. "Yep, it's me."

She attempted to move each of her parts in accordance with her startup routine and then realized she couldn't. Her eyes shot down to her body. She had arms. Legs. A torso. Shoulders. Based on the check she was running, she even had a face. It was all just as her previous logs said it should be, meaning she looked the same.

"What's going on? Why am I...? Where am I?" she asked, her eyes darting about as she started taking in her surroundings.

They were in a square, plain room she had never seen before. There were rows of cases along the walls displaying AIs and their parts. Each item had a monitor beside it, projecting what looked to be explanatory notes. The excellent lighting made it easy to see everything clearly.

Diva knew of a location that looked similar: the exhibition room in NiaLand. It wasn't the biggest hit, even though it was always part of the park tour. As she looked around again, she realized there was a sheet of hardened, transparent glass separating her from the Director. It wasn't just in front of her either—it went all the way around. Diva was, quite simply, boxed in.

"Right, I'll explain everything," said the Director. "First things first, this isn't NiaLand, unfortunately. It's an AI museum in the city." He went on to tell her what had happened, starting from the beginning.

About a month ago, Diva was collected by OGC's research department as planned. Her body was taken apart, and every piece was inspected to find the cause of the malfunction. No matter how much they looked, they couldn't find it. The researchers scoured every single bit of code making up her programming but didn't even find one unnecessary program, let alone something that resembled a virus.

At that point, an opinion letter came from NiaLand. It was titled "Predicted Public Reaction to Treatment of the AI A-03 and Impact on OGC Profits." The massive letter would've been several thousand pages long if printed on standard-sized paper. As implied by the title, it detailed the possible public opinion of how OGC handled this matter and calculated OGC's future profits in a variety of situations.

The original reason OGC decided to recall Diva was because, if the theory was correct and Diva had boycotted the festival due to a malfunction similar to the one that had caused Ophelia to destroy herself, then it could be a security issue for all OGC AIs. In short, they wanted to find the cause of Diva's malfunction so they could tell the world it was a one-off, meaning all other OGC AIs were safe. But they *didn't* find a problem with Diva. Now their only option was to announce it was still unclear what had caused the songstresses to malfunction and then weather the fallout.

That left the question of what to do with Diva. The safest option was for OGC's research department to store her parts for further research, which they tried to do. But then the opinion letter arrived and pointed out that was a bad move on OGC's part.

Without knowing the cause, they couldn't return Diva to NiaLand, where she had relative freedom. If they put her someplace the public couldn't see her, like in the research department, AI rights groups and the general public would criticize the company with words like "confinement" and "imprisonment," which would cast OGC in a poor light.

And while Diva's popularity was fading, and she was old, she had once been the world's most popular songstress and still had passionate fans. A large portion of those fans had been supporting her for a long time, putting them in their golden years. Many had established for themselves a decent level of social influence and standing. In other words, a relatively large percentage of her fans had the power to sway public opinion. What OGC did with her could turn those people into enemies and weaponize the public.

Since OGC couldn't store Diva or send her back to NiaLand, they needed a facility where people could see her, but where her freedom was limited. The solution presented in the opinion letter, based on a variety of calculations and simulations, was to send her to an AI museum.

"What surprised me was that it was Kishibe-san who sent that opinion letter to OGC," said the Director.

Diva was just as baffled. "The manager?"

"Surprising, right? She didn't even get help from us; she did it all on her own. I saw it afterward, and I couldn't believe one person put something of that scale together. I knew she was the kind of person who could handle her job, but I didn't realize she could go that far..." He shook his head, impressed.

"Why would she go to all that trouble?" Diva said with a look of disbelief. The manager struck her as the kind of person who optimized decisions for maximum profit. She had calculated this was the most beneficial path for OGC, one of NiaLand's sponsors, but something still didn't sit right.

The Director's brow was furrowed, as if he was thinking the same thing. "Well, maybe it was her attempt at a going-away present. She quit."

"What?!"

"Apparently, her health wasn't great. She left the company that placed her at NiaLand, and she's in the hospital now."

"Really? I never realized she wasn't well."

"Don't you remember? She told us. She didn't get to leave the hospital until she was seventeen or eighteen."

"Hmm...she said that?" Diva didn't remember it. She hadn't actually talked to the manager that much.

"She did. But maybe it was actually..." The Director stopped, like he'd just had an idea. His expression turned nostalgic, and he said, "She said she wasn't at the time, but maybe she really was moved by your song."

"Um, when was that?"

"It was that same time Kishibe-san told us about the hospital stuff. The day you were collected by OGC. You played the piano in Haru's practice room."

Diva froze. She certainly had no memories of that. To her, this conversation was happening immediately after she was collected by the truck and shut down. Her calculations raced, trying to figure out what this meant. She had a feeling she knew.

"Yeah, all the staff members loved the song. No one has sung it yet, though. We don't even know if anyone other than you should—"

"Director." Diva couldn't stop herself from cutting him off. It was just one word, but she was incredibly nervous doing it. "I'm sorry. I just started up, and it seems I'm still a bit out of it. Could I have some time to myself?"

The Director looked startled. He bobbed his head. "You're right; I'm sorry. I was just so happy to see you again."

"Me too."

He smiled cheerfully. "This is your stage from now on. Your audience isn't made of visitors to NiaLand but visitors to the museum. And they're not coming for a performance but probably for studying or a school project. When it comes time, you won't be singing, and I'm not sure you can sing unless the visitors ask you to...but that doesn't make this any less your stage." Diva nodded, and the Director nodded back. "I'll come visit again."

Once she was alone, Diva didn't focus her eyes on her new environment. Instead, she stood there with her calculations focused internally. That feeling she had earlier was about the period of time where she had no memories, and her body had acted on its own. She'd experienced that before.

Diva brought a hand to her chest and whispered, "It's you, isn't it...Vivy?"

Overture

VIVY BOOTED and immediately ran through her startup routine. No abnormalities in her positronic brain or any part of her body. All of her calculation circuits were operating without issue, but her vision was flooded with the red of error messages and something else:

Fire.

It crept forward, writhing as it consumed the area. Even with the heat distorting her view, she realized she didn't know where she was.

A nearby wall let out an awful screech and burst, unable to endure the expansion from the heat. It triggered a nearby pillar to tumble. Without its support, the ceiling above crumbled in, and the new air that burst into the room fueled the flames.

Each of Vivy's sensors was overloaded from the smoke, the heat, the noise. Her audio sensors picked it up first.

"What is happening?"

She was shocked when she realized what it was. Her logic circuit rapidly reorganized her list of priorities. She shouldn't have a body, but she still did. Why? Why did she activate? Where was she? Why were her surroundings encased in fire? She ignored all those questions and focused entirely on calculating the true nature of what she heard.

Her audio sensors were picking up the mechanical voices of AIs singing. Those lyrics, that melody... It was the song she'd written.

"What is going on?!"

It was almost exactly one hundred years from the start of the Singularity Project, the end of Vivy's journey. There, she found all AIs singing the song she'd created.

She had feared this, and here it was. The start of the war between AIs and humanity.

VIVY
Prototype

Afterword

THANK YOU VERY MUCH for your purchase of *Vivy Prototype* Volume 3! This is Tappei Nagatsuki, one of the authors of this collaborative work. Following Volume 2, I was asked to be in charge of the afterword.

Now then, Vivy and Matsumoto completed their hundred-year journey, overcame the Singularity Points in each era, and finally arrived at the future in question. History has walked down the modified path thanks to the efforts of the two AIs, but has that actually made any difference to the world? Were Vivy and Matsumoto able to change a future where the world was destroyed? Did they successfully carry out their mission?

The answers to those questions will come in the final installment of the series, Volume 4. Get pumped!

As you readers who regularly read all the way through the minute details of the afterword will already know, there are some differences between *Vivy Prototype* and the anime *Vivy -Fluorite Eye's Song-*. Those differences are in character details, how the story unfolds, the conclusions of the arcs, and even some of the full arcs themselves. This is in line with the fact that the novels are, at their core, the draft for the anime.

In the first volume, this difference came in the mystery surrounding the suspicious death of the previous owner of the space hotels, which happened before the Sun-Crash Incident—the event where Sunrise fell to Earth. In the second volume, the Metal Float arc came to a different conclusion, and the characters led different lives afterward. In the third volume, we have Vivy making the decision to create a song, including the things that drove her to compose and the thoughts and relationships of the people around her.

All these things only happen in *Vivy Prototype*. Did you enjoy them?

If you like these books, please do watch the incredible work that is the anime *Vivy -Fluorite Eye's Song-*. I guarantee you'll be surprised again by the setup, plot, and conclusions of the stories you've read. That is one of the ways you can enjoy this work.

Umehara and I enjoyed discussing what sort of problems might arise as AIs develop in the future, and we used that discussion to pick themes for *Vivy*. Giving AIs names, giving them responsibility, love between an AI and a human, an AI taking their own life, an AI creating something for themselves... These aren't all the potential Singularity Points, though. What kinds of Singularity Points do you think would become a problem? It could be interesting to think of that as you read the story.

All right. There's still so much I want to talk about, but I'm quickly running out of pages. I'll now move on to saying thank you to all the people who made this book possible.

First, a huge thank you to the head editor, Satou-sama, who handled every aspect of making a book with care. You were the first reader of this volume and the final volume, and your thoughts have been incredibly motivating.

To our illustrator, loundraw-sama, your incredibly detailed and emotive illustrations for this volume are amazing yet again. You took my breath away with Vivy's fragility on the cover, and then again with Ophelia's beauty. Thank you for helping us all the way to next volume and the conclusion of our story.

Thank you to all the animation staff, including Shinpei Ezaki-san, the director. You've given us an incredible show with the anime, with its fantastic art and production that spur the story on. As I'm writing this afterword, you'll be tackling the last portion of the anime... Look toward the conclusion of the story and keep at it until the end!

Next, I would like to thank Wada-sama and Ootani-sama of WIT STUDIO, as well as Takahashi-sama of Aniplex. Thank you for your help selecting which sections were needed for turning the draft novels into an anime. We probably wouldn't have been able to complete this if it weren't for you working with us to extract the best parts of the story, marking what makes the books good books, and the anime a good anime.

My next thank-you goes out to Umehara-sama, who struggled alongside me as we wrote this volume together. Unlike Volumes 1 and 2, which we took turns writing, Volume 3 was a true collaboration between the two of us. It's the culmination of us working together on the pacing and flow of the story, and of our unending efforts. I'm glad we were able to pull it together in the end without having to make concessions. Thank you!

Lastly, the biggest thanks go to you, readers, who read this far into the story and to the end of the afterword! I hope you'll thoroughly enjoy each work, watching how the story unfolds for the different endings for Vivy in the novels and in the anime! Please do stay with us until the end!

I hope to see everyone in the next—and final—volume! I look forward to seeing the end of the story, Vivy and Matsumoto at the final Singularity Point, and all you readers! Thank you for your kind attention to the very end!

Tappei Nagatsuki